THE GREAT OÑATE

Not until then did the chief cattle thief, the great José Oñate, appear upon the scene. He was a man of mark. He could not have walked on the stage of this world unnoticed even as a slave. In a far land, his conversation would have changed the minds of cannibals. His wisdom always would have unlocked the heart of the sternest tyrant, and his hands, a little later, would surely have opened the seven sealed doors of his treasure chambers. Women could not resist his wiles. Men could not resist his weapons.

If he were a robber, it was plain, not that he loved money unlawfully gained, but money gained by dangerous methods. Nothing in this world had spice for him if it were unseasoned by danger. He had dipped his young hands, already, in a hundred fortunes and, when they were his, he had cast aside the spoils readily. He gave to his companions, to his friends, to his acquaintances, to the beggars beside the road. When the hands of all these were filled, it was said, he then gave to his enemies.

The appearance of this man was such that, at a glance, all eyes instantly understood the metal of which he was made; that is to say, he had the look of steel that will cut steel. In addition, upon the face of him he was gay, vain, cheerful, inconstant, and as keen as a hungry hawk on the wing.

MAX BRAND

TWO SIXES

LEISURE BOOKS NEW YORK CITY

A LEISURE BOOK®

April 1999

Published by special arrangement with Golden West Literary Agency.

Dorchester Publishing Co., Inc.
276 Fifth Avenue
New York, NY 10001

ISBN 0-8439-4508-7

TABLE OF CONTENTS

WINKING LIGHTS

Frederick Faust's working title for this story was "Two-Speed Conifrey" which was perhaps more appropriately changed to "Winking Lights" by the editor of Street & Smith's **Western Story Magazine** *before it appeared in the issue dated 1/6/23. In the serial, "Tramp Magic," published almost a decade later in six installments in* **Western Story Magazine** *(11/21/31 - 12/26/31), Faust introduced one of his most engaging characters, a confidence man known only as Speedy. In fact, when this serial first appeared in book form, it simply bore the title* **Speedy** *(Dodd, Mead, 1955). Nine short novels also featuring Speedy appeared subsequently in* **Western Story Magazine,** *including "Speedy's Mare" (3/12/32), "Speedy's Bargain" (5/14/32), and "Speedy's Desert Dance" (1/28/33). In many ways Two-Speed Conifrey, although arriving earlier in the mountain desert, bears more than a little resemblance to the subsequent character and is certainly possessed of a similar artful brashness and willingness to accept a challenge, no matter how daring.*

I
"SOMETHING HAD TO BE DONE"

THEY WERE LIKE THE EARS OF A MULE, THOSE TWO, sharp-sided hills that jutted up on either edge of the little plateau. So great was the similarity that Conifrey, as he rode into view of them, broke out into hearty laughter. He reeled in the saddle and clasped his ribs with delight. Then, as a cowpuncher will, he stopped his horse and

1

rolled a cigarette. This was worth a moment of smoke and consideration, even though he was supposed to be hurrying ahead of the party at this moment to warn Bud Custis against their coming and to see that kitchen preparations would be equal to the occasion.

His laughter had hardly died to a chuckle, however, and his smoke was not half rolled, when a dry voice remarked from the side: "What might be tickling you so much in the short ribs, stranger?"

Two-Speed Conifrey turned his head, still chuckling, with the slowness that had gained him his nickname. An old employer had once said of Conifrey: "He's got two speeds...one is all-fired slow, and the other is dead stop." In this leisurely fashion, then, Two-Speed Conifrey turned his head and observed in the shadow of the rock a great, black horse, unsaddled and unbridled, and grazing the sunburned bunch grass of the plateau. Next to the edge of the hill, saddle, bridle, and pack were piled, and against the pile reclined a big-chested, long-limbed, dark-eyed man.

"Hello," said Conifrey. "Don't you see nothing to laugh at around here?"

"If I did," said the other, "being polite by nature, I'd keep my laughing inside my stomach." And with this, he grinned broadly.

Conifrey thoughtfully rubbed his chin. It was not the first time that people had laughed at his long, lean-featured face with the humorous mouth and the oddly sad eyes.

"Well," he commented, "I guess it ain't the first time that a gent has had to swaller his laugh." And he grinned in turn, feeling, with some justice, that he had earned the right. "But, speaking for myself," he continued, "a good laugh is better to me than a day's pay."

"Sure," said the hero of the dark eyes, removing his hat and running his fingers through hair as silky black as his eyes themselves. "I know some folks are that way. Which sort of reminds me of something that I heard when I was a kid...that a loud laugh is a sign of an empty mind."

A desire to dismount from his horse and smite the stranger rose in the mind of Two-Speed Conifrey, but, as often happened with him, he allowed the impulse to evaporate in contemplation. The sun was comfortably warm between his shoulder blades and to dismount would be labor. So, instead, he turned his thoughts to the huge electric torch with which the stranger was now toying, a great tube ten times the size of the ordinary pocket light. He lit the cigarette he had finished rolling and touched a match to it, the smoke as sweet incense in his nostrils.

"I see you carry your own headlight with you," he remarked.

"By way of telling folks that I'm coming," said the big man, and yawned. "Besides, I use it for talking, being a silent sort of gent by nature."

"I ain't noticed you being particular backward with your lingo," said Conifrey. "But how come you can talk with it?"

The other paused. "Look here," he said. He snapped on the switch. A spot of strong light showed against the shadow on the rock beside him. Then he covered and uncovered the mouth of the torch rapidly with his hand, and there was a swift play of the light against the rock. "That's the shortest way of explaining," he said.

"That light meant something," said Conifrey. "Am I right?"

"If you was a sky pilot in a pulpit"—the big man

yawned again—"you couldn't've said a truer word."

"Thanks," said Conifrey. "That's a job that I ain't been picked for until now."

"You're welcome," said the other. "Which I might say that you're plumb easy to please."

"I see that you're a great hunter," said Conifrey.

"Me?" queried the other, rolling over up on one elbow.

"For trouble," explained Conifrey.

The big man sat up.

"Sure I am," he said. "But I don't have much luck. Maybe you could put me on a hot trail."

Conifrey grinned. "I could," he said. "If you was to see some of the growed men in my part of the country...but me, I'm only sort of a choir boy."

The stern light vanished from the eyes of the stranger. A sneer curled his lips as he sank back once more and pillowed his head against a knapsack.

"That's why they give you that sort of a hoss to ride, I guess," he said, and turned his glance disdainfully over the gaunt and bony outline of Two-Speed Conifrey's mustang.

"You don't like this hoss, maybe?" said Conifrey with silken gentleness.

"Do you?"

"Son, you ain't looking at him close enough. This old roan has snaked me a hundred and twenty miles in twenty-four hours."

The other opened his eyes. Then he laughed. "Anyway," he said, "I see that they don't neglect the education of the choir boys in your part of the country. Speaking by and large, that's a man-sized lie for a boy to tell."

Conifrey had started to roll another cigarette, but now

4

he dropped the makings, fluttering toward the dust. He stretched his long, thin arm, straightened himself in the saddle, and yawned. It was not at all to his liking—violent exercise on such a morning as this—but something had to be done. He dropped to the ground with a cat-like lightness. He had made a slouched figure sitting in the saddle, but it was a new man who stood beside the mustang—not heavy to suggest strength, but, compared to the big man, he was as a greyhound is to a mastiff.

"I spent a month chasing that Simon hoss," he said as much to the mustang as to the stranger. "He was running plumb wild. We worked the others down in a week. I spent three weeks longer working on Simon. Nope, he ain't much for looks, with that tucked-up rump and that ugly head of his, but he'll run from sunrise to sunset, and, if you put a couple of hundred pounds in the saddle on him, it don't make no difference. He just nacherally laughs at work."

"A month of the kind of chasing you give him might've just been good exercise for a decent hoss," said the stranger. "Wouldn't have raised a sweat on Sir Charlie, yonder."

"You call your hoss Sir Charlie?" asked Conifrey.

"Is there anything wrong with Sir Charlie?" asked the other.

"The only Charlie I ever knowed," said Conifrey, "quit cold when it come to a pinch."

"Meaning to say that my hoss would do the same thing?"

"Meaning to say that he's got sort of a foolish look to his eye," said Two-Speed Conifrey.

The big man sat up. "I dunno just how to take that," he declared.

"I dunno just how you would," said Conifrey.

The stranger blinked and stared at Conifrey. It was odd, indeed, if this tall, slender fellow was other than he had seemed. But indubitably there was a challenge in this last remark, so he rose to his feet, truly an impressive figure.

"Talking loose and free about my hoss," he said, "is sort of talking loose and free about me."

"Then," said Conifrey, "it looks like I'm killing two birds with one stone."

An oath dropped from the lips of the black-eyed man. "Son," he said, "are you feeling sort of tired of living?"

"I'm feeling sort of in need of exercise," said Two-Speed Conifrey.

"Well," said the other, his wonder changing to a scowl, "here's a starter for you." And he struck as a coiled snake strikes—with inescapable speed. It quite fooled Conifrey. He had expected a heavy leisure of movement in such a ponderous fellow. This lightning blow crashed through his erected guard that he had whipped up. The burly fist was deflected from the point of the jaw at which it was aimed, but, glancing down, it struck Conifrey's chest. Even though deflected, it had power great enough to lift him from his feet and hurl him back, sprawling, to the ground.

"Now, you fool," said the big man, "that'll teach you to pick fights with gents of your own size and...."

The last word stopped short. Conifrey had tumbled to his feet with amazing lightness, and he ended the sentence by slicing a left swing into the face of the larger man. He lacked some forty pounds of the weight of the other, but he had, instead, the instinct of the natural hitter. It was a crushing blow that landed on the cheek of the big man. Astonished, the fellow gave back a half step, more stunned by amazement, perhaps, than by the actual blow.

Conifrey slipped in and pounded both hands against the body of his antagonist. It was like beating at a barrel. It made the wrists of Conifrey ache, but it brought only an angry grunt from his antagonist. The next instant the man's clutches were on Conifrey. He lifted his lighter foeman as though the latter were a child and dashed him to the ground, flinging his bulk down afterward to crush Two-Speed Conifrey with his fall. But he struck dirt and rocks instead of a human body. Conifrey, half stunned by the shock, had presence of mind enough to roll from under. He whipped away in the nick of time and came, reeling to his feet, to face another lunge from the black-haired man.

The latter came with a wild roar. His fury had been growing by the moment as the contest dragged on. Now the continued opposition had thrown him into a frenzy. The blow that he aimed at Conifrey's head seemed powerful enough to crush the skull, had it landed. Conifrey ducked it and sprang away.

He was amazed and bewildered. "Look here," he shouted, "have we got any call for trying to murder each other?"

It was like calling to the wind. The giant swerved from the rush that he had missed and came on again, his face suffused with passion.

II
"THE END FOR TWO-SPEED"

IT MADE NO DIFFERENCE THAT THE FIGHT HAD STARTED from foolish badinage. The important thing now was that this overbearing and insolent fellow was in a murderous rage because the resistance had been so much prolonged. Conifrey threw off his good nature like a cumbersome cloak. He began to fight desperately. He met that headlong rush with a straight arm blow that licked out like a leap of flame when the draft heads down the chimney. After the one stroke, Conifrey side-stepped, saw the giant go by him, and struck again. That second blow did damage. Conifrey saw the other stagger even as he turned. And, though he came back to the charge with as much fury as ever, his mouth was slightly agape, and his eyes were rolling.

It was child's play to avoid that charge. Conifrey leaned, smote his right hand into the pit of the other's stomach, and, then, as the black-eyed man doubled with a gasp, Conifrey rose as a spring snaps straight and jerked his hard, left fist into the other's face.

This time the latter went back on his heels. A tiny, crimson trickle came from his nose and mouth. He had been cut by a grazing blow beneath the eye. His brain was lost in a black fog of fury.

Conifrey stepped in closer and closer, and, with each mincing step, his fists flew home. They spatted on that dripping countenance as though he were slapping with his open palm. His own hands were splashed with crimson to the wrists. In vain, the big man struck with roundabout blows. He began to shake his head to get away from that blinding spray of fists. He cuffed clumsily down. He roared in a brute fury of impotence. But not a blow went home, for Conifrey was ducking, dodging, and swaying like a will-o'-the-wisp, and the flailing fists glanced past him.

Suddenly, the big man whirled with a shout of animal anger. Conifrey knew what it meant. He had heard it before and had learned to dread it—and to love it. It

8

meant that the ultimate test was coming—that this giant would take his life in his hands to kill or be killed. He saw the other go to his pile of equipment. He saw the big man reach for the saddle. Then the giant spun around, dashing the blood from his eyes and swinging the Colt into line. Already it was barking. In true cowboy fashion, the big man was shooting as soon as he had his gun out of the holster. One slug cracked a white-faced stone in three segments. Another covered the boots of Two-Speed Conifrey with dust. Then Conifrey fired. He was loath to shoot. He could tell by the very fashion in which the stranger had first gripped his weapon that this was no dexterous expert with such a tool. But there was nothing for it, save to kill or be killed—or to have a random bullet crashing among the lean ribs of the mustang, Simon. So he twitched his own Colt out of the holster and made his snap shot—not at the head or the body, that would be sheer murder. He fired, instead, at the right upper arm. A third bullet from the other's gun had just flown past Conifrey's side. Now the weapon slid unregarded out of the fingers of the big man, knocked up a puff of dust where it fell, and the big man passed his left hand to his right upper arm while he glared at Conifrey in stupid amazement.

Then he understood. He had fought like a savage and fought to kill. Defeat had sobered him with strange suddenness.

"Well, friend," he said, and his quiet voice was in odd contrast with his gashed face, "you should have shot for the head. Hanged if I ain't played like a wild man and a fool. I've got what's coming to me. Only, Lord, Lord, why did I pick this day for a fight?" He turned his eyes with yearning to the east and across the wide, shallow valley.

9

"I'm plumb sorry," apologized Two-Speed Conifrey. "But some of my friends are coming along, and we'll take care of you and see that you get to the doc in Lawson. Now let me have a look at that arm. I'm a pretty good hand...if the slug didn't break the bone."

The bone was safe. Luck had stood at the side of the big man in that, at least. The bullet had entered close to the elbow, missed the bone, and issued again in the back of the arm and close to the shoulder. With water from their canteens, Conifrey cleansed the wound. He was busy bandaging it when Ned Dolan and the rest of the men with the wagons came up.

Explanations were not needed. In five minutes the big man was ensconced in a wagon and made as comfortable as could be. Then Ned Dolan called Conifrey to one side.

"'Speed," he said, for Two-Speed was far too long to serve as a nickname. "How did it happen?"

"It just come about," Conifrey said mildly.

Ned Dolan was so angry that his sun-browned face was tinged with purple blood. "What did I send you ahead to do?" he asked.

"To ride on and get things ready for the boys," confessed Conifrey.

"Which it looks like you been more busy getting your own little corner in hell reserved for you."

"Which it looks like I ain't been real sensible, Ned," admitted Conifrey sadly.

Ned Dolan turned away. He dared not trust the first words that were on the tip of his tongue at this moment. Finally he was able to confront his hired man again.

"'Speed," he said, "I ain't never going to forget a lot of the good things that you've done for me."

"Aw, the devil," said Conifrey, covered with

embarrassment.

"There was that time that crazy Portugee got me cornered...."

"Drop it," said Conifrey.

"That's what you done to the Portugee." Dolan grinned. "Well, I won't keep lingering on all the good things that you've done, 'Speed. If it comes to a pinch for anything from roping a cow to fighting a man, I'd pick you out sooner than any man I ever seen. You're all in the clear, 'Speed, for real life-or-death work, but when it comes to everyday, keep-plugging, never-say-die work, why, you ain't worth a continental, old man."

"I know it," said Two-Speed Conifrey with deepening gloom.

"When you busted loose and tried to turn Kansas City into a three-ringed circus, 'Speed, did I quit you cold?"

"You didn't," said Conifrey.

"Did I go bail and get you out of jail?"

"You done that thing, partner."

"When you shot the cigar out of Judge Hanlett's mouth because you didn't like the decision he made on that fight you had with Cree Jackson, did I let the judge send you to the pen?"

"No," groaned Conifrey more solemnly than ever.

"Did I go and make love to the judge's daughter till she got plumb kindly, and then did I get her to beg you into the good graces of Hanlett?"

"You done all them things," said Two-Speed.

"Did I sit down with you about ten times and talk from sunset to dawn about how you'd ought to get rid of that meek way of yours that makes folks think they can ride right over you? Have I pretty near got down on my knees and begged you to act up a little rougher so's you wouldn't have to fight to prove you was a man?"

11

"You've sure talked." Two-Speed sighed.

"But I've talked myself out," said Ned Dolan. "Here I send you on ahead to get things ready, so's we'll have some chow when all the boys come in, fagged out and tired. Instead, I find you adding up gents for us to pack on into camp with us, sore toes and busted heads and all."

"It's pretty bad," conceded Conifrey.

"'Speed, I'm through."

"I'm sure sorry, Ned."

"I think you are, and so am I. And so will all the boys be sorry. They like you pretty near as well as I do, and, if they knew you were going, about five of 'em would want to go with you. So you stay on here behind, and, when we start ahead, you just fade out."

"I'll do that, Ned."

"And if you're ever broke or in trouble, you'll know where to send for help…."

"I'll sure send to you, Ned."

"Good bye, 'Speed, old man, and may the Lord take care of you better than you take care of yourself."

"Thanks." Two-Speed grinned again. "Maybe the Lord'll take your advice. I sure hope that He does, Ned. And what about José Carneff when he comes back in the spring?"

"Hang it! I forgot about him and his gang. They'll raise the devil now that you're gone."

"You tell 'em that old Two-Speed Conifrey is lying back to windward just waiting for them to start something, and, if they rustle as much as one three-months' calf, I'm going to come back and tie 'em all together and drop them into the old river. Send 'em just that message from me, Ned."

"Suppose that they call the bluff?"

12

"It ain't a bluff," said Two-Speed Conifrey with perfect soberness, and he looked Ned Dolan squarely in the eye. After that, he went to see his victim. The latter greeted him with a battered smile.

"I'm feeling considerable better," he announced. "I was beginning to think that I was going back to no more'n half of the man I used to be. But they tell me that I been tangling up with Two-Speed Conifrey and…."

"Has that name got clean away down here? Well, partner, I've come back to say again that I'm sorry you got banged up this way."

"It ain't the banging up of me," said the other gloomily. "That ain't what counts. It's what you've done to the whole…." Here he stopped, flushing.

"Banging up of the whole of what?" asked Two-Speed.

"Nothing," said the other.

"Nothing it is, then," said Two-Speed. "So long, partner."

"So long, Two-Speed."

III
"A NEW SIGHT FOR CONIFREY"

"IF FIGHTS WERE DOLLARS," SOLILOQUIZED TWO-SPEED Conifrey as the procession of wagons and horsemen dropped out of sight among the deeper hills, "I'd be rich. But the way things are framed up, a gent that does the fighting ain't got a thing on his side but bad dreams after all the work is over."

So, having fulfilled to the letter his promise to Ned Dolan that he would drift gradually out of the picture so that none of the cowpunchers could suspect that he was deserting them, he reined Simon around. The wise mustang tossed up his head and pressed his ears a little flatter along his neck. He knew that this turn to the rear meant a longer journey before he reached his next feed of barley. The spurs of his master touched his flanks. Two-Speed Conifrey never pricked deep with his spurs. The spurring was simply a reminder that once before they had fought out the battle together and that on another occasion the man had won. And he had won in such a fashion that Simon, the wise, never forgot. So he made the best of a bad proposition, presently, and trotted away among the hills at a steady dog-trot, just faster than a walk. That speed suited Conifrey. He liked to see the desert float around him slowly, slowly. He liked to see the hills approach with dignity and retire behind him again at a smoothly regulated gait. He liked to hear the soft and steady crunching of the hoofs in sand or gravel.

So he worked back to the scene of his encounter with the stranger. As he looked upon the place of conflict, for the first time his mind went back to the parting words of the other man. It was not for himself that he cared, apparently, but without him the whole affair would go to pot. What was the *whole affair?* Whom did it concern? What was the odd business that made a man bring a huge, electric torch into the desert and then camp among the hills with his knapsack under his head, as though waiting? For what could he be waiting?

There are too many mysteries among the mountains for the head of any lone cowpuncher. Two-Speed Conifrey, who had heard prospectors tell their yarns of mystery, their stories of haunted mines and wild adventures; Conifrey, who had swung far south and heard odd Indian tales in Indian tongues south of the

14

Rio Grande; Conifrey, who had lived and hunted and worked and fought through the mountains since his childhood, shrugged his shoulders and went on. Let the dead past bury its dead.

He came on rare hunter's luck in the late afternoon. A deer moved behind some shrubs. Conifrey had out his rifle in a trice and killed his game with a long shot. The rest of the afternoon and the evening he spent cleaning and skinning and cooking the meat. He would take only the skin with him and one meal in the stomach. The rest of the body must go to rejoice the buzzards and the coyotes. Yet the country that lay eastward ahead of him was new. He had never traveled in that district before, and he was determined that, if a famine march lay ahead of him, he would start it as well fortified as he could be. A more painstaking man would have carried a quarter with him. But Two-Speed Conifrey disliked such work. As usual, he preferred taking a chance to doing what might seem like work.

He had finished his long meal. His fire had died down to a glimmering. His dishes were tended to. And his cigarette was fuming busily between his lips. Looking west, the tall mountains rolled dim as smoke, only vaguely distinguishable where they blotted out the low-lying stars. He looked east of the valley, and there his attention focused on a swiftly winking light. Conifrey watched in quiet wonder. After dinner is not a period during which the brain functions smoothly and swiftly. He noted that the light worked with a peculiar rhythm. A short flash and then a longer one. A long and a short, then a quick jumble of shorts and longs too rapid for his eye.

He shook his head, made another smoke, and looked back to the light. It might be ten miles away. It might be

15

more. But what on earth made it wink in this curious fashion, just as the electric torch of the big stranger had winked against the shadows of the rock earlier in the day? The instant that similarity came to him he stood up with a muttered exclamation of surprise and interest. Now that he thought of it, the parallel was exact. The big stranger had said that the winking light meant words, words spelled out by symbols of light. Was this, then, part of the affair that he had "banged up" by disabling the stranger? Did that winking light to the east expect an answer from the opposite hills where he had had his fight? Was it for this that the stranger had been waiting patiently, delaying until the night should bring him his message?

That was logical enough. Two-Speed Conifrey made up his mind on the spur of the moment that he would get to that far-off, winking light and find out who was sending the message. Even as he came to this determination, the signaling, if it were indeed that, ceased. Conifrey took note with care of the conformation of the hills from among which the light had been flashing. And he took note, moreover, of the steady shining of a fixed star just above and beyond the point from which the light had shone.

After that, he saddled Simon swiftly. The darkness could not make his sure hands falter or stumble with the straps. A moment more, and he was riding east. No jogging trot satisfied him now, and Simon did not even attempt that slower pace. As though he knew that a night march must be a swift march, he stretched out his ugly head and swung at once into a steady lope. A wolf could hardly gallop with more frictionless ease than Simon as he rocked forward, putting the miles steadily behind him.

The hills grew constantly more sharply defined where their heads butted up among the stars. In a little while Conifrey had topped the first low ridge. Descending the farther slope, he noted that the guiding star was lost to him, but still he kept on at a steady pace. He had an inborn and well-trained sense of direction that constant practice had brought well nigh to the sharpness of an instinct.

So he came up the second slope and nearly ran into the house. The mud-gray walls melted into the night colors. Conifrey, with a grunt of surprise, reined Simon back and strained his eyes through the darkness to make sure of the outlines of the building. Now that he had seen it once, it became easy to make out the whole extent of the place. He was simply at the unlighted side of a dwelling of great size. Indeed, it was one of the largest homes Conifrey had ever seen, and he wondered at it. It was built after the Spanish-American school, with low walls of thick adobe and with deeply inset, tall, narrow windows. He could make out these details easily enough, and even by the starlight he could see that the house was finished, in point of workmanship, far better than any he had ever seen. All that side of the house was blank of light. Even the tower that, at one end, projected upward the height of another full story above the rest of the structure was devoid of even a lantern.

Conifrey could hear that murmur which is made of many voices blended by distance, and now he skirted around to the farther side. He did not simply turn the corner of the wall, but he doubled straight back on his tracks, and then rode around in a generous loop that brought him, eventually, toward the dwelling from the opposite direction. He found enough to reward his caution. The dwelling had been built on the extreme

17

western verge of the cultivated ground of the ranch. All to the east were tilled fields. Yes, water had been brought here in some manner. Perhaps great artesian wells had been sunk, and the water was brought to the surface by powerful pumps. At any rate, here it was. Through the dusk, Conifrey inhaled an indubitable proof in the heavy, sweet odor of alfalfa hay. When he squinted against the rolling skyline, he saw stack after stack swelling up from the ground, hundreds and hundreds of tons after the last mowing, now waiting to be baled.

To Conifrey it was a thing of wonder. He was used to naked desert, naked mountain ranges, where the cattle browsed industriously from one withered and sun-blighted tuft of bunch grass to the next. To him this wealth, pouring up from the ground, was a magic, an unexplainable, thing. It troubled him a little, and he looked carefully, suspiciously around him as a man will do when he is in strange country.

Here to the east of the ranch house were more signs of wealth. There was a tumble of barns and sheds, sweeping away from the house. There were corrals filled with mules and horses, not the undersize animals with which he was familiar, but great, long-legged, heavy animals, each capable of tugging a ton and a half in road work. And the odor of sweat from their day's work was still heavy as a vapor about them.

There were men at work here and there, throwing out hay from racks. What manner of rancher was this who could make his men work for him until the dark had come? He circled past lighted windows in the barns, and, inside, he had glimpses of other men at work, scraping collars or digging out padding to make a free place for sore shoulders or repairing broken places in the harness. One might have said that these were independent ranchers, each working for himself and not for the day's hire, but all of them were Mexicans. It was still more miraculous that such a leisure-loving people could be made to labor after this fashion.

These observations were made not in a glance but as Conifrey cautiously worked his way, as though through enemy's country, up toward the ranch house. He came at length to the house itself and dismounted under the shadow of a great, arched gate that opened upon a patio within—a patio of spacious lawns and a showering fountain and many lights, playing softly among the shadows. Conifrey was filled with awe, and he had hardly courage to hail a soft-footed servant hurrying across the patio.

"Hello, stranger," said Conifrey. "What's the chance of bunking here tonight?"

The man wheeled toward him, then came forward slowly, and raised the lantern he was carrying. He peered earnestly into the face of Conifrey.

"Wait here," he said at length, and disappeared into the house.

"And what sort of a house is this?" muttered Conifrey with a scowl that the night covered. "What sort of a place is this where they look at a gent that needs a bed like he was a snake?"

IV
"LAGRANGE, THE CRUEL"

THE DIFFICULTIES OF SECURING A LODGING WERE NOT yet over, however, for presently a tall man, dressed in white and with hair as blanched as his clothes, came out onto the patio and approached Conifrey. He stepped to the gate and paused there, looking keenly at the stranger.

"I am John Lagrange," he said at last.

"My name is Conifrey," said Two-Speed. "I'm glad to know you, Mister Lagrange."

"Thank you," said the other, but he acknowledged Conifrey's introduction with a nod instead of a handshake. "My man tells me that you wish to put up with us for the night?"

There formed in Two-Speed Conifrey's throat one of those drawling and infuriating retorts for which he was famous and that had led him, one after another, into his series of single combats. But he swallowed the speech before it was uttered. Indeed, the more difficult it seemed to win past all of these guards to the interior of the house, the more determined he was to continue his effort until he was successful

"That's what I want," said Conifrey. "The point is that I started from Lawson the other day...."

The man of the house raised his hand.

"Mister Conifrey," he said, "I am sure that you must have come a long distance and that you need shelter for the night. I see the signs of travel on your clothes and your horse, also." Here he stepped out from the gate a little where the light from the interior glowed clearly upon the down-headed form of Simon, with the dried sweat streaking his hide here and there. "Your horse, also," continued the other, nodding as though the picture of Simon were reassuring to him, "offers similar proofs. For such honest travelers, I am sure we can make a room and a welcome."

It seemed to Conifrey that there was an unnecessary emphasis upon the word *honest*, and again he had to swallow one of his irate impulses.

"All right," he said, "I'll put up my hoss and be right in."

"Not at all," said Lagrange. "I shall have your horse cared for."

Here he struck his hand lightly against a brazen bell that hung beside the gate. As the jangle died out, he turned his keen eyes upon Conifrey again. He seemed to be relenting from his former austerity.

"Mister Conifrey," he said, "you will wonder at the precautions with which I have surrounded my house. I can assure you that at one time my home stood open to the four winds, and every guest they blew into my precinct was doubly welcome." He paused, and still at every intermission in talk his glance took the opportunity to probe his guest more deeply. "That time is now long since past," he continued. "I have learned in a school that teaches by the whip...the whip." He repeated this word with a bitter and almost snarling emphasis. "What I have learned," he said, "is that every man one meets is a new man, and that, whereas one man is grateful for the good that is done him, another bites the hand that feeds him...like a dog...like a dog!" He changed his manner suddenly. "You are a stranger to this region?" he asked.

"Never rode through here before," said Two-Speed Conifrey.

"Otherwise," said Lagrange, "you would have known of me, and I dare say you would not have applied here for shelter. But, since you have come, you are very welcome." He turned and waved to a Mexican who now appeared behind him. "Take the gentleman's horse," he said, and indicated Simon with a gesture.

"Between you and me," said Conifrey, "I think that I'd better take care of my own hoss. He's sort of used to

21

my touch."

"Hurry," said Lagrange to the Mexican, who was holding back somewhat.

In dread, under the very eye of the master, the poor peon attempted to catch the bridle rein of Simon. As he reached, Simon reached also, with his long, yellow teeth. They clicked a fraction of an inch from the throat of the other, and the Mexican turned with a wailing yell and danced away through the gate. Simon did not follow but merely cocked an ear tentatively after the fugitive. Lagrange grew dark with anger.

"Pedro!" he called.

The peon came, trembling, into view once more.

"How long have you been in my service?"

"Eight years, *señor*, and my father before me, ten years, and his father before him…."

"You and your father need serve me no longer," said Lagrange. "There is no place in my house for a coward or for his father!"

Pedro, transfixed with horror, could only stammer. "But the mother, and my wife and our children…*señor*…what will become of them?"

"Have you been well paid and well cared for while you served me?"

"Yes, *señor*."

"Have I guaranteed your future?"

"No, *señor*."

"Then I tell you to go. By the morning let me find no trace of your tribe. Either be gone or else"—and here there was a gleam in the eye of Lagrange—"go at once and take charge of Mister Conifrey's horse."

Pedro, as he saw the cruel alternative that was offered him, quaked again. On the one hand was the tigerish mustang. On the other hand was the tigerish master. His trembling right hand rose. Upon his forehead and over his heart he made the sign of the cross. Plainly, he already felt the tearing teeth of Simon in his flesh, the stamping feet of the mustang upon his bones. But better this than to send his whole family—his mother, his father, his wife, his babies—into the world as beggars.

Conifrey was sickened by the spectacle. He stepped a little closer to Lagrange.

"That poor devil will be chawed up in a minute," he said. "Are you figuring on letting this go through?"

Lagrange turned on him a glittering eye.

"I could tell you a tale of a man who was not called back," he said, and he turned again to regard the approach of the Mexican to Simon.

The mustang had flattened both ears along his neck and watched the coming of the man with a devilish interest. Yet, it seemed to Conifrey that there was less wicked cruelty in the eye of the horse than in the eye of Lagrange himself as the master looked on at the approaching conflict. Still the Mexican with short and shorter steps, to be sure, kept straight on until it was plain that he was throwing himself away. And there rose in the mind of Conifrey the picture of a certain horse thief who, knowing the wonderful qualities of Simon, had attempted to steal that tireless horse during one night. His smashed and wrecked body had been found the next morning, and the muzzle and the fetlocks of Simon were red. He remembered that, and then he called out sharply. The Mexican stopped short, glad of the reprieve. Simon, in the very act of springing forward like a cat, halted and tossed up his head as though a stern hand had wrenched at the reins.

"Show me the way," said Two-Speed Conifrey to the Mexican. "I'll take care of this hoss if you'll show me where to put him. I'll see you later, Mister Lagrange."

The latter made no answer, but with his black brow he watched them go off together through the night.

Pedro, in the meantime, was pouring forth his thanks into the ear of Two-Speed Conifrey. He was not a coward, he assured Conifrey. No, for he had proved his courage more than once, with gun in hand or with knife in hand. And he would prove it again if the occasion arose. But he had one weakness, and that was for bad horses. In his childhood, he said, he had been thrown and trampled by an outlaw mustang, and since that time....

Conifrey let the words drift into his ear without giving them the slightest heed. He had heard the tale before, and he had heard it more than once. It was always the same. But, for that matter, even a brave man might well hesitate before approaching Simon, the terrible. After the mustang was put up, Pedro threw down a huge feed of excellent grain hay, then brought a heaping measure of oats. Simon was not used to such fare. Good enough for him were a few mouthfuls of moldy, old hay at the end of the most terrible day's march. Enough for him to be turned out to graze a meager bellyful on whatever sparse grass grew near his master's uncertain camp. Now he sniffed these unasked riches suspiciously, then buried his head in the good provender. Conifrey and Pedro stood back to smile at the exhibition.

"And what's wrong, friend, with the boss?" asked Conifrey suddenly of Pedro.

The latter opened his eyes wide, then gave the courteous retort of all Latin peoples. He shrugged his shoulders and made a gesture of ignorance.

"But," insisted Conifrey, "why should a gent want to

see you chewed up by a strange hoss? This Simon hoss of mine is a regular man-killer. I seen one gent all mashed to a pulp. He didn't have no face left at all when Simon got through with him. Same thing might have happened to you, if you don't mind me talking straight to you."

Pedro closed his eyes and quivered from head to foot in dread. Then he glanced uneasily over his shoulder. "You ask me, *señor*, why he should wish to see me beaten under those hoofs?"

"Right." Conifrey nodded.

"When a man has been starved, *señor*," whispered Pedro, "is he not glad enough to see other people hungry?"

"Eh?" said Two-Speed Conifrey. "Now what d'you mean by that?"

"If a dog bites a man," whispered Pedro, "does not the man hate all dogs ever after?"

And with this enigmatic rejoinder, he came to a silence and would say no more, no matter how Conifrey tried to persuade him. But it was plainly to be seen that, though he dreaded his stern master, he did not hate him. He feared him, but he half sympathized with even the cruelty from which he himself had almost suffered.

V
"LOCKED IN"

LAGRANGE WAS GONE WHEN THEY RETURNED TO THE house, but another Mexican servant met them with the word that the master regretted a sudden necessity had taken him away for the moment on business, and that he must leave the escorting of the guest to a room to one of his servants.

To Conifrey it was the keenest of disappointments. He had been hoping against hope that in another interview with old Lagrange he might be able to come to some clue, no matter how slight, that would help him toward an understanding of this strange man. But he could only follow his guide to a room on the side of the patio, a spacious room where he was asked if he could think of anything that would make him rest more easily during the night? He could think of one thing, indeed, and that was an opportunity for five minutes' uninterrupted talk with Lagrange, but he recognized the futility of asking the impossible. He started at once making ready for bed.

Those preparations went no further than the removing of his boots. When that was done, he sank into a chair near the window and fell into a brown study. There was a rose garden beyond the window. Delicate scents poured through to him, but, when he attempted to lean out to inhale the perfume more freely, he found that his way was blocked. Perhaps, in the old days, when this great house was first built, there had been a need for a thousand precautions. At any rate, the window was guarded by a criss-crossing of thick iron bars, the roots of which were sunk in the adobe. He tried those bars separately, wrenching at them with all the strength that lay in his long, sinewy muscles, but he could not budge one of them. He could not evoke a single groan of loose iron against its holding mortar.

He sat down in the chair and pondered the events of this singular day. The fight with the big man in the pass had not been so unusual. There was something about Two-Speed Conifrey's manner that readily provoked fights. He seemed to carry about with him a red flag that challenged other men in battle. But all that had followed the fight had been strange, indeed. It was as unusual as was the fragrance of those roses in the life of Conifrey. He decided that he could not sleep. His brain was far too active. He must take another turn through the patio and listen to the whispering of the fountain. Then, after a look at the stars and a few deep breaths, he might be able to sink to sleep.

He put on his boots again, but, when he tried the outer door of his room, he found to his amazement that it was locked on the outside. Conifrey stepped back with the hair pricking on his head. There was no real reason for this sudden burst of fear. It might have been mere accident that had caused the outer bolt to fall into place when the servant closed the door after him. Suppose he were to call out and raise an alarm?

He decided at once that this would be folly. If Lagrange had some reason for wishing to imprison him in this room, he would endanger himself the more by letting the others know that he was aware of his imprisonment. If he remained quiet in his place, the danger would blow over. Certainly, Lagrange could have no real reason for desiring to injure him. It was only to circumscribe his movements during the night that the door had been locked. Yet, Conifrey could not be sure. Other possibilities were suggested. The wild and over bright eye of the old man, his quick and explosive temper, the singular passion with which he spoke—these things surely pointed toward irrationality. And it was one of the features of insanity that the afflicted man entertained a suspicious hatred for those who came near him if there were anything unusual about them. And might not the rich rancher be in that condition?

His wealth, his isolation here among the Mexican

ranch hands, would have secured him from arrest and confinement as a public menace. The more Two-Speed Conifrey thought of it, the more sure he became. A man with such a house and such wealth at his disposal should have a flood of relatives, guests, pouring that spacious patio full of music, of laughter, and the pleasant sounds of voices instead of that silence of which Conifrey had been aware from the first.

To Conifrey, listening now with his head raised intently, it seemed that there was something terrible in the quiet that lay over the whole place. Was it, indeed, possible that so little sound could come from all those scores of horses and mules he had seen not so long before? Silence lay like a weight over the ranch of Lagrange. And Conifrey, at a faint noise near his window, whirled to face that direction with his eyes dilated, his fingers working stiffly over the butt of his gun. Nothing was there. A gust of wind had merely blown a branch of a tall rose tree against the bars of the window. Or had the shadowy silhouette of a man actually stood close before those bars just the instant before, watching the prisoner, grinning in at him?

Conifrey blinked and gasped. This siege of quiet terror was becoming too much for him. The next alarm made him jerk a revolver out of the holster and drop to his knees, swinging the weapon up above his head, ready to shoot and shoot to kill. For he had heard from the ceiling just above, the distinct sound of a lock clicking. It was not the lock of a door closing over him in a second story. It was a noise of a lock within the floor. Of that he was certain.

No wonder, then, that he backed away to a corner of the room and waited. If only the room were dark. But, if they chose, they could strike him down from the window. Or, on the opening of a trap in the middle of the ceiling, they could strike him at will from the shadows beyond that aperture.

But perhaps all of this was only a ghastly game. Perhaps that white-haired, keened-eyed, old man, quite mad, indeed, stole about through the house, and with those stealthy and ominous noises threw his guest into a nightmare of fear and, in the meantime, watched and grinned from safety. Somehow, this thought was yet more horrible than the dread of actual danger. The fear of fear for its own sake became most appalling. But Two-Speed Conifrey finally made himself walk out in the center of the floor, from which point he stared up at the ceiling. He could make out the outline of the trap door now. It was a faint crack, very dimly traceable through the plaster. Only a master craftsman could have joined the surfaces so deftly. The sight of the shadow of a door excited Conifrey to determined action at once. Trap doors cunningly concealed in ceilings could not be explained away so easily as the careless locking of a guest's door from the outside.

He rolled back his bed. He climbed on the foot of it until, with his feet resting on the rail, he found that his hands could press against the plaster above his head. Then he started to work with his knife, first sinking a deep trench in the plaster all around the faint crack that suggested the presence of the door. Next he began to pry away the plaster itself. It was ruthless work, and, if he found nothing, it would be difficult, indeed, to apologize to Lagrange the next morning. But Conifrey had little thought for Lagrange or the morning. He was too busy digging toward the heart of the odd, little mystery into which he had inadvertently stepped. Now the plaster peeled away readily and eventually exposed a smooth surface beneath, not of laths but of carefully joined boards not more than two inches in width—singular material for the ceiling of a room. It would have done for a flooring.

He cleared the remaining plaster hastily, throwing down the lumps, as he brought them away, onto the bed where the sound of the fall was muffled. What he eventually saw was exactly what he had surmised at the moment when he first glimpsed the crack—what was revealed to him was a solidly built door that had been sunk into the ceiling. With both hands he pressed up against it. The bed creaked beneath the strain, but that was the only result. He spread out his feet, and, having secured a better purchase, he strained up with all his might. There was a groan, and then a sound of wood splintering underfoot. Then above him he began to get results. The panel against which he was thrusting with all his force now gave a little, sagged, and with a sudden lurch gave way altogether. The trap door shot up with a faint scrape of metal against metal. The release from the pressure, coming so quickly, threw Conifrey off balance. He toppled to the floor, but he managed to check himself and land lightly. When he looked up through the square opening, he saw the midnight blue of the sky and the pale twinkling of a dozen stars.

It was a vast relief to Conifrey. Had that opening looked up into nothingness of black—had there been a range of low attic above his room—he would have felt that the black gap was a veritable cannon's mouth yawning toward him. But the stars—all at once he could have laughed at the danger around him. He was free. He was in his own country under the stars.

Now he started toward the aperture. Once more he clamored onto the foot of the bed, but this time he hooked his hands on the edge of the hole and drew himself carefully up. It was ticklish work, for there was barely enough room for his shoulders to squeeze through. But he managed it, and presently he had drawn himself up and stood on the roof of the mansion. Mansion, indeed, it was. He had never realized its size so keenly as he did now that he was on top of it and could examine the roof line. Every portion of that roof was covered with a green and flourishing garden, with little paths winding here and there, and with even a little fountain tossed up at one side, showering a delicate outline of spray across the faces of the stars.

As for the trap door, it had risen in the center of a path paved with red flagstones. Conifrey closed the door beneath him. It would be a luckless moment if he ever returned to that cunningly contrived prison. And then, for the first time, it occurred to him that, if he had really been a guarded prisoner, he could never have escaped so easily.

VI
"RICHARD MASON ARRIVES"

FOR THE MOMENT THE THOUGHT MADE CONIFREY blush to the very eyes. He recovered some of his equilibrium when he recalled the manner in which the door to the roof had been locked above him. That click of the closing lock had certainly come from this trap door, the bolt of which he had just forced up through the tiling and so broken his way to escape. No matter for what reason, Lagrange had seen fit to close his guest behind a locked door, a barred window, and he had even gone so far as to see to the locking of the secret door to the roof. As he reviewed these details, Conifrey lost the embarrassment that had, for a time, made his face hot. He had taken one step toward freedom. Now to follow those first steps with others and regain, finally, the back of tireless Simon and the range of the open mountains that meant home to them both.

But here a sudden play of light and voices, approaching the patio on the farther side of the house, made him steal to the edge of the roof. There was a fence along the roof's edge built as a sort of parapet. Behind this he knelt and peered anxiously into the patio itself. All lights were out now in the enclosure. It was black as a deep well until a yellow shaft from a lantern splashed on a pillar beside the gate. Then more light followed. Men came out to the arcade, surrounding the patio, men with lanterns that were soft blurs of light. A gradual radiance filled the little court, and, finally, into this gathered light stepped the man. A jumble of horses had been halted just outside the gate. There were the voices and the clinking spurs of men, dismounting, until at last two big Mexicans, armed with revolvers in their hands, stepped inside the gate and hastily faced back. After them he came. He was not more than twenty-five, perhaps, and he was the finest-appearing man that Conifrey had ever seen. Tall, magnificently built, wide-shouldered, slender-hipped, in spite of his hands tied behind him, he walked with the high head of a conqueror. Bound and guarded as he was, he had all the manner of the victor, and he seemed more formidable without a weapon than any two of the formidable train that now pressed in at his back.

Conifrey had passed through a wild series of adventures in his lifetime. But he had never seen, he was sure, such an aggregation assembled. They were mostly Mexicans, like the rest of the servants of

Lagrange. But these were not the humble-minded peons such as Conifrey had already seen around the ranch. These were huge fellows. There was hardly a one of them under the romantic height of six feet. Most were well above that figure. They were well nigh pure Indian in blood, and they were well nigh pure Indian in the little thrill of fear and aversion they inspired in Two-Speed Conifrey.

He no longer regretted that he had broken so rudely from his room. He was only sorry that he had stayed to look at this scene, instead of making with all haste across the desert. Yet he could not leave now. A fire of curiosity consumed him. *Who was this handsome youth? For what crime was he brought here? At whose command had he been apprehended?*

As though to answer the last question, at this instant a door on the farther side of the patio opened, and the silver-haired form of Lagrange advanced toward the center of the court. Two servants accompanied him, each so eager to light the way that their lifted lanterns shone full upon the face of Lagrange himself, and thereby Conifrey could examine him closely. What he saw was a face fused with rage and joy combined. The old man walked with his head thrown back a little and his raised face gleaming. He advanced straight to the other. The prisoner halted to await this meeting. The guards stood back in a thick circle to watch, and the two who had apparently been most closely assigned to him took him, one by either arm, and jabbed the muzzles of their revolvers into his ribs.

What had he done? What was his peculiar prowess which could fill so many armed and dangerous men with fear they did not trust to the ropes that held his hands or to their own numbers or weapons?

Lagrange, now, had come to a halt. One hand was dropped upon his hip. The other caressed his chin slowly.

"And so, Richard," he said, "at last we meet, after so many efforts on my part."

"You have spent money and men enough," said Richard in a clear, steady voice whose sound affected Conifrey at once with sympathy and admiration. "You have me here at last. I suppose I may say that you've paid the price for me."

"For a dozen like you!" exclaimed Lagrange, his face suddenly suffused with passion. "I have paid the price of ten good men rather than one paltry boy."

Richard bowed as though an honor had been conferred upon him. "But, as a matter of fact," he said, "these good fellows of yours, these neat-handed cutthroats and assassins, have treated me all the way to your house as though I were ten men, instead, as you say, of being one boy."

Lagrange nodded. He was watching Richard with the most intent interest. Now, at a signal of his lifted finger, the light bearers raised their lanterns so that a stronger flood of light fell upon Richard's face. Still Lagrange studied his prisoner calmly, with a sort of detached, impersonal interest.

"The old Mason blood is in you," he said. "It is undiminished. Time does not rust it away. The years have not changed it, I see." He paused, and in a softer voice he went on: "I can almost see and hear Tom Mason standing before me in his youth...."

"A youth that you ruined," interrupted Richard Mason.

Lagrange raised his hand, perhaps because he did not care to bring up such a subject before so many listeners, or perhaps he had already tired of this strange meeting.

"You will give me your word," he said, "that you will not attempt escape."

"And then?" suggested Mason.

"And then these ropes will be removed from your hands."

"Ah?"

"Yes, Richard, I shall hold you with no stronger bond than your simple honor."

The younger man bowed his head. When he raised it, it was to say: "If I give my word, shall I also have the liberty to see her...to see Beatrice?"

Lagrange rubbed his hands together. "You hark back so far toward the past?" he said with a chuckle. "Good Lord, my boy, have you been fool enough to build on that chance meeting and a foolish girl's enthusiasm of a single week?"

It seemed to Conifrey that Richard turned pale.

"A foolish enthusiasm of a single week," he echoed. "Very well...perhaps it was no more than that."

"Perhaps? Do you actually doubt?" Lagrange asked and laughed. "Why, my boy, if she were truly interested, why should she not be here? My Beatrice, full of storm and fire...she should be here on her knees as the old romances will have it. She should be weeping and begging for your life. But where is she, Dick? Where is she?"

"She is a hundred miles from here."

"Wrong...very wrong! She is in this very house."

"And at liberty to go where she pleases?"

"Do you think I am the jailer of my own daughter?"

"Then," said Richard Mason, "I shall never again trust the word of a human being if she has forgotten me."

"A bitter speech," said Lagrange, "and a very youthful one. But, shall I have your word not to attempt an escape, Richard?"

"You have my word," said Richard. "Why should I wish to?"

Lagrange stepped back with a faint exclamation of satisfaction.

"Untie the ropes," he called fiercely to his servants. "Do you treat white men like dogs?"

It was the fury of exultation rather than mere anger. But the ropes were hastily torn from the wrists of the prisoner. He shrugged his shoulders, stretched his strong arms, then turned and looked at his guards. They shrank under his glance. And Two-Speed Conifrey saw their guns jerk up and saw the lantern light quiver on their uncertain barrels. Plainly they feared this young fellow as though he were an incarnation of the devil himself.

Who was Richard Mason? And what had Richard Mason done? And by what authority did Lagrange send out his men and use his money to hunt down this victim? Why was it, again, that Richard Mason so quietly accepted his fate as though it were his due? But Conifrey could not yet resign himself to the delightful torment of striving to solve the problem. His eyes and his ears were too busy drinking in the scene below.

"Will you have dinner?" inquired Lagrange.

"No," replied Richard Mason.

"After all this riding, you are not hungry?"

Mason turned and actually smiled into the face of his captor. "I am not in the mood for eating," he said.

Lagrange nodded. "Put up your guns," he said to the guards. "The word of this man is better than bonds of steel. He will not attempt to escape."

Reluctantly, very slowly, the revolvers disappeared

into the black leather of the holsters. As the weapons were put up, the big fellows shrank farther and farther away from their captive. Plainly, they wanted no more business with him upon such even terms as hand to hand.

"This way, then," said Lagrange, and he and Richard Mason stepped out of view into the steep shadow that dropped like a curtain from the arcade. For another moment, Conifrey pored over the busy figures in the court where they swirled together like leaves in pools of wind, all talking and gesticulating at once.

Men and women, the house servants of Lagrange, slipped out and formed in circles around the big, harsh-featured cavalrymen, with the dust of their journey powdered thick over their red bandannas. They became busy rolling cigarettes. They accepted drinks and tidbits from the hands of their admirers. And, little by little, they consented to unbend. They began to tell details of the chase that had resulted in the capture of a prize so very great, apparently, that every man of them found honor enough for himself without robbing a companion.

Conifrey strained his ears. Here was his chance to make out the mystery, or at least a large portion of it. But he could not hear clearly enough to catch any sustained sentences. There was only a jumbled jargon. Most of it was in Spanish, too. He understood something of that language, to be sure, but an excited Mexican can talk more swiftly than the beat of the wings of a wild duck. There was only enough to tantalize the mind of Conifrey as he strove to bind together into logical meanings a fragment caught up here, caught up there, from the sea of swiftly changing talk that filled the courtyard. At length he gave up in disgust. Let the dead past bury its dead. It was not for

37

him to delve into the affairs of others whom he did not know.

He crossed to the opposite side of the house, and there, looking up to the tower on his right, he saw that from the upper window a long and powerful light was stabbing out toward the westward in pulses, quick and irregular pulses such as those he himself had seen from the hollow hand of the valley earlier in the evening.

VII
"TWO-SPEED INVESTIGATES"

ALL THOUGHT OF HIS OWN ESCAPE FROM THIS singular house at once left his mind. For a time he stared up, fascinated, to the pulsing of the light in the dark of the night. Surely, here was a ray that was searching for a response from the west, such a response as the stranger of the pass could have flashed back with his light, spelling out letters and words. Conifrey hesitated.

Down yonder was a window ledge. It was child's play to drop to it, thence to the ground. But to linger in this odd house might mean peril of the most deadly kind. That instant of hesitation was all. In another moment he was stealing down along the edge of the roof. All could not have been more comfortably arranged to assist in his progress. There was a narrow, decorative balcony of soft stone swinging around the side of the tower and directly beneath the window that looked toward the west. Onto this balcony he stepped. He stole along it, careful of noise, until he reached the black aperture of the window, and through this he cautiously peeked. All he could see was the great, round circle of glass, all ablaze with light. It was winking away merrily, sending out its rapid succession of long and short flashes in such a manner that Conifrey was dazed by them.

He drew back to consider. There was no light in that tower room. For all he knew, there might be a dozen people lurking there. He searched the western hills toward which the signal was being directed. But there was the wink of no answering light out yonder. He made up his mind. Someone from this place was striving in vain to get in touch with the man whom he had shot earlier in the day. *Was it not possible that the signaler who apparently was working from covert in this little tower room was, in fact, an enemy to the powers that were in the house? But how could he find out?*

To call out or to show himself foolishly would probably be to invite a Forty-Five caliber slug crashing into his body. So he acted on the spur of the moment with the first wild thought that darted into his head, as he usually had acted in crises throughout his life. He caught the ledge of the window sill. He half leaped and half hurled his body through the open window, his arms spread wide, his head down. He heard a strangely soft and shrill cry from before him. Then his shoulder crushed into a body that toppled before him.

Instinct taught the flying hand of Two-Speed Conifrey to find the throat of the man in the dark. His other hand caught up the fallen electric torch, and he shone its current of light into the face of—a girl!

Conifrey pitched to his feet as though he had been hurled back by a tremendous blow in the face. The girl leaped up to confront him with a wicked little automatic, glittering in her hand. The gleam of light on the metal of the gun was not a whit less ominous than the angry glistening of her eyes.

As for Two-Speed Conifrey, there had been many

times in his life when he found the burden of work more than he cared to undertake, but this was the first time in his life that he had ever stood aghast in the middle of a fight, unable to stir hand or foot, mentally paralyzed by the mere sight of his foeman. Had the girl been ten men, and each of the ten armed, Two-Speed Conifrey could not have been rendered more thoroughly helpless.

"Put up your hands!" gasped the girl.

He obeyed, blinking at her.

"Get into that corner!"

He backed obediently into the designated position.

"Tell me what you are doing here."

"Lady, just…just looking around," stammered Conifrey.

"You lie to me!" she said, still furious, and she stepped closer to him.

He had seen other women of the mountains handle guns before, but none who used a weapon with such absolute familiarity and ease. She held her gun like a man held one; she held it half carelessly as an expert may do. But the glance of Conifrey was not centered on the mouth of the gun as she advanced. He was fascinated by the face that terror and the shock of surprise had made snow white the moment before, and into which the color was now suddenly flooding.

"You were sent by John Lagrange," she cried.

He shook his head.

"You were," she insisted. "You're the man he's had spying on me all these days. And now that I've caught you…!"

She paused, but the pause came from her inability to make an end that would be terrible enough for the presumed spy.

"Lady," he said, "I'm telling you the truth."

"You coward," she answered. "You coward, to hound a helpless woman as you've hounded me."

A faint smile twitched at the lips of Conifrey.

"Do you dare to laugh at me...to my face?" she asked fiercely.

"I couldn't help smiling, ma'am," said Two-Speed, "when you called yourself helpless. You see, you don't no ways look the part."

Slowly, she lowered the gun. A look of bewilderment passed over her face. "No," she said, "you aren't the type that John Lagrange uses for his errands. But who are you?"

"My name's Conifrey," he said.

"Conifrey? I've never heard it. But...you may lower your hands, though I warn you I'm watching every moment."

"Thank you, ma'am," said Two-Speed Conifrey.

His memory flashed back to a score of famous battles in the past. What one of those warriors of fist and knife and gun would have believed their eyes if they had been able to look in and see him cornered by this mere child?

She was rubbing her throat meditatively. There was a rosy flush on the delicate skin where the long fingers of Two-Speed Conifrey had seized her and crushed her to the floor.

"I'm sure sorry for mussing you up this way," he apologized.

She shrugged her shoulders. Her own physical hurts were forgotten. Her eyes were busy with the problem of this stranger and what he meant by being here.

"You've come here broke, intending to hunt through the house and pick up what you could," she said. "You saw a woman in this room, and you thought that it would be easier to begin with her than with a man."

Conifrey flushed darkly to the eyes. "D'you really think that?" he asked.

She hesitated again. It was plain that she was by no means sure of him.

"No," she confessed frankly at last, "I'm not sure. But then, who on earth are you, and why did you jump through that window at me?"

"I was leaving this house," said Conifrey, "but, when I seen that signal of yours, playing out of the window, I made up my mind that I'd got to see who was working it. I come up to the window and looked through. The inside was plumb black on account of the brightness of that signal light. I was tolerable sure that there was something queer about it on account of something that had happened earlier in the day. If I showed myself and asked a question, I figured that I'd get a slug through the brain. So I thought I'd take a dive tackle. And I done it. But when I seen that it was a girl...." He shrugged his shoulders. "I just made a misplay, lady, and I'll be going on my way, if you'll let me."

"Stay where you are!" she commanded eagerly. "What was the other thing you saw today?"

While he answered, he kept the most scrupulously careful watch upon her. "Up yonder in the hills," he said, "there's a place where a couple of crests come up beside the top of a little plateau. It looks a pile like the top of a mule's head and ears."

She nodded, curious, but apparently feeling no interest in the place he had named.

"I came up there," said Two-Speed Conifrey, "figuring that I'd cut right through to the other side because I was in a hurry, but up there was a gent that seemed like he was inclined to argue about nothing in particular and everything in general. Him and me had a falling out that led to downright trouble, and in the end, I'm sorry to say, he went down with a slug through his right arm."

She shook her head. "But what has that got to do with this little affair of the electric light and the signals you say I have been sending…which, of course, is absurd."

"Because the gent up there in the hills had another great big torch like yours. Threw a light like the headlight on a train, pretty near."

"Oh!" cried the girl.

She was seriously interested now, to be sure. Her eyes shone at him with terror and bewilderment.

"Tell me what he was like."

"Big," said Conifrey, "and dark-eyed and fine-looking, of the sort…."

But there was no need to go further. She had cried out softly in wonder and dismay.

"But that was Chuck Kennedy."

"Was that his name?"

"You've never heard of him?"

"I disremember hearing of him. This range is sort of south of where I mostly ride."

"But everyone's heard of Kennedy. Why, he's never been beaten.… I know…I know! You caught him at some cowardly advantage…."

Conifrey flushed more deeply than ever and stiffened.

"But he can't have been shot. Oh, I picked him because I knew that nothing could budge him from the place…not twenty men. And now…now…."

She threw away all the advantage that had rested with her. She raised her hands to her head and broke into tears, not the soft and easy weeping of a woman, but a heart-racking abandon of grief that shook her body from head to foot, like the despair and anguish of a strong man.

43

VIII
"WITH A PRICE ON HIS HEAD"

CONIFREY WAS AMAZED. AND, BEING AMAZED, HE naturally drew out the makings for a cigarette. He had rolled his smoke and lighted it before she seemed to realize that she had given up her captured man. She started erect with the tears still streaming down her face and jerked up her gun once more to take command of the situation. But then she saw that Conifrey was quietly watching her, smoking, with his gun hanging peaceably in its holster. She put up her own weapon with a gesture of despair.

"Then everything is lost," she moaned. "Everything is helpless and hopeless. And it's because of you...." She struck her hands together, then tore them apart in an agony of grief. "But, after that, what brought you here? Oh, don't tell me that you made Chuck confess that...." She stopped, the dreadful thought choking her.

"He didn't say a word," said Conifrey. "He was plumb game. When I camped down in the hollow, I looked up here and I saw the winking of a light. It looked the way his light had flicked against the rock in the shadow when he was practicing. I got curious and came on here. I met Lagrange. He talked sort of queer to me, but he put me up. And, after I got in my room, I found that they'd bolted the outer door. It got me sort of excited. I'm a gent that likes the open, d'you see? So I come up through a trap door in the roof, and here I am. I seen a procession coming in with the gent they call Richard Mason...."

"You saw Dick. You saw Dick," she breathed.

"Might it be," said Conifrey, deep in thought, "that your name is Beatrice?"

"Yes. And poor Dick…he asked for me?"

"He did."

"What did they tell him?"

"That he didn't amount to much in your life. That you were sort of tired of the idea of him. Y'understand?"

She leaned against the wall near the window, very pale, apparently half faint.

"What did he say to that?" she whispered at length.

"Not much," said Conifrey. "He just lowered his head, and they walked out of my sight."

She drew a sobbing breath. "Oh, how he must hate me…how he must despise me," she said at last.

"Speaking personal," said Conifrey, "I've got to say that he didn't act like he hated you none too much. I sort of figure him with reverse English on that idea."

Suddenly she brushed past him, half running toward the door.

"Ma'am," said Conifrey, slipping in before her, "can you give me the low-down on this here proposition, figuring that maybe I might be of some sort of use to you before you get through with the game?"

"You? You can't help me. No, no, no. No one man can help me. But I had intended that thirty fighters should come. My message would have brought them."

"Is that the message you've been trying to send out of this tower window to Chuck over yonder in the hills? And was he to sort of relay it along to a place where the men would've been ready…?"

"Yes, yes. But don't stop me. I must go to him."

"Suppose that a fast rider was to leave the house now and start…."

"Could he bring back riders before dawn?"

"Dawn?"

"Yes, dawn. The finest man who ever rode a horse

through these mountains will be dead before morning. Dick…poor Dick…will be dead."

"Wait," insisted Conifrey. "Something can be done. There's something I can do."

"Save your own life," said the girl. "The devil himself lives in this house. If you have a horse, go get into the saddle, ride until the horse drops dead under you. Take another and ride again. Speak to no man of what you've seen or heard. And so you may save yourself, but twenty like you could not save Dick Mason from what will happen before the morning."

She was gone. She had twitched the door open and was gone with a swift clicking of heels and a whispering of skirts down the stairs. Conifrey took a pace or two in pursuit, but then he drew back. There was no use trying to force his help upon her if she did not want him. So he stood in the dark with the picture of her growing brighter and brighter in his mind's eye. There was no other like her. There never had been another like her. In all the infinite years to come, there would never be another to fit into her place. Conifrey, dim-eyed and with bent head, pondered. *How perfectly she loved this Richard Mason.* There was a jealous pang in Conifrey's heart as he thought of it. *Why not wait until the morning came and young Dick Mason has passed beyond this world and out of the ken of the girl forever?*

With that, there arose the picture of Mason as he had walked across the patio with his head so high, his eye so bright, and his hands bound behind his back. Surely, there was a man among men. It lifted the very soul of Conifrey to think of him. And surely, too, there was a man with the voice and the carriage and the mien and the face to win a girl's heart, even such a girl as this lovely Beatrice. In contrast, he summoned up the

46

familiar picture of his own face—lean and brown and ugly of feature. Of what use was it for him to sigh? He gritted his teeth. He called himself a nameless idiot. Having done this, he managed to breathe more freely.

What should he do now? Richard Mason was to die before morning. And, as one brave man feels for another, Conifrey felt for the doomed one. As a curious mind yearns to get at the shadowy heart of a secret, so the mind of Two-Speed Conifrey fairly ached with an anguish of desire to investigate when he thought of the mystery that had drawn him this far. The wise thing, doubtless, was to take the advice of the girl and ride as fast and as far from this haunted ranch as horseflesh would carry him. That being the logical thing, what more natural for Two-Speed Conifrey than deliberately to reopen the door through which the girl had disappeared. He eyed for an instant the black well of the stairway beneath him. Then he started down in pursuit—not of her alone, but of the well-being of Dick Mason, and, above all, he went upon the trail of the mystery of the Lagrange Ranch.

The stairway was a narrow and winding affair, circling elusively back on itself again and again. It was a noisy staircase as well. But Conifrey went down as noiselessly as the underside of a snake slides over polished stone. He reached a door. He sensed its presence in the darkness and put out a hand in time to avoid crashing into it. That door, when he turned the knob, opened upon a lighted hall. Conifrey, when a single shaft of the outer brilliance struck into the darkness where he stood, became as cautious as a wolf poaching in a corral filled with colts and the man scent along the fences. Then he let the door fall open as slowly as it would have moved had the catch of the lock

47

slipped and a draft fanned it ajar. Finally, it had reached a width of eight inches. From this aperture he could reconnoiter. The door opened upon a perfectly blank and empty hallway. The walls were painted creamy white. Upon the floor were no coverings. Truly, it would be a noisy place to investigate. In the darkness, Conifrey pulled off his boots. The stockinged feet would be safer—far safer.

At length, he stepped out, freely, boldly, and cast an imperious glance up and down the hall. There was no one in sight, just as he had been led to believe by his reconnaissance. On the opposite side of the hall, at a distance of some paces to the right, there was a door that opened upon a room filled with greenery—a sort of semi-indoor garden or green room. This he decided to make the goal of his next trip and started, therefore, toward it. He had hardly taken the first step to cross the hall when he heard a heavy hand fall on the lock of a door nearby and knew that he would be discovered before he could possibly reach the refuge he had picked out for himself. Conifrey leaped back. He was several strides away from the door out of which he had come. Otherwise, he would have retreated through that opening. But, as it was, he had only a shallow niche against which to flatten himself, a scant six inches of projecting wall to shelter him. The idea was ridiculous enough to make him grind his teeth. It was one thing to be caught. It was another to be caught playing the trick of a silly child.

For a moment the man who had opened the door at the end of the hall did not enter. He paused there, listening to a companion, who was saying in Spanish: "Go quietly. Tell no one what you are hunting for. But try to find the *gringo*. If you can catch him and bring him back safely, the master will give you a hundred dollars in gold and a new horse…that chestnut you wish for your own. But bring him back with a safe skin if you can."

"No other way?" asked the man at the door.

"Another way…yes," said the man who was repeating the order. "But by the other way you get only fifty dollars and no horse. Hurry now, *amigo*. Search everywhere through the house. There are small chances of catching the *gringo*. He is probably gone. He knows something, and he has gone to tell. I myself saw his empty room and the hole he made in the roof. The dog is strong as a bull. *¡Adiós!*"

The door closed. The first man turned down the hall. Conifrey saw that it was one of those big-shouldered Mexicans who had formed the escort of Dick Mason when the latter had been brought into the patio under guard. The big fellow advanced slowly, his head bent, his thoughts perhaps on the hundred dollars he hoped to spend rather than a dream that his goal might be so near to him. He came close. Conifrey dared not breathe. He was near—yes, he was passing—and now Conifrey saw the big fellow suddenly stop, gasp, and whirl toward him, reaching for a gun at the same instant.

IX
"WHILE CONIFREY LISTENED"

IT WAS WITHOUT EVEN A HAND EXTENDED THAT Conifrey leaped. With legs thrusting against the floor and hands pushing out from the wall, he fairly cast himself through the air at the big Mexican. Twisting sidewise as he flew, he gave his shoulder to the chest of the other. Down went the Mexican with a gasping cry of terror and surprise. The gun that he had torn from his holster spun, clattering across the floor. His head, as he fell, struck with a loud click against the stones of the floor. It would be more than a few seconds before that hero regained his feet, Conifrey was sure, and, since he felt that he had disarmed his man, he himself rolled cat-like to his stockinged feet and darted away through the open door that led into the green room.

But the bones and the head of that Mexican seemed to be made of a most flexible and durable substance. A shock that would have half killed a normal man had no effect upon him except to raise a yell from his lips that split through the ears of Conifrey like a keen knife's edge. And a knife itself followed. There was a twitch at Conifrey's shirt. Past his lowered head darted a long-bladed weapon. Conifrey, as he sped through the green room door, glanced back and saw that the other was on his knees, to which he had risen in his eagerness to drive the knife home. That was all Conifrey saw of him. The wall shut out his view from that point, but the wild cry of the Mexican followed him—vivid as a betrayed shaft of light that pointed out his flight.

Others had heard the alarm. Doors were opening and slamming. Padding footfalls, or the click of riding boots, scurried here and there. Men were shouting to one another. And Conifrey looked around him for a means of escape. He knew that this was the finishing touch. It might well have been, as he could see now in retrospect, that Lagrange had locked his guest in the room simply so that guest might not be able to see anything of what happened in the house during the night. But now that Conifrey was known to be loose, Lagrange had offered a reward for his apprehension—a large reward for the living captive—a small reward for the dead body. What manner of man was this Lagrange, who made laws of his own and placed prices upon the heads of men as though they were outlaws fit to be hunted?

There was no exit to that green room other than the door through which Conifrey had come. He tried the curving side of green glass. It was of solid slabs, very thick. He turned, looking for an instrument with which he could break a way out, and his eye lighted on a little, stone bench. At the same time the forms of two Mexicans burst into the green room. The rewards they had been promised had made them frantic and careless of life. In their headlong eagerness, they collided and stuck in the entrance, shoulder to shoulder. In that instant, Conifrey had his revolver out. He aimed carefully. His first bullet twitched the hat from the head of one and left the long hair streaming wildly. His second chunk of lead took a piece out of the corner of the adobe wall and sent it crashing into the face of the other man. But so swiftly were those two shots placed that both men recoiled as one, with yells of surprise and terror. For a moment, no doubt, as Conifrey watched them topple backward, they would think themselves no better than dead.

He caught up the stone bench he had noted a moment before. It was a good hundred pounds in weight, but in the lean and sinewy arms of Conifrey it was a small thing. He whirled it and crashed it into the side of the green room. It knocked out a solid wooden rib with its impetus and tore out two huge sections of the glass.

Outside, Conifrey peered into an alley between the edge of the house and a tall garden wall. It was lit by the stars and a yellow shaft of lamplight, falling through one of the open windows and spilling in a splash of orange upon the painted surface of the wall opposite.

That open alley of garden ran for a considerable distance, then turned a corner of the house. The end was out of sight. Might it not be a closed trap for him?

After taking a few paces, he shrank back and crouched in a shadowy corner of the room. Tumult crammed the house full of sound.

"This way! Through here!" called half a dozen voices in Spanish, and there was a charge of the big Mexicans, the fighting soldiery of Lagrange, through the door of the green room. They came running low, some with a gun poised in either hand, some fighting mad and carrying only a knife. They shot past Conifrey and swarmed into the garden. There the noise of their voices poured away, paused, then began to wash back. Other men had gone into that alley from the house, and presently Conifrey heard the calm voice of the master calling.

"He's not in this place...of course not, you idiots. There are his tracks out of the green room. And where do they lead? Straight for the garden wall. He jumped to that wall, climbed to the top, dropped to the farther side, and made off...and, unless I'm very badly mistaken, he's still running as though the devil were behind him. Juan...Poncho...and a few more of you, take your horses and make a dip out yonder. Bring him back alive, mind you, if you can. At any rate, bring him back, or you'll never be allowed to forget this night and your clumsiness. And you, Juan, to be knocked down like a blind fool...!"

There was a stamping and rushing of feet as half a dozen men made off to obey these orders. Juan was left almost tearfully protesting that a demon had dropped upon him from the ceiling of the hall by pure magic. He was silenced with a terse word, and he set after the others.

"And now I want silence. No talking in the halls or outside the house," said Lagrange. "I want perfect peace and quiet. Don't let me catch gabblers talking louder than a whisper. Remember!"

There was a sibilant murmur of "*Sí, señor,*" and the crew dispersed.

It was not until they were entirely gone that Conifrey dared to emerge from his dim corner, stood up, straightened his limbs, and stretched the cramps out of them. After that, he could not help smiling at the simpleness of the stratagem by which he had outwitted this clever Lagrange. Yet there was an easy explanation. Lagrange had been so long surrounded by fellows who dreaded him like an incarnation of the devil that he could not imagine being bearded in his own lion's den.

Conifrey, now that the scare was over, felt that he had purchased through that moment of danger a comparative freedom of movement. No one would expect to find him within the limits of the house, and to what one does not expect, one remains at least partially blind. He stepped out into the garden alley again, where the plants had been crushed and trampled by that blind hastening of feet toward the manhunt. Down the alley he continued to the window from which the stream of light poured across the garden strip. He paused here and looked through squarely into the set and stern face of Lagrange, standing inside the room with folded arms. Conifrey shrank. Then he discovered that those fixed eyes were not fastened upon him but upon the distance. So Two-Speed Conifrey slipped to the side and there waited and watched.

Lagrange, blinded partly, no doubt, by the greater light within the room to all that was without, and blinded still more by the intense vigor of his own thoughts, now turned away and faced the other person in the room. That other person was Beatrice, standing slender and small and defiant beside the farther door. The window was inches ajar. Every word they uttered was plainly audible to Conifrey.

"You have thought it all out carefully?" said Lagrange.

"Very carefully," replied Beatrice.

"And you are determined?"

"As fixed as life or death," she said in a high manner.

"As fixed as that?" sneered Lagrange. "Then I tell you what you may do. Go out before dawn…when the first red is in the sky…and you will have the opportunity of seeing your lover die."

"Dad!" cried Beatrice, and started a pace toward him.

He warned her back with a raised hand.

"As you have already reminded me," he said, "I am not truly your father. Adoption cannot put my blood in your veins…my cruel blood!"

"At least," she cried, "you are my father's brother."

The voice of Lagrange trembled with emotion. He raised his head. To the astonishment of Conifrey, the features of the stern, old rancher softened with holy sadness and exaltation.

"I am the brother of that good, that great and noble man," he said. "I am the brother of William Lagrange, heaven be thanked."

"Ah," said Beatrice, "is there anything nearer to you than the love of my father?"

"Nothing," said Lagrange.

"You have given your life to doing all that you thought he could have wished."

"I have, to the best of my powers."

"But suppose that he looked down on us now. What

54

would be in his mind? Do you think he would want you to do what you are going to do?"

"Would he not?"

"Let you murder a man who has done you or him no wrong? No, he would rather die himself."

"You are sure of his mind, my dear," and Lagrange sneered. "I know how he hated the Mason blood...all of it. There's poison in that name. There was poison in it for your father."

"Because they hounded him wherever he went. But he would never have struck an innocent man."

"No Mason is innocent. They are born guilty."

"Except Dick."

"Beatrice, you are a child and a fool. I had rather see you dead than the wife of Richard Mason."

"Name one wrong thing he has ever done."

"What wrong thing had Richard's father ever done until he murdered your father...my faultless brother? May the Lord never forget or forgive that death. I...."

He could not finish his speech. He made a turn through the room before he could speak again.

"I swore on my bended knees that I should never have finished until I had hounded down every Mason. I have done the work I laid out for myself. One by one they have gone. I have followed them relentlessly. Only one escaped me until almost the end. But I killed the first Richard Mason at last. And now I have that devil's own son in my power."

He threw up his hands in a sudden exultation. "It is the judgment of heaven!" he cried in a shrill, half-choked voice.

"There is always money in the judgment of heaven!" stammered Beatrice, shrinking away from such passion.

"You little, empty-headed fool!" thundered Lagrange.

"Do you still think you can shake me?"

"Oh," moaned Beatrice, sinking, half fainting, into a chair, "oh, I know this thing only…that, if he dies, I shall die after him."

"I have heard other silly little idiots say the same thing. It's an old story…that women will die of broken hearts. But in a year they have forgotten."

"My mother died," said Beatrice.

The old man muttered a sort of muffled shriek. He jerked up his hand until Conifrey shrank, expecting to see the blow fall on the body of the girl. But the hand of Lagrange dropped weakly to his side.

"Your mother died after the murder of her husband," he said. "She died. And who killed that sainted woman? He who killed William Lagrange. The same bullet served for two. Do you ask me, then, to spare the son of the murderer? Was your own infant brother spared by that slaughterer?"

X
"TOO STRONG FOR BEATRICE"

CONIFREY FELT HIS BLOOD RUNNING COLD AS HE guessed at the tale of fiendish cruelty all of this implied.

"It was the work of a feud," said the girl. "In those days, every Mason hated every Lagrange. There was no need for a challenge given. Merely a glance was enough to call for guns. And my father was killed in a fair fight."

"It's a lie," said Lagrange. "Not ten men like the first Richard Mason could have killed such a man as my brother!"

"Nevertheless, the facts are known."

"What facts?" cried Lagrange. "Yes, it is known that

Mason went to the peaceful home of my brother. He shot him at the threshold of the dwelling after he had called him to the door. Then he burned the house and with it the helpless body of your brother."

The girl covered her face as though to shut out the sight of that tragedy.

"Only the good grace of heaven provided that your mother and you, Beatrice, were not in the house, or you would have died at the same time. Yet you ask me to spare one of that ten-times-cursed blood."

"Will you hear me say ten words?" she pleaded.

"If you must, I shall listen."

"Isn't it more than probable that when Richard Mason called my father to the door of the house, he gave him time to draw a gun and defend himself? And then, when my father fell in the fight, Richard Mason mounted his horse and rode away, while the poor baby inside the house pulled over the burning lamp from the table afterward, and so the house went up in flames?" She gasped. "Oh, it is too terrible to be told, but surely you cannot mean that Richard Mason deliberately burned that house to kill my baby brother."

"Cannot I mean it? But I do mean it. With all my heart and my soul I am convinced that is the truth. He was not low enough to kill the child with a bullet. But he found it in his devilish brain to set fire to the house, feeling that the murder might then be explained away just as you have tried to explain it. Yes, he saw even in the child a Lagrange who might one day grow to be a man, and a Lagrange grown to manhood they dreaded worse than the fire of perdition. And so the thing was done. And after it was done, you ask me to be merciful to this new snake in man's skin...this Dick?" He altered his tone. "But, no, my dear, this is your weaker, more

57

foolish self speaking against the voice of your wiser instinct. Come, come! Recall that it was your own message that brought him to the trap. Am I not right? You surely have not forgotten that. Without your message to bait the trap, it might never have closed over him."

"Ah," she said, "you would never believe. You could never understand that I loved him every moment...that I was never unfaithful to the thought of him."

"Never? Then unravel the riddle for me. You cannot do it, Beatrice."

"It was when you discovered that we had been writing letters to each other...when you discovered that Dick and I were in love."

"Calf love!" thundered Lagrange. "The insane attraction of a ...."

"A love that will never change," said the girl.

He snapped his fingers in the air. "Go on," he commanded.

"You threatened then to have Dick put to death by your men. You sent for the Mexicans from the mountains. Before they came, you remember the evening when you told me the details of the death of my father and my baby brother?"

"I remember. I had never told you everything before. I had not guessed, then, at your adroitness in explaining truths away into a mist of fiction."

"But that evening I pretended I agreed."

"You mean that even then it was pretense?"

"Even when I declared that I could help...that I would write a letter which would be the bait for a trap to catch Dick."

"Impossible!"

"Do you think so? But don't you see...when I knew

that those terrible manhunters were ready to start on the trail of Dick, to get him alive or dead…better dead…I saw that I must do something quickly to prevent it. What could I do? I could not send word to a sheriff. If the sheriff made an inquiry before the killing of Dick took place, it would be easy for you to say that you had nothing to do with that band of Mexicans. They were simply a hunting party which had started of their own volition."

"Yes," nodded Lagrange, watching her curiously.

"So I saw that I could not appeal to the law to tie your hands, and I thought of another way. I told you that before Dick died I wanted to tell him face to face that I have merely pretended to care for him from the first. I did not want him to die thinking that I have ever been truly interested in him. I wanted to see him face to face and tell him those things. In order to see him face to face and alive, I would draw him into a trap…if you would agree to bring him here alive from that trap. Do you remember?"

"I remember."

"But you couldn't see through it. You know so little about women that you really thought a girl could do such a cold-blooded thing!"

"I only knew and still know that anything a Lagrange can do to rid the world of a Mason is well done and worthy of praise."

"So I wrote a letter to Dick," she said. "I told him that I was ready to run away with him, and that I would meet him a week later at the old, abandoned shanty under Mount Prospect. I showed you the letter."

"I remember."

"And you swore that, if he came to that place, where your Mexicans would be waiting for him in ambush, they would overpower him with numbers and bring him safely back to this house."

"I swore that, and I lived up to my promise. But how does all of this prove that you were not trapping your lover in fact, Beatrice? Or was it madness on your part?"

"Madness, perhaps," she said softly. "I should have trusted to him to escape from them. But I knew those Mexicans. I knew they were like bloodhounds on the trail, and tireless. It seemed a death sentence for Dick if they started to find him. So I did this other thing as part of a wild plan."

"What plan?"

"I went to the foreman."

"To Chuck?"

"Yes."

"You got him to resign?"

"He was ready to resign before I went to him. You know that he was tired of his work here."

"Tired of taking orders. The independent young fools these days never know when they are located for their own best interests. But go on."

He sat down close to her and facing her, intent on her face in his consuming interest.

"I told everything to Chuck...everything that was going to happen."

"You dared to do that?"

"Yes."

"To get his help for Dick?"

"Yes. You never knew that Dick had saved Chuck's life in a flood on the Little Silver."

"Ah, that was it?"

"Chuck was a selfish fellow, but he could never forget such a service as that. When I told him what was threatening Dick, he agreed to do all he could to help. And we worked out everything between us. First of all, he was to resign from his place."

"Which he did?"

"Yes. Then he was to ride across country as fast as he could to Lawson. You know how well known and popular Chuck is there. He's ridden in a dozen posses. At least fifty men are there who would follow him at the drop of a hat."

"I've heard that, of course. Matter of fact, Chuck was never tired telling about what he could do and how many men he could raise."

"Chuck was to arrange a signal with these friends of his in Lawson. One of them was a signaler during the war. If he got a call from the hills, he was to gather the others and start for a certain place in the hills as fast as they could come. Do you see?"

"I begin to, by heaven."

"They were to arrive here, thirty, forty of them, perhaps. They would find Dick. They would set him free. And, when Dick left, I would leave with him."

"A neat scheme," said Lagrange. "And how were they to know when Dick was brought in here?"

"They were to know when Chuck flashed the signal, and Chuck was to wait in the hills to the west of us, across the valley, until he got a flash from me."

"From you?"

"I was to signal from the tower window."

"By heavens, I see it."

"And you see, too, what I said before was true…that I have loved Dick from the first…that with the letter I was only trapping him so as to get him out of the mountains and save him from the Mexicans. I could not simply warn him to run away, because such a man as

61

Dick doesn't run from danger, no matter how many men are coming against him."

"So I'm to expect a cloud of light cavalry descending on the house at any moment?" asked Lagrange, setting his teeth.

"Do you think I'd be telling you this," said the girl sadly, "if there were still a ghost of a chance that my plan might work?"

"I suppose not, Beatrice."

"When I made the signal tonight," she said, "as soon as Miguel rode in on the black horse with word that the others would be up in a few hours, bringing Dick…as soon as I had that message and went up to send the signal across to Chuck…there was no answering flash."

"Because the air was too thick…too much dust in the air to let the light travel through?"

"I thought of that. But I noticed the sky and the hills at sunset. They were as clear as crystal, and even by the starlight I can see the hills clearly from the tower. No, the air was clear, but Chuck was not there. The most unlucky chance had taken him away." She struck her hands together and groaned when she thought of it. "But at least," she went on, "even if Chuck is shot and badly hurt, there is enough life left in him to give the warning when he goes to Lawson to send men. They may come too late to save Dick, but they would hang his murderers!" And her eyes flashed at Lagrange.

"Including me, my dear?"

"Including you," she challenged him. "My plan fails in one way, but it works in another. If Dick Mason is killed, *you* will be tried for murder."

"Perhaps," and Lagrange smiled. "In that case, I shall have a full twenty witnesses ready to swear that Dick Mason came as a free visitor to my house, but that in the middle of the night he had a brawl with one of the Mexican hunters, a shot was fired...ah, it was very sad...but a nameless man killed Dick Mason, poor boy. And who will disprove such testimony as this, Beatrice?"

She lowered head. Plainly, he was too strong for her.

"But now another thing," said Lagrange. "How did you know that Chuck was shot while he was waiting for your signal in the hills?" He rose and towered over the girl. "Tell me that! What messenger brought you such word?"

XI
"ONE CHANCE IN A MILLION"

"NO ONE," BREATHED BEATRICE. "ONLY THERE WAS no answering flash when I sent the signal and...."

"And you guessed the rest?"

"Yes."

Lagrange smiled on her with perfect disbelief.

"There has been a messenger here," he said calmly. "Someone has brought you the word of the shooting of Chuck. And that messenger"—he hesitated ever so little—"was the stranger, Conifrey. Am I right?"

She stared at him. Then: "Conifrey?" she repeated vaguely.

"My bad luck followed me to the last," said the rancher. "This evening a wandering cowpuncher came in and asked for a place to sleep overnight. This night of all nights when I needed to have no one but my own men around me. He might have known that...yes, it must have been that he knew of the old custom that makes the Lagranges open their door to any man who knocks. He knew that, and he came to take advantage.

This, Beatrice, was your messenger…this fellow was one of the henchman of Chuck?"

She shook her head and set her teeth as though afraid that she might answer against her will.

"However," said Lagrange, "putting all that to one side, there remains the very important affair of this Dick Mason. I must see to that, and so, good night, Beatrice, my dear."

He bowed to her from the door, but the gesture struck the girl suddenly full of life. In an instant she was on her knees beside him. Her arm was around his bony knee, and the other hand was thrown up imploringly to him.

"For heaven's sake," she panted out. "For the sake of mercy. If you kill him, you kill me!"

"A Lagrange who dies for the sake of a Mason deserves death," he answered bitterly.

He tore her away and thrust her to a distance. Vainly, she struggled after him. The door slammed in her face, and she lay on the floor, twisting and stirring with agony as if she had been struck a mortal blow.

Conifrey could not endure inaction after that. There was something in him crying out for movement as the suffering body cries out when the thirst-stricken sees the cold blue of water. He put on his boots and knocked up the window with a blow of his hand. Then he jumped lightly through the aperture. By the time he had turned, the girl had started to turn her face to confront him. She uttered no cry as he came before her for the second time on this night. She merely backed farther into the corner and watched him as one fascinated. Still the great trouble that shadowed her mind, shadowed her eyes also, so that she seemed to be seeing Conifrey only in part.

"You still here," she murmured. "But they said that

they were chasing you with horses across the hills."

"I never left the house," said Conifrey, smiling in spite of himself. "I heard Lagrange giving the orders to hunt me. I was six feet away when he was speaking."

"You know, then, that you are in terrible danger if you stay here?"

"I know that. I have even heard the amount of the cash award for bringing me in, dead or alive."

"Then what sort of madness keeps you here?"

"I told you," said Conifrey, "that I saw Dick Mason led across the patio?"

She shuddered and returned no answer. How utterly she loved the youth.

"And since then," said Conifrey, "I've heard that he's to be butchered before morning."

"If it takes my own testimony to do it," cried the girl in an ecstasy of sorrow and anger, "those who kill him shall die for it!"

"Look here," said Conifrey, "did it ever come home to you that there might be a way to help Mason without using force or without waiting?"

The very whisper of hope was enough to make her eyes brilliant.

"Instead of waiting until the man is dead, save him first?"

She shook her head. "The whole house, the whole region of the hills is thick with Lagrange's men. They are chosen fighters. They would do a dozen murders a day for the sake of the name of Lagrange, and feel that they had nothing on their conscience. They have lived with and for the Lagrange family so long that the command of the master takes the place of conscience with them. Take Dick away from among such guards as those?"

"Listen to me," said Two-Speed Conifrey. "There was a money prize offered to all that same gang of Mexicans to get me. But here I am alive and tolerable healthy, talking to you. Doesn't that mean something?"

She hesitated, then nodded to admit the force of this argument.

"The point is," sad Conifrey, "that they all figure just the way you do. They don't expect that anything can possibly happen. And that way they tie their own hands. You know how it is. They try to be careful, but, when there isn't anything they fear, they can't keep their eyes very sharp."

"You hope to rescue him?" said the girl.

"Why not make the try?"

"Because he has given his word that he will not try to escape."

"He'll change his mind when he sees a chance."

"Ah, you don't know Dick Mason."

"Then," said Conifrey, "we'll get him at the point of a gun. We'll stop him that way. We'll make him come by force, with his hands tied behind his back."

She shook her head, but it was an automatic sign of dissent, for her eyes were beginning to brighten more and more with the faint coming of hope.

"But even suppose we should get him outside of the house?" she said. "What could we do then?"

Conifrey was deep in thought. "While I do my best to get him away, you must manage to go out and saddle three horses…and one of them has got to be my Simon."

"The stables are guarded night and day," said the girl.

"The stables guarded?" groaned Conifrey.

"Yes…always."

Conifrey shook his head. To attempt to escape on foot would be worse than useless. It would mean only an illusory few moments of liberty and then a double pain of capture. That capture would be to Dick Mason death and to Conifrey death, for by that time he would know far too much to be allowed to live. And yet, it was better to make the effort. Suppose that they might wind away into the hills, might they not find a refuge among the rocks where they could hold off even a great number of besiegers until help arrived?

But, even as he formed the picture in his mind, Conifrey shook his head and knew that it was hopeless. What rescue would come? And under that burning sun without water, with only revolvers and one rifle to hold off scores of rifles, they would have a wretched existence of a few hours and then perish miserably.

It was hopeless, but in spite of himself he could not draw back.

"Lady," he said, "there's one chance in a million. But we've got to take that chance. We've got to get out of here, on foot, and travel west."

"On foot!"

"I know. There isn't any hope. Still, we've got to do it."

He found that she was looking at him with deepest wonder.

"Who are you?" she said. "And what do you owe to Dick or to me?"

"Nothing," said Conifrey, "except what every honest man owes to a lost cause. The next thing is to find the room where Mason is kept prisoner."

"I know that room."

"Where is it?"

"Only three rooms beyond this, around the corner of the house."

"Opening onto the garden?"

She killed the hope that had grown up in his mind.

"There are guards even on the garden side."

"And others in the halls?" said Conifrey.

"Of course."

"Still, we've got to try the garden. Come through the window with me. We'll do what we can. No man can do more."

XII
"WHERE RIGHT IS RIGHT"

SHE FOLLOWED HIM, IF NOT IN CONFIDENCE OF success, at least readily—as though she hoped in the heat of action to forget that solid gloom that had closed over her mind. Conifrey slipped through the window first and dropped lightly to the ground. The girl followed. He caught her beneath the elbows as she dropped, and broke the force of her fall. Then they went down the garden strip, staying close by the wall of the house until, as they approached the turn of the wall just beyond, Conifrey waved the girl back and slipped ahead alone. One glance around the corner showed him the danger that lay ahead. In fact, he did not need a glance. The voices of the two Mexicans told him all that he needed to know.

"Get two packages of paper," said one in Spanish.

"Yes," said the other. "I'll be back in two minutes."

That fact registered heavily in the mind of Conifrey. Two minutes to beat down the remaining guard—a task that must be accomplished in utter silence—then to wrench away some of the iron bars that closed the window even as the window of his own room had been secured, and, last of all and far from easiest, bring Mason out into the open and start their flight.

The remaining guard now came whistling very softly toward the corner. Conifrey with a raised hand gestured toward the girl and, turning his head, saw her sink to the ground shadows by his warning. He himself crouched still lower. The guard stepped past the corner of the wall. He loomed huge above him, made yet more bulky by the large *serape* thrown about his shoulders. He turned, and, as he turned, Conifrey acted. He rose, stood stiff and straight. Holding the revolver by the butt, he struck his victim on the side of the head with the barrel. The heavy metal thudded against the skull. Down went his man without a groan. Conifrey dropped to his knees and listened for the heartbeat and the breathing. Yes, the fellow was living, but it would be more than two minutes before he opened his eyes and spoke again.

As Two-Speed rose to his feet again, the girl was beside him.

"The first step!" he said to her, and then laid his hands on the iron bars of Dick Mason's window.

They were sunk as deeply in the mortar as had been those bars that closed the entrance to the room he himself had occupied, but there was this difference—either a softening of the mortar in which the bars were fixed or else a desperate increase of Conifrey's strength, for, as he twisted and strained, he felt the iron begin to stir in its sockets, begin to crunch a little leeway through the mortar. He stopped his labor. In five seconds of strain he had collapsed the effect of a day's work.

He began again, fiercely, powdering the edges of his teeth with the force with which he ground them together. And that convulsion of nerve power and muscle power brought a reward. One iron sagged out and came free at an end. The other end dropped out by its own weight. But this was only one bar out, and no grown man could pass his body through the aperture that was thus made. There must be another bar torn away, and where should he find the strength to do it, now that he was weak and trembling like a frightened girl from the terrible strain of his work?

Yonder came a form that cast a black silhouette upon the window. The curtain was drawn aside. There stood Dick Mason above them.

"Dick," cried the girl in hushed voice.

"Beatrice," he whispered.

He dropped to his knees and thrust out his arms to her. She pressed her body against the bars. Conifrey turned his head.

"Only help to tear away another bar and you're free," he heard the girl pleading at last.

"If only I could," answered Mason, a whisper with a groan in it.

"Dick, you must. This man's strength is gone."

"Heaven bless him, but I cannot raise a hand to help myself. I have given my word."

"You have given your word to a wild wolf, Dick. Do you know what he intends to do?"

"Well?"

"He will have you led out and shot down before morning. He will have you murdered, Dick!"

"He dares not do that. Not even Lagrange dares do that!"

"Ah, you don't know him."

"But this is the Twentieth Century."

"Not in this house."

"Beatrice, you aren't serious?"

"I swear I am. So take hold of this next bar...you within and me without...we can surely tear it away."

"I have given my solemn word of honor," said

Mason. "I cannot lift a hand to free myself from this room. Once outside…ah, that would be a different matter."

"For my sake, Dick."

"Hush," said Conifrey. "I've been standing here like a fool. We don't need his help. We've got a tool that will work for us."

With his shaking hands, he raised the iron bar he had just succeeded in tearing loose. He placed it under the next bar and set the point of his lever against the masonry. One jerk and the end was loosened. Another thrust at the lower end, and there was a gap opened large enough for a man to step through easily.

"Now," said Conifrey.

"Dick," called the girl.

"If this is breaking my word of honor, may heaven forgive me," said Dick Mason, and he dropped through the gap and landed lightly beside the other two. For an instant he clung to the girl, and she to him. Then there came a harsh voice to the side, rousing them.

"Miguel! Where are you? Here are the papers," called the returning guard. "The devil take such a sleepy-headed fool as you. Why don't you answer? Miguel, if…?"

Here he turned the corner and was struck, at the same instant, by two pile-driver hands clenched into fists of iron. One smote him on one side of his head, the other landed on the opposite side. And the guard sank softly to rest upon the damp ground.

The three turned on one accord and fled across the garden. There they scrambled up the wall. Conifrey, lithe as a cat in climbing, was at the top first. Mason, from below, thrust up the burden of the girl. And so she reached the hands of Conifrey and was lifted over. They

71

gained the open ground on the farther side with greater ease, and still no alarm had been given behind them. They had covered in a breathless rush the first two hundred yards away from the house and were rapidly going downhill before a gasping, half-strangled voice cried out from far behind them.

"Help! They have murdered me! Help! Help!"

"It is Miguel,' said Conifrey, grinning in spite of his fear. "He has had a bad dream in his sleep."

"Now run as we've never run before," gasped Mason. "Beatrice, run just behind me. I'll show you the way over the smoother ground."

ⓥ ⓥ ⓥ ⓥ ⓥ

What saved them from certain capture by the swooping horsemen of Lagrange, they did not know until many a weary day later. And then they learned the strange truth. Lagrange himself, highly excited and strained more than he could stand by the events of the night, had given way under the new shock when he learned in one flashing stroke of intelligence that both Beatrice and Dick Mason had slipped from his hands. And the Mexicans who had brought him the tidings, and who had waited to take their orders from him, had seen him turn purple, gasp, and then sink to the floor, speechless. For twenty-four hours he could not speak, and, when he could utter a sound at least, one half of his body was withered by paralysis. He gave his order for pursuit many and many an hour too late.

Dick Mason and Beatrice and Two-Speed Conifrey were already in safety. It was a wild run that night, with Beatrice exhausted, supported on either side by the men, begging them to go on and let her stay behind. But there was a reward for all the agony of that effort. At least, it seemed to Conifrey that there was an ample reward when he stood up at the wedding of Dick Mason and Beatrice Lagrange a month later. But he would not take the foremanship on the Mason Ranch that was offered him. He chose to ride out of their lives on Simon as swiftly as he had come into them. But he came back once a year. For five minutes he would look into their faces, hear their voices, and then he would be gone again.

THE BEST BANDIT

*Frederick Faust completed this short novel in September, 1931, and titled it "The Tender Feet of Randal." This title was changed to "The Best Bandit" when it was first published in Street & Smith's **Western Story Magazine** (3/5/32). It has since appeared from Audio Renaissance in a single cassette audio version read by Barry Corbin. In this story Faust created two of his most formidable outlaw characters—Jeems Loring and José Oñate—but perhaps even more memorable than either of these is the fragile and most resilient Maruja Flandes.*

I
"THE BEST MAN"

IN THE DAYS OF THE CHISHOLM TRAIL, GREENSVILLE was betwixt and between. On the map it was nothing that you could put your finger on, because it was neither Mexican nor American. You see, at that time, where Greensville stood, the Rio Grande had the wobbles. Part of the year it hooked an arm around Greensville, leaving a strip of dry land that connected it with Mexican soil. The rest of the time it washed across this strip, and the town was then linked up with the American side. It would have taken the work of three investigating committees from the United States Senate, and half a dozen emissaries from Mexico to settle the rights of ownership, but no senators, no emissaries were ever dispatched. The reason was neither the United States nor Mexico wanted Greensville. Who will go clamoring for a nest of wasps?

To be sure, the inhabitants of Greensville were nearly all fair women and brave men. Only in a world-wide search would you have found the counterpart of such beauty and such courage. The ladies were as kind as they were fair, the men as generous as they were brave.

Yet, neither the Mexican *Rurales* nor the Texas Rangers desired to have dealings with the people of Greensville. Three brave marshals and five equally brave sheriffs had died in that no man's land. As for Mexican officials, they were not counted, and, since the river was the favorite cemetery of the town, how could history keep tabs or run up reckonings at a later time?

As a matter of fact, there was nothing to be said in favor of owning Greensville. For one thing, nobody in the town wanted to be owned. They all preferred, while they were in the place, to be people without a country. Many a cutthroat, forger, counterfeiter, gunman hurried to Greensville and heaved a sigh of relief when he walked those dusty, narrow, winding streets. If valiant officers of the law dared to venture into the town in pursuit, their careers were glorious, perhaps, but exceedingly brief.

It was never a large town, but the cost *per capita* of life in that place was higher than in any spot on the globe. Faro and roulette wheels soaked up a great part of the coin. Then there were the saloons, one for every other sort of building in the place. There were also eating houses where French wines could be had. They were good wines, too, good and almost priceless.

Small though it was, no one could have put Greensville under a hat. There was such eruptive force in the place, it had burned itself to the ground half a dozen times from sheer excess of the joy of life. For fear lest it should burn again, it had been built the last time, about three years before, chiefly of canvas and tin and boxwood. Those three fiery years had weathered and aged it so that it looked like a gypsy camp, and an old one, at that.

Into that town one day rode Randal Dale, fair and young, tall and straight, with an engaging smile, a gentle manner, and the look of one who loves and trusts the world because the world never has deceived him or done him harm. He was clad in clothes that smacked of the East. He spoke in a voice and in language that announced him to be one of the educated few. Greensville drowsily opened one eye and looked at the youth, calmly winked that one eye shut again, and continued to sleep until the evening.

Randal Dale found a hotel, put his pack in his room, and looked to the lodging of his horse, a handsome, gentle creature, tall and straight and reliable. After this, Randal Dale walked back into the hotel and talked to the proprietor. The latter had only one eye because, some cruel people said, he had seen too much evil to retain both optics. He sat behind his desk, with a pair of greasy hands stretched out idly upon his knee.

"Can you tell me the name of the best man in town?" asked Randal Dale, with that gentle, trusting smile.

The proprietor raised both brows, then lowered one brow over his good eye, and squinted at the questioner.

"What might you call a good man?" he asked.

"A good man?" asked Randal Dale, apparently amazed.

"Yeah," said the other, "there's gents that are good at faro, and some that are better at poker. There's some that know how to handle soup, and some that like powder better. There's good drinkers, good hunters,

76

good wrestlers, good boxers, good sleight-of-hand artists, pickpockets, thugs of all kinds, gunmen. Then, on the other hand, you might be meaning the best churchgoers, or the best preachers, or the ones that pray the best. I dunno what you mean."

"I dare say that I mean what you would mean by a good man," said Randal Dale. "I believe that all humanity agrees about certain of the fundamentals of life. I'm sure that you could name the best man in Greensville."

The hotel proprietor hooked a thumb under the single band of the suspenders that kept his trousers up to the hips. Then he said: "All right, you go up to your room, and I'll send you the best man in Greensville...to my thinking."

Randal Dale thanked him and straightway mounted to his room, having left with the proprietor, for safekeeping, a roll of greenbacks. And Tubby Graham, the hotelman, sent for the "best man in Greensville according to his thinking." In the interval of waiting, he made a careful estimate of that roll of greenbacks.

Jeemy, or plain Jeems Loring, if one stopped to think about it, was the best man in Greensville in many ways. He was the best poker player. He was the best shot. He was the best horse wrangler. He was the best spinner of long yarns. He was the best plain liar. He was the best fancy liar. He was the best killer. He was the best gunman and general, all-round killer. Having all these "bests" to his credit, it was hardly strange that Tubby had picked him out as the best man in the town of Greensville.

Jeems Loring came in presently, in response to the message from his friend, Tubby Graham. Mr. Jeems Loring was neither tall nor short, neither old nor young.

He had very wide shoulders, a very wrinkled forehead, and a very long, outthrusting jaw. Moreover, he wore, continually, the smile of one who knows more than he ought to know.

He rested a hand on the desk, and said in a confidential tone that was habitual with him: "Look here, Tubby, what's the deal going on now?"

"Easy money," said Tubby. "Have a cigar?"

"I don't use that kind of poison," declared the other. "Not when I'm talking with a two-headed wolf like you. Whacha want?"

"The best man in town," said Tubby.

"Yeah? Take it from me, that might cost you some money," said the other.

Tubby chuckled. "You dunno what I mean," he said.

"No, because you won't talk," declared Mr. Jeems Loring. "What's brewing in you?"

"Easy money," said Tubby tantalizingly.

"How much?"

"Scads."

"How much is a scad?"

Tubby looked doubtfully about him, as one tempted to do evil, but wishing to do it in private. Then he reached back of him, jerked open the door of the hotel safe, and pulled out a well-filled, chamois bag. In this there was a paper package, containing a closely packed stack of greenbacks, that he now held up for inspection. Then he cast an eye around the lobby and, with haste, returned the money to the safe and slammed the door after it. He was panting a little when he faced Jeems Loring again, and, drawing out a big bandanna, he mopped his face.

"Well," said Jeems, "you had the coin in your hand. Is it real?"

The other opened his eyes. Then he sneered.

"Is it real?" he repeated.

His friend shrugged his shoulders.

"Go on," he said. "Explain."

"There's a poor simp, a tenderfoot," said Tubby, "that's just come to town and asked if I could find him the best man in Greensville." He laughed before he was able to end his sentence. "So I asked what did he mean by *best*, and he said undoubtedly the same sort of *best* that I would have in mind. And he smiled at me, the poor boob. And I said that I'd get a-hold of the best man in Greensville for him, all right, according to my way of thinking. So here you are, brother. All I want is a split."

"You had the dough in your hands," said Jeems.

"I can't do that," said the other. "I got a reputation. I don't rob people."

"No, not that way. You don't take their coin out of your safe," said Jeems. "But suppose that I stick you up, right now, and clean out the safe?"

"It wouldn't work," said the other regretfully. "Because everybody knows that I'm your friend. They'd smell the plant, right away."

"Are you gonna go and get all complicated?" asked Jeems sadly.

"It ain't complicated at all," said the other. "Go up and have a look at *it*. It's in room seventeen. You don't need no letter of introduction. Just you go on up, and have a look, and say that I sent you."

"It sounds like a phony deal," said the best man in Greensville, "but I'll go and waste a little time on your idea, anyway."

II
"WET BEEF"

WHEN JEEMS LORING WAS INVITED, IN ANSWER TO HIS knock, to enter room seventeen, he saw the bright face of Randal Dale bowed over a large sheet of paper on which the boy was making rapid notations with a fluidly moving pencil. The bright face looked up and smiled at Jeems.

"Tubby, down yonder, sent me," said Loring and waited.

"Ah! I'm glad to see you," said Randal Dale.

He got up, as he spoke, and shook hands heartily, showing Jeems to a chair. The latter remembered to take off his hat, which he dropped on the floor.

"I asked the proprietor who was the best man in town," said Randal Dale, "and he's sent you to me. It's a pleasure to have you with me, Mister…?"

"Jeems Loring," said the man-slayer.

"Mister Loring," said Randal, "I've determined to go into the cattle business."

"The which?" says Loring, somewhat startled.

"The cattle business," said Dale, "because, obviously, it's the best business in the world."

"Is it?" Jeems asked.

"Why, of course it is," said Dale, bright and surprised. "Look at this. Just take it over a ten-year period. You have a hundred cows, say, and in the first year they have a hundred calves, and in the second year a hundred calves. That gives you a herd of three hundred in two years. Then, in the third year, the first lot of calves have calves of their own, so the herd increases to five hundred. And there you are!"

"Where are you?" said Jeems Loring.

"Why, at five hundred. Every three years, the herd will increase fivefold. Take a nine-year period, to make it come out even. There is a fivefold increase three times. Or, from one hundred to five hundred, from twenty-five hundred to twelve thousand five hundred. Why, think of a vast army of cattle like that produced in nine years from a hundred cows."

"Yeah, that's a lot of noise to think about," said Jeems Loring.

"Nine years seems a long time," said the boy cheerfully. "But I have patience. I can make a bigger beginning, by a great deal, than a hundred cows. A thousand cows, say, or even more. Think of it! That would be a hundred and twenty-five thousand head of cattle in the course of the nine years."

"Yeah, it's something to think about," agreed Jeems Loring.

"There's only one puzzling thing about it all," said the boy.

"Is there?" asked Jeems. "You go on and tell me what it is, will you?"

"Why, it's this. I only wonder that everybody else in the world doesn't get the facts as I do, and immediately begin to raise cattle. Why don't you do it yourself, for instance?"

"Why, I dunno," said Jeems, honestly enough, "but maybe I never thought about it. And maybe it was just that I heard yarns about rustlers cleaning you out one year, and a famine stamping you out the next. Then a plague comes along the third year to kill what you got left. Or, if you have a real good year, everybody else has a good year, too, and the dog-gone market is flooded. Your price for beef comes down so low that it ain't hardly worth while to make the drive north over the trails to the market."

Randal Dale listened at first with astonishment, and then with a shake of his head and another smile.

"I understand how it is," he said. "You're one of the very honest people who understand that young men ought not to be given too much encouragement in the beginning. I realize that. I like you all the better for showing me the gloomy side of the picture. But I know that the brighter side is the true side. And now, Mister Loring, I'll tell you what I wish. I wish that you'd work for me."

Loring looked at him quite a time. "How long?" he finally asked.

"Oh, forever."

"I might work," said Jeems, who had lost all his money at faro the night before, "for sixty a month so long as we get along with one another."

"Sixty?" said Randal Dale. "No, no! I couldn't think of offering the best man in Greensville less than a hundred."

"Couldn't you?" asked the gunman, thrusting out his long jaw, for he began to suspect that perhaps everything was not as smooth and clear, here, as it appeared on the surface.

"Why, no," said the boy. "You'd be my foreman, of course. And the first thing that I'd ask you to do, would be to hire a dozen more men for me."

"What kind of men?" asked Jeems.

"Your kind of men," said the boy. "That is, if there are any others half as good as you are. Exactly your kind of men, Mister Loring."

"If I work for you," said Jeems, "leave off the mister, will you? Call me Jeems, and you can wear Rancie for a moniker, as easy as anything else. Folks down here, they don't like to get snagged on formal names, not a little bit."

"Don't they?" asked the boy. "My real desire is to learn the manners of the country as soon as possible. Of course, you may call me Rancie, Jeems."

Jeems Loring left his employer with a prepayment of a hundred dollars in his trousers pocket, and found Tubby behind the desk.

"Look a-here, Tubby," he said, "this here tree is full of ripe fruit. All that we gotta do is to give it a shake."

"Didn't I tell you? Am I a sucker that can't use my own eyes?" asked Tubby.

"You told me, all right. Now, brother, I'm gonna frame this fall guy and frame him good and hard. But the first thing is for me to hire a dozen more men as good as myself."

He indulged in a vast grin.

"Get 'em," snapped Tubby, with the decision of a practical businessman, closing a good deal. "Get 'em as close to yourself as you can, so long as you don't crowd yourself out of first place."

"The kind of a first place that I rate," said Jeems, "it ain't easy to elbow me out of. Who'd you know about town?"

"You know as good as me, except you might not know that Sam Paley and Alabama Joe Hixon are both sleeping upstairs in a back room right now."

"That pair of snakes? Who've they poisoned today?"

"They ain't been poisoning nobody, and they're looking around for something to get their fangs into."

"I can use 'em both," said Jeems Loring, and hurried off upstairs to see them.

He got them easily for fifty a week. They might have to do a little cattle work, he said, but there would be something more than monthly pay in the job at the finish.

Then he circulated through Greensville and selected ten more of the same type. He was the thirteenth man. When, at the close of the day's work, he thought over the list that was due to report for service the next morning, he assured himself that he had found the twelve toughest men in the toughest town in western America. That is to say, the twelve toughest men in the world. There was not a one of them that was not a tried-and-proved horseman, a thoroughly stanch warrior with knife and gun or even empty hands. They were not all of pure American blood. He had an Indian half-breed that should have been living on the Navajo Reservation, except that his criminal record had automatically expelled him from that peace-loving but stern people. Loring also had a pair of renegade Mexicans, well seasoned. They were experienced in all the downs of life, together with a few of the ups that follow successful pieces of knavery on a large scale. He had a Portuguese wanderer, along with an adventurer from France out of a noble family, a French-Canadian from the Northern woods, and a Swede with a grin like a hungry cat's. The rest were Americans, even more unsavory than the foreigners. All were well known to him, either through practical experience or by eloquent reputation. He was satisfied with them, when he thought them over, and carried his report back to his young employer.

Again, he found Rancie Dale sitting in his bedroom and working at columns of figures on another large sheet of paper.

"In fifteen years…," began Dale.

"I got a dozen boys that you couldn't match in fifteen years of hunting," said the foreman of the gang. "You oughta see 'em. Not pretty, mind you, but dog-gone efficient."

"Efficiency," Rancie said. "That's what we want.

84

Really efficient men, able to ride and handle cattle."

"Yeah, or men, even. They could handle men even better than they could handle cattle."

"Could they?" murmured Dale. "That's wonderful. Now we must buy the cattle, you know."

"What kind of cows d'you want?" asked Loring.

"I want your advice," said Rancie Dale. "But I heard somebody speaking today about very cheap cattle to be had from Mexico, cattle that can be driven north over the Chisholm Trail and fattened on the way. Wouldn't that be a good idea?"

"Greaser beef," said Jeems, "ain't any cheaper than *gringo* beef, unless it's wet."

"Wet?" said Rancie, with a deprecatory smile and a spreading gesture of his hands. "I'm afraid that I don't follow that. Wet beef?"

"Yeah, wet beef." Jeems pointed through the window toward the darkening face of the Rio Grande.

"South of the river," he said, "you can pick up beef for a quarter of the price of the north-shore stuff. If you know how to go about it, and if you can pay cash."

"Why, I can pay cash, all right," said the boy. "D'you know how to go about getting the beef?"

"I'll start tomorrow," said Jeems.

III
"RANCIE RIDES"

JEEMS DEPARTED THE NEXT MORNING, SOME TIME before the sun was up, and made a fifty-mile circuit before he returned. He not only rode, but he stopped here and there and talked. The people with whom he talked were in little Mexican *fondas*, or in outlying shacks among the hills, or tucked away in the densely populated small towns. Each man was a picture worth looking at. They might not have possessed the reputations that distinguished the twelve worthies he had picked up the day before, but in appearance they were far more formidable.

They were the dealers in "wet" cattle. They stole here and there, and they always had a few head, or a few thousand head, tucked away somewhere, ready for the rush through the Rio Grande. On emerging from its waters, they were bought, head by head, for what appeared only a song to a Yankee, but what seemed to be solid sunshine to a Mexican cattle thief.

The orders of Jeems had been very lax. Exact numbers were not estimated by his employer. It was simply a *lot* of cows that he was told to arrange for, and this he interpreted liberally. He engaged for seven thousand, but he would not be offended if there were a few thousand more. After all, he wanted to deploy all the money that he had seen locked up in the hotel safe and about the disposition of which Tubby had been so foolishly recalcitrant.

He saw Tubby when he returned, late in the evening.

"I got it fixed," he said, "and, if we can get the fool to unlimber all his coin and make it down to the bank of the Rio Grande north shore, I'll arrange to have him relieved of it painlessly before morning. Going to be ready for the play in twenty-four hours, Tubby. And I'm glad that I got that gang together. This kid, he's just been doing my thinkin' for me."

It was, in fact, entirely clear that they would need to have plenty of men if they were to handle the Mexicans who were to bring their cattle to the river and make them swim across. It seemed to Jeems, whose love of great exploits sometimes almost swept him off his feet, that this was a deal out of which he might make a handsome fortune. He considered it at length. Once the Mexicans ran the cattle across the river, he would wait until the majority had got over. Then he would start the great herd north, and, when the Mexicans demanded payment, he would give it to them in the only form he thought Mexicans either deserved or appreciated; that is to say, he would pay them in lead, in wholesale quantities. He was so pleased by this idea that he felt a song rising in his heart at the idea.

As for the cash in the safe of his friend, Tubby, that money he would secure with as little personal violence as possible. He did not dislike young Rancie Dale. He had, in fact, a kindly feeling for him, as much as he was capable of feeling toward any human being. For out of the fool head of Rancie had arisen this magnificent scheme into the mind of Mr. Loring. How much there might be, all told, in the safe of Tubby, in that single heavy stack of greenbacks, he could not guess. But Tubby, as we have seen, with great patience had flicked over the corners of the greenbacks and had made a fair estimate. Between a hundred and seventy and a hundred and eighty thousand dollars, honest Tubby estimated, was in that pile.

Jeems Loring, when he thought of this, did not regard himself as a criminal. For there is a point at which murder, for instance, ceases to be murder and becomes glorious war, and there is a point at which common stealing ceases to be theft and becomes statesmanship. He felt that work on such a scale as this could not be called crime. He wanted to lift his chin, and he did lift it. He wanted to look the world proudly in the eye, and he did.

He could see that there were difficult points to be

considered. As for Rancie, he hardly mattered at all or for that matter, any action that he might take. What was important, however, was the handling of the Mexicans. They were almost certain to come in great numbers, and no matter what the storybooks may say, Jeems Loring knew that a Mexican with a grievance can fight like a wildcat, and no mistake. He depended upon the hand-picked quality of his dozen rogues, all of whom could fight, all of whom loved battle. In the fracas, blood would be shed, but what of that? The more Mexicans killed, the simpler the future. The more of his own men dropped, the fewer would remain to share in the split.

It was only too bad that he had to get this priceless tip from Tubby. Tubby would have to have a good rake-off. Yet the fat man was almost worth his price, considering the fact that he had named the great Jeems Loring as the best man in Greensville. On the whole, it appeared to Jeems Loring as a satisfactory world, but, when the morning came, he received a shock—indeed, a distinct shock.

When he laid the full story of his day's work before the boy, as full a story as his employer's ears could endure, young Rancie Dale declared that he must ride south of the river to see the gathering of the cattle. Wait on the north bank while they were brought into a great dusty focus in the late evening, and then poured through the funnel of clever riders toward the river? No, no! That would never do for Mr. Rancie Dale. He had to go where he could see the animals in their native habitat, as it were. He was strangely stubborn. He smiled, as usual, and made his deprecatory gestures with both hands, as though sorry for an attitude in such marked contrast to the usual pleasing ways of Rancie Dale, but, however that might be, he was immovably fixed in his determination to cross the river and mingle with the native Mexicans.

Jeems Loring had lived long enough in this world to know when he was dealing with a man who could not be argued from his point. The whole scheme that Jeems had formed might be bungled by this headstrong decision of his employer, but he saw that it would be a very delicate matter to win him away from his idea. So Jeems accepted it, feeling that his wits were equal to this new necessity. He sent out word to his host. He appointed the proper hour, and, in the fire of the middle day, that cavalcade of fourteen rode through the muddy waters of the Rio Grande, unobserved, and headed south.

Mr. Dale wondered why they did not take the bridge—and he wondered aloud, so that Jeems was forced to explain to him that they never bothered about the bridge, when the water was as low as this. Dale accepted the argument, it appeared, until one of the men, the Frenchman, laughed loudly.

"Why did that man laugh?" asked Dale.

Jeems explained loudly: "He laughed partly because he's a laughing jackass, and partly because he ain't got any sense. For another thing, there's a greaser on the other side of that bridge that's looking for his scalp, and I hope he gets it."

It will be seen that Jeems Loring could, on occasion, be very severe.

The Frenchman made a motion toward his gun, thought better of it, and shrugged his shoulders. After all, in certain ways it will be remembered that Jeems Loring was the best man in Greensville.

So they went on through the blinding heat and the stifling alkali dust that burns the lining of the nose and parches and cracks open the lips. They went on steadily, with little conversation, pulling the silken folds of their bandannas over nose and mouth, and breathing through these.

Rancie Dale did not seem to be much troubled either by the heat of the sun or the steady racking of the horse beneath him. If this was a surprise to the great Jeems Loring, it was nothing compared with the real bewilderment felt by him and the rest of his chosen cutthroats when they witnessed the smooth ease with which Rancie Dale backed his horse.

Alabama Joe Hixon explained to his riding companions: "You take a whole lot of these here tenderfeet, and you'll find out that they've been stuck on the back of a hoss every day since they was six years old, and what they sit on is just a piece of leather that ain't got anything to stick to. They're what you call an English saddle, and an English saddle ain't a saddle at all. It's just a shiny piece of leather, polished up so's the hoss can shed you all the easier. Off an English saddle, a gent rolls easier than a drop of water off a duck's back.

"And that's likely what the kid learned to do his riding on. No wonder that he can sit in one of these here Mexican saddles like he was in a chair, though, if the mustang begins to act up, you'd see Rancie starting right up for the sky. He looks like a regular hoss wrangler, just now, but let the pony give him some fireworks, and he'll come all apart."

The opinion of Alabama Joe was accepted, but still there was a touch of respect in all their faces as the men looked at the straight back and the easy carriage of the boy.

"If he's half the gent that he looks in the saddle," said one of the half-breeds, "it's a damned shame to roll him like old man Jeems is sure to do."

"Anybody that's a real man can take care of himself,"
declared Sam Paley.

They had reached this easy compromise with
conscience when, out of the southern horizon, they saw
a dim mist that heightened into a wall, tall and white,
and through the lower rollings of this approaching fog,
they were presently able to make out dim forms moving.

"There's some of Rancie's cows!" said someone.
"The party is gonna begin."

IV
"THE PARTY"

THE PARTY BEGAN VERY SIMPLY AND EASILY TO THE
eyes of the 'punchers and rascals gathered behind Jeems
Loring. To young Rancie Dale, however, it must have
appeared more than strange to see the wild men who
brought up the herds all through that day. Sometimes
there were not more than a hundred cows in a bunch,
but in one bunch nearly three thousand came in.
Everywhere around the southern horizon, the columns
of white smoke arose and stood, trembling in the upper
sky, melting and then growing closer and closer, higher
and higher until, at the base of the moving columns, the
dark forms of the cattle began to soak through into the
straining vision of the watchers.

They were a wild lot, those cattle. Most of them had
come far and had been driven mercilessly all the way,
but, though they were red-eyed with anger and with
thirst, they were not spent. They had plenty of passion
in them, plenty of vigor. And their sharp horns were
always threatening to this side and that. They were
much smaller, on the whole, than the cattle handled on

the ranches north of the Rio Grande. They were smaller
much leaner, and likely to be a little rough-backed and
very ewe-necked.

Their fleetness of foot amazed young Dale. When a
patch of them broke out of the edge of one of the large
herds, the cowpunchers had to sprint their horses at full
speed, in order to overtake the fugitives and work them
back into the crowd.

"Are they dangerous?" asked young Rancie Dale.

"Dangerous?" said Alabama Joe. "Why, if you was to
hook a pair of horns onto the head of a grizzly bear, it
wouldn't make him less dangerous, would it? And them
things can do anything that a grizzly can do. They got as
much strength in their paws, and, if they miss you with a
swipe with a front hoof, they try a sideswipe with a back
foot hard enough to stave a hole through an iron barrel.
If they miss with all four feet, they'll bite a hole in you
with their teeth. When their feet and their teeth go back
on 'em, they got the horns throwed in, all extra. I dunno
where you was raised, son, but around the parts that I
know best a long-horned lump of a Mexican steer is
called mighty dangerous, I can tell you!"

Young Rancie Dale heard, and, as he listened, he
opened his eyes until they were as wide and as innocent
as the eyes of a girl. The men were growing familiar
with this look, however, and they were able to control
their mirth somewhat. They simply smiled askance at
one another.

They had many other occasions for smiling before
that day ended, and seven thousand cattle, more or less,
were gathered, milling and bawling and screaming like
wildcats and buffalo combined.

For Rancie Dale rode everywhere, admiring
everything with the same bright and open eye. He said

that it was a wonderful sight, but that he did not understand why all the poets in the world did not come to admire this glorious spectacle and write down in words its terror of thundering, clashing hoofs, the white rolling of the dust storm, the flashing of the horns through the mist, those polished horns, beautifully curved like an antique bow.

Rancie Dale expressed himself in words very similar to these, and Jeems Loring and his twelve poisonous companions listened, looked darkly on one another, and endured. Even though they all expected to make a tidy little fortune out of the spoiling of this tenderfoot, it was hard for them to endure until the ending of the day and the final gathering of the herd for the drive across the river.

There was still a batch of three hundred cows, more or less, outlying, when the sun began to redden and puff out his cheeks in the west. And now the rosy glow of the sun's light stained the dust clouds above the milling thousands of cattle and above the heads of the Mexican riders who circled the edges of the wild horde, shouting, singing, laughing, whooping, sometimes rushing to a distance to head off and turn back the outbreak of a band.

Not until then did the chief cattle thief, the great José Oñate, appear upon the scene. He was a man of mark. He could not have walked upon the stage of this world unnoticed even as a slave. In a far land, his conversation would have changed the minds of cannibals. His wisdom always would have unlocked the heart of the sternest tyrant, and his hands, a little later, would surely have opened the seven sealed doors of his treasure chambers. Women could not resist his wiles. Men could not resist his weapons.

If he were a robber, it was plain, not that he loved money unlawfully gained, but money gained by dangerous methods. Nothing in this world had spice for him if it were unseasoned by danger. He had dipped his young hands, already, in a hundred fortunes and, when they were his, he had cast aside the spoils readily. He gave to his companions, to his friends, to his acquaintances, to the beggars beside the road. When the hands of all these were filled, it was said, he then gave to his enemies.

The appearance of this man was such that, at a glance, all eyes instantly understood the metal of which he was made; that is to say, he had the look of steel that will cut steel. In addition, upon the face of him he was gay, vain, cheerful, inconstant, and as keen as a hungry hawk on the wing.

José Oñate appeared upon a coal-black charger that wore on its haunch a brand that was never printed by a Mexican branding iron. He wore upon his shoulders a little Mexican jacket, brightened by great quantities of gold and silver lace. About his narrow hips flowed a sash that had cost two generations of patient labor and once had adorned the altar of a church. Silver trimming gleamed down the seams of his trousers. At his flaring stirrups there were golden bells—bells of real gold, too. Finally, to finish off his costume, a splendid cloak blew back behind him or drooped over the arching tail of his horse.

He came attended by four men, like a chief who cannot ride abroad unattended. And what a retinue it was. Each of the four looked worthy to be a chief, ruling over a fierce tribe of fighting men. Each of the four was worth naming. Beginning with the least, they were, first, Pedro Iribas, in whose blood was a plentiful admixture of Apache days inherited from those times when the terrible Indians used to ride south following the Mexican moon and whitening their trail, north and south of the Rio Grande, with the bones of dead cattle and dead men. Pedro Iribas was gaunt and somewhat bent in the shoulders. Hair had never grown on his face, but it was covered with small punctures, as though the hair had been plucked forth by the roots. His nose was small; his forehead was broad; his eyes were overshadowed by deep brows; and upon his great mouth there was a continual smile that might have been caused by weariness, or pain, or ferocity, or perhaps a mixture of all three. He was the oldest of the three, a man of great cunning, capable of leading others in battle, as he had repeatedly done, capable of long retreats and brilliant attacks, capable, also, of all the thousand devices with which the red men of the old days conquered their opponents on the prairies or in the mountains.

At his side appeared Ricardo Girones, a man without color in hair or skin; his eyes, alone, had a dull gray color or, rather, a hint of color, but eyebrows, hair, and skin itself were simply dust. He was an albino. He possessed a sort of horrible beauty, with a feminine smile and a rather feminine manner, but no observer was surprised to learn of his bloodthirsty cruelty.

Antonio Cuyas looked like any other peon, with a round face and a brown skin. When one came closer, one saw that his eyes were red and yellow about the pupils, as though they had been inflamed by constantly facing a strong wind. Antonio Cuyas had been longer with the great Oñate than any other of his followers. Treacherous in his dealings with other men, Antonio Cuyas feared his master more, even, than he loved his own well being.

Finally, fourth and greatest of the lot, there wa Arturo Llano, known throughout the length and breadth of Mexico. It was strange to think of such a man being a follower. All sorts of infamous achievements had been laid at his door. Yet, he actually surpassed rumor; he was one of those few men who had performed more than was credited to him. He was a big man, with a pair of well-squared shoulders, such as one often sees in a military man. And a soldier he had been, to be sure until the murder of his officer set him adrift. Ever since he had remained a fighting man, and, whether it were battle arranged on a large scale or simply a quiet little knife fight in a dark room, he was sure to be equally zealous, equally at home. The scars he had received were on his body as well as his face, but the face itself had been bullet-furrowed or knife-slashed no less than six times. Hence, it followed that though he had been a handsome, smooth-shaven fellow in his youth, his face was now covered with mustaches, beard, and side whiskers—a thick growth, but neatly trimmed.

Arturo Llano was the right hand of José Oñate. All four were a part and parcel of him. It was said that he possessed all of their peculiar virtues and all of their peculiar vices. They were himself divided into four separate parts. Yet, it was said, if all the four united against him, there was in Oñate more ferocity, more strength of mind and body than in the precious quartet.

Even Jeems Loring quailed a little as he saw the five coming.

"Jumping Cæsar!" said the great Jeems. "It's the old boy himself and his four house pets. There's trouble in the wind."

V
"A LAMB AMONG WOLVES"

THERE WAS TROUBLE AHEAD, INDEED. FOR THE FIRST thing that Don José suggested, after a most cordial greeting to all of the *gringos*, was that since the seven thousand head of cattle had been collected, it was time for some hard cash to be paid down on them—not the whole amount of their agreed value, but fifty percent of the total sum. He said this not to the purchaser, Randal Dale, but to that other and more famous man, Jeems Loring.

Loring answered: "You see how it is, José. These are wild cows, and who's gonna tell which way they're likely to run? After half the coin was paid down on 'em, they might turn around and run straight for the hills."

Don José smiled gently at the *gringo*. He said, in quite good English, with only an occasional wrong construction and only a slight lisp in some of the consonants: "There are all your good men and all my good men, ready to hold the cows together."

"Yeah," responded Jeems Loring, "but take it this way. Some of your boys don't speak English, and some of my boys don't speak no Mexican. Suppose they got all confused and started drivin' the cattle different ways. Look what a mess that would be."

Don José smiled again, deliberately, and looked Jeems Loring up and down. They had known one another—or about one another—for years. Each was a certain dubious kind of hero. Each knew the exploits that made the other famous. Perhaps no two men in the world more thoroughly yearned to gain further fame and reputation, each by putting the other down. But they avoided giving offense. Ordinary battles they would accept with delight, but for one another they preferred courtesy until, in the course of time, a pinch should come that would force matters to a conclusion. Not until that moment would the battle come.

So José Oñate, watched and listened to by his four main adherents, merely said: "There might start a stampede, it is true. Still, I have a great many hungry men, and some of them want their pay and wish to get back into the hills. They want their price for their cattle. That is all. Then they will go. Not all their money, but a part of it. You know, *señor*, that they are men of hard work. They cannot throw time away. They must return quickly to their duties."

Jeems Loring grinned, but not widely. He knew what sort of work the rascals employed by the great Oñate were usually engaged in. They wanted to return hastily to the mountains, no doubt, because down here in the lowlands they were likely to be too nakedly in the eye of the law. Mexican law was inclined to be a hit-or-miss affair, in those days, but, when it hit, it landed hard. Half a dozen grim-faced, gaudily uniformed *rurales*, expert with horse and gun, were liable to turn up at inconvenient moments and explode the penalties of the law like poison gas.

Loring slowly shook his head. "Friendship is friendship, José," he said, "and I'd like to please you by makin' a part payment now. But business is business, too, and you know that we bargained for payment when the cows climbed the north bank of the river."

Don José did not frown. He merely steadied his glance upon the American. And his four followers, of one accord, each picked a man and, in like manner, steadied glances upon their possible foes. It was a cold, still moment. Jeems Loring did not lose countenance, but there was an icy tingle up his spine. Then he said: "When it comes down to a pinch, José...."

He did not finish that sentence, and perhaps it was a lucky thing that he did not. At any rate, the tenderfoot, young Rancie Dale, broke in: "And why not pay what they want, Loring? I have the money with me in cash."

Fire shot from the eyes of José Oñate, as from the eyes of a hunting cat. "Good," he said.

Jeems Loring turned a look of disgust on his employer. "That's all right," he said. "That's quite all right. You got the money, brother, and nobody doubts it, but there ain't any use making your greenbacks into a flag and wavin' 'em around in the open air. I tell you what...this here Mexican sun is so strong that it's got a lot of fading power."

The innuendo was not any too subtle, but it did not reach the bland understanding of the boy. He said: "Is that so, Loring? But still, I'm not waving the money about, you know. I have it safely inside my coat pocket."

Jeems Loring snarled with disgust, and shrugged his shoulders. "You go and do your business in your own way, then," he said. "I've had my say. Now you play your own hand, brother."

Don José was the very essence of courtesy. He bowed to Rancie Dale and said: "There is the old *hacienda* where *Señor* Flandes now keeps a *fonda*. You can see the sun blink on the windows, yonder, beyond the dust."

"Yeah," said Loring. "It's blinking on those windows as red as blood."

There was a meaning in his voice, but again the meaning missed the cheerful mind of Rancie Dale.

Now Don José put in with: "Four of us, then, should be enough. We can settle everything. I and Arturo

Llano, you, *Señor* Dale, and my old friend, Jeems."

He drawled out the last word in a strange voice, and Jeems Loring squinted his eyes narrowly and peered, or strove to peer, into the interesting mind of the Mexican.

Perhaps he would have refused, but now the boy was saying: "Why not here, Don José? I have the money with me. I can count it out to you. It's ten dollars a head, isn't it? Wonderfully cheap, I'd say, and I have a lot more money than that with me."

A sort of stifled groan that sounded like despair came from the lips of Jeems Loring.

Then the groan was cut off midway, as he glanced at the handsome face of José Oñate and saw the man wink broadly, slowly, significantly.

A new thought flashed across the active mind of Loring. And he winked back.

"You know, *Señor* Dale," said the Mexican bandit, "that in my country we mix friendship with business. We put the two together, because we find it very unpleasant when we have to count *pesos* to no accompaniment but their own clinking. Now, in that *fonda*, there is some good, red, Mexican wine, and brandy, too, if you will have it, excellent cigars and cigarettes. And it seems to me, *señor*, that I can breathe the scent of roasted kid as it turns on the spit in the kitchen of that *fonda*. Shall we not go there to finish our little business?"

"Why, of course," said Rancie Dale cheerfully. "Of course, we'll go there."

He laughed in happy, cheerful anticipation. A moment later, a Colt revolver shone in his hand, and he began firing. His target was a lank desert rabbit that had cuddled down in a bunch of grass all this while and suddenly, like his foolish kind, unable to endure the presence of the danger, had bolted out into the open.

Once, twice, and again, Rancie Dale fired, his face set, a frown of determination upon his brow, but the bullets struck widely about the little, swerving streak of fur and speed that was bolting away toward the horizon. The others smiled grimly upon one another. Then, that *conquistador*, Arturo Llano, drew a gun, with casual grace, and fired once. The jack rabbit flung up high into the air, fell to the ground, and was still.

The joy and admiration of the boy knew no bounds. He smote Arturo Llano on the shoulder, thereby forever wounding the dignity of that gentleman, and exclaimed: "Why, that's simply magnificent! And at such a distance! What chance would even half a dozen men have if they tried to ride you down, *Señor* Llano? Tell me that. What chance would they have?"

Señor Llano looked him straight in the eye, twirled one end of a pointed pair of mustaches, and finally forced from his throat a faint murmur that might have been taken for disgust with this boyish fool of a *gringo* who did not know the proper manners that should go with men of the frontier.

"They wouldn't have much chance," said Jeems Loring. "Not if they shot a gun the way you do, Dale. Ever practice with it?"

"Practice?" said Rancie Dale, his good humor not in the least troubled by the last sarcasm. "Oh, yes, I've practiced with a revolver a great deal. For hours and hours, in fact." He laughed a little. "But rabbits are hard to hit."

"So are men," snapped the disgusted Jeems Loring. "Don't forget that, son. A Mexican is the hardest thing in the world to plaster with lead. They can make themselves smaller than a knife edge, and they can come

101

at you, dodging faster than a snipe that's flying down wind, and don't you forget it."

"A very strange thing," said Rancie Dale, opening his large, blue eyes. "Of course, I won't forget it."

Loring was already at the side of Don José. He said quietly: "You see how it is. There's two of us, and there's two of you. But the fool of a kid don't count. He's nothing. It's me against you and Arturo, and that's too much, if a pinch came. You know what I mean?"

Don José nodded. He was grave, and he straightened himself a little in the saddle as he answered: "Between you and me, Don Jeems, there does not have to be lying, eh? If you come over to the *fonda* with us, we work together…you and I and my friend, Arturo. Look, my friend, there is enough fruit hanging on that tree to fill all our pockets. And it hangs very low. Even a child could pick it."

Sudden, smooth joy slid over the face of Jeems. "Yeah," he said, "a kid could pick it off the highest branch. No half-wit, like him, deserves to carry that much freight around with him. José, I'm gonna trust you and make a try of it."

VI
"TROUBLE ON THE WIND"

TELL ME, SINCE TIME BEGAN, WHAT CROWD OF MORE perfect ruffians ever gathered together to prey upon one poor, wretched boy? Any one of the three appeared in himself ten times more than sufficient to overcome any resistance that the tenderfoot could offer. But there they were, banded together—the great Arturo Llano, Jeems Loring, famed through many a land and, last and most deadly of all, that man-queller, José Oñate. All of these banded together for the plundering of one boy!

They distributed the task of holding and watching the herd through the night to the overseership of Paley and Alabama Joe, and to the attention of Cuyas, Girones, and Pedro Iribas. Then the four cantered away at the rocking gait of a Western horse, reaching the *fonda* at dusk.

It was not an attractive place from the outside, and the nearer it came, the less attractive it appeared. It stood naked to the bitter heat of the summer, without the suggestion of a tree about it. There was not even a hill for it to stand upon to take any chance breezes that might wander by. There was only a little swale of sand about it, making the place appear a little higher than it was, in fact. It was simply a blunt, square, white-washed lump of a building dumped down upon the desert. There were two stories. That was all, unless one chose to give consideration, also, to the tangle of fencing at one side of the house and a few sheds that were falling to pieces. These were signs that at one time considerable bodies of cattle must have been handled from the ranch house. There was no verdure, yet it was certain that there must be at least a good well about the place.

The house was old, indeed, built with very massive walls, for it is not easy to raise adobe walls to the height of two tall stories, unless the sun-dried bricks are heaped up like a great mound, rather than a mere wall. Into these walls were sunk a few casements, a very few, and these were so small and deep that they looked rather like lookouts of a fort than windows of a house. For the heat of the sun would be besieging this place through nine long months of the year.

Time was telling on the old place; the thick wall of whitewash that had accumulated on it in a thousand paintings had crumbled away near the ground. For five or six feet above the base, the walls were eaten slightly away from the outside and were the color of plain mud. Winter rains would account for that.

Altogether, young Randal Dale never had come near a place that raised fewer expectations in him than did this lonely outpost, but, when they drew up in the very front of it, at the shout of Don José, a battered old door that filled in an archway in the middle of the wall opened its two groaning panels, and the men rode into a large, enclosed court. It was a naked place, as naked as the outside of the building, but the effect was quite different, for around it ran a clumsy, adobe arcade, and above the arcade appeared larger windows, set in the deep casements. It looked to young Rancie Dale like a cross between a modern barn and an ancient castle. A sense of time and of romantic adventure breathed through the place.

A peon, bare-legged, was leaning against one panel of the gate, slowly walking it shut behind them. Looking out through that diminishing exit, Dale saw the fog of dust, rising above the milling cattle and turning dull crimson against the rim of the sky. He made out the dream-like dimness of the moving cattle, the riders circling on the verge of the great herd, and now, as the second panel of the gate shut out that picture, he heard the lowing of the thousands boom across the air, while the ground seemed to tremble beneath his feet as he dismounted.

The host himself now appeared in the court and was bowing and waving to them with affability, but with a good deal of dignity as well. Servants appeared, active, ragged house *mozos*, who took the horses by the bridles and held the stirrups as the guests dismounted.

Rancie Dale understood Spanish very well, indeed. He understood, also, a good deal of the Mexican dialect, but for a time he found it hard to follow the chatter of greetings and orders, as Don José made himself at home and ordered an excellent dinner with the best red wine that the inn had to offer. The host, immediately after, was considered important enough to be introduced by name, and it appeared that he was Bartolomé Flandes. He shook the hand of Dale and assured him that the house was at his disposal, at the disposal, in fact, of all of the good friends of José Oñate. He, Flandes, would now busy himself with the arrangements for their dinner, and his daughter would take them into the garden. They could walk there, or they could sit and drink an appetizer in the garden, if they chose.

They would walk, said Don José. Llano, twisting at a mustache, exclaimed: "*Señor* Flandes, what man in the world is such a fool that he would rather sit and drink, than stand up and walk with the *Señorita* Maruja?"

That was well enough. One expected that a fellow like Don José, or fire-eating Arturo Llano, would be extravagant in speaking of almost any woman. But Randal Dale pricked up his ears when he heard Jeems Loring mutter: "I seen her once, four, five years back. She was only a spindling brat about fifteen then, but god damn it if she didn't stop a man like a bullet between the eyes."

At this, in an arch of the arcade that surrounded the patio, a small door opened, and there Dale had a glimpse of the garden beyond, green and glistening faintly in the evening light. In the doorway itself stood Maruja Flandes. She startled him as though a light had been flashed into this eyes. Why had not the others prepared him for this unexpected beauty, not black and olive-brown, but golden and blue, and tan that was richer than bronze? He looked at her, smiling, and suddenly his heart laughed in him joyously.

She took the hands of the others; she welcomed them in a quiet, gentle voice, and then Randal Dale stood before her and received a second shock. He had conceived of her, through the mist of the evening light, as a slender, child-like, winsome creature, and he was wrong. He had thought of her as something that will fit easily into the heart of any manly man. But now he saw that she was quite a different affair.

True, the hair was golden, if it were not too red to be called by that name. And the eyes were blue, but she was no clinging vine. A hundred and thirty or thirty-five pounds of whalebone and sun-dried muscle cannot be made into a clinging vine. And that was what she was. No matter how comely, here was one likely to challenge any man in the riding of a horse or the climbing of a mountain. Her hand grasp was firm, with the strength of the muscles behind it. Her very eye was not that of a woman, either overconfident or overly shy, but a level, steady glance that went against his face like the scrutiny of any man—not an altogether too friendly man, at that. It took his breath away. "Confounded masculine creature," he murmured to himself, and stepped into the garden with the others.

The beauty of the garden itself disarmed him almost at once. It was built against the back of the house and surrounded by a tall wall of adobe bricks. The top of that wall had broken down with the process of time and looked like the ruin of old battlements. Even the garden itself appeared old and battered. At the farther end of it, only half screened behind a badly worn hedge, he could make out the power beam and the white circle of dust in which the power mule walked in lifting up water from the well. That was the water, no doubt, that had made this once a good site for a ranch house. That was the water that made the pool in the center of the garden, with its flat, green floats of leaves and the water lilies crimson and yellow and white, giving off a sweet odor. That was the water, too, that had newly drenched all of the garden ground, so newly that one could still, with an attentive ear, hear the sound of the soil that was yet thirstily drinking, deep and deeper, down to the smallest roots of the bushes and the vines.

It was, indeed, a battered garden, but this was the best moment to see it, when the dusk covered the bruises of time and allowed one to enjoy the fragrance of the flowers and their dull sheen. There were monstrous blossoms here that Randal Dale could not identify; there were blooms that looked like full moons, shining through clouds, and others that burned through the dimness like flames.

Dale came out of a trance to hear the brisk, rather hard voice of Arturo Llano, talking with the girl. The other men had fallen back a little, giving Llano precedence, in walking down the garden path with the girl.

Dale heard Jeems Loring saying: "Well, José, it looks as though your side-kicker, yonder, wanted to settle down and start a home, eh?" As he said this, he laughed a little.

"Why do you laugh, Don Jeems?" asked the Mexican. "My friend, Arturo, would be a good husband to her. He is not one of those who can love more than one woman in his lifetime."

"They'd have a kind of a peaceful life, wouldn't they?" suggested Jeems Loring. "What I mean is, with the *rurales* knocking on the front door every Monday and on the back door every Tuesday. Yeah, they'd have a peaceful life." He laughed again.

"You know, *amigo*, that happiness is something to be plucked here and there," said Don José. "If it withers in your hand after a few moments, why, let it wither. Everything dies before very long, including ourselves."

"Well, that's an answer," said Loring. "That's a kind of an answer, anyway. But you know what I smell in the air?"

"Tell me," said Don José.

"Trouble," said Jeems Loring. "I can smell it on the wind, as sure as ever a fox smells wolf and starts home with his brush down."

There might have been more talk. But now a *mozo* came scurrying and stood panting before them to announce that dinner was ready.

VII
"DINNER AND DYNAMITE"

IT WAS A STRANGE DINNER. *SEÑOR* BARTOLOMÉ Flandes sat at the table with them, sipping red wine from a massive, old goblet, but tasting no meat. His daughter moved here and there, into the kitchen and out again, overseeing the service. There was that same roast kid, concerning which José Oñate had prophesied. In addition to that, there was a stacking of tortillas and red-hot beans, prepared as only the artists of Mexico knew how to cook that fiery sauce with peppers, green and red. There was plenty of wine to wash down this meal, and there was little talk while the food was being absorbed. There was only a very occasional sharp glance of curiosity directed toward young Randal Dale as he consumed one helping of the beans and then passed his plate for another. While he ate a portion that would have wrung tears of pleasure and pain from the eyes of even the hardiest Mexican, it was noted by all that there was not so much as moisture about the eyes of Rancie Dale. He declared that he never had eaten the dish before, but to his thinking it was the best he had ever tasted.

"You know, *Señor* Dale," said Flandes, the host, "although you say that you have never been in Mexico before, yet you are able to speak Spanish, and Mexican also. How does that happen?"

"When I was a youngster on my father's place in Virginia," said the boy, "a man came and asked for work. He was different from anyone we had seen before. He spoke a rather bad English, but we couldn't tell his nationality, and he wouldn't talk about it. But he got work, quickly enough, because he turned out to be a fellow who could stick on the back of the worst horses on the place. There was only one trouble about him. The horses that he could ride were hardly any easier for others after he got out of the saddle. He had an art of his own, in sticking on the back of anything that wore horsehide, and he didn't care at all what sort of a saddle was up. A mere blanket was equally good for him, it seemed. I've seen him stick on a bare back when any of the other boys would have been thrown from a good saddle.

"Well, after a time, a police officer showed up and began to ask questions about this new man of ours, whom we used to call Dick. The policeman was asking for a certain Ricardo, who was a Mexican, and wanted for killing three men."

"A-ha!" said Flandes, Llano, and José Oñate all in a

breath. Jeems Loring grinned broadly.

"Did they get him?" asked Flandes.

"You see," said Rancie, "I guessed at once whom they wanted, and so I slipped away, got to the stable, and warned Dick. I called him by his Mexican name, and I thought for an instant that he would put a knife in me, but then he seemed to realize that I was a friend, and I told him where to hide out on the bank of the creek, in an old cave where we youngsters used to play pirate, you see."

"*Señor*, I see that you are a man to have for a friend," said Flandes.

Dale, with a smile, waved the compliment aside. "For three or four weeks, the police were hanging around, searching," he went on, "and I had to slip out from the house with food and bring it to my friend, Ricardo. He lived close in the cave, and lived pretty well, too, and I think that those days were about the happiest in my life, because he used to talk to me by the hour about Mexico and his old life. I used to get out of bed at night and go out to him, and he'd sit in a sputter of lantern light and tell me stories that raised the hair on my head.

"He had done a good many things that were outside the law, you see. He was an expert robber, and he loved a revolver almost as much as he loved a knife. He used to show me how he handled a gun. Sometimes we walked out into the hills, and he would give me exhibitions of shooting. He was wonderful with a revolver. He was an expert, as you people all seem to be." He looked about the table and flattered them with an all-inclusive smile. "But with a knife," said the boy, "he was a great artist."

"Ah?" said Flandes. "What could he do?"

"Well, I used to throw up apples, and he got every

110

apple while it was sailing through the air. He used to hold the knife in the flat of his hand and stare at the target, and then there would be a sudden flash, and a line of light would leap from his hand straight into the target, whatever it was. They were small knives with weighted handles. Have you ever seen such things?"

Flandes looked at Don José, and José at Llano, and all the three of them smiled with understanding. It was plain that they had seen exactly similar things and understood all about them.

"What became of your friend Ricardo? Did he have a last name?"

"Oh, yes. His last name was Briguez."

"Hah? Ricardo Briguez?" cried out Don José.

"That was the name he told me," said the boy.

"A short man with a scar slanting up over one eye and disappearing into his hair?" continued Don José.

"Yes. Did you know him?"

"Yes, I knew him," said José Oñate. "I knew him very well, too." He broke off speaking and looked rather gloomily straight before him.

"I knew of Briguez, also," said Flandes, with equal soberness of tone. "And he got away from Virginia and the police?"

"A friend of my father's ran freighters to Central America," said Rancie. "I knew him, and I took a chance and opened up with the whole story. He was interested. So we smuggled Ricardo down to the docks and shipped him away. That's the last I ever heard of him."

"The last?" said Flandes, frowning.

"Yes. I never knew what became of him."

"That's not like Briguez," broke in Llano. "He never forgets a kindness done to him. Never!"

111

"You know him? He is still alive?" asked young Randal Dale.

"I know him. A good many other people know him. He has changed his name a few times, but he is still Ricardo," said Llano. "If I ever meet him again...." He stopped. His face was fierce.

"He may have written back to me," said Rancie Dale, "and the letter may have gone astray. I don't know about that. But now, Don José, can't we talk business and get things finished up?"

The meal was ended. They had only the red wine before them, and fruit.

"As good a time now as ever," said the Mexican. "You could make the half down payment...that is, five dollars for each head, and there are about seven thousand. Have you as much as thirty-five thousand dollars with you, *amigo*?" He spoke softly, but his eyes burned so that he hastily glanced down to the table.

"Thirty-five thousand?" said the boy. "Yes, I have that much and a great deal more. I don't see why I shouldn't pay you the entire amount at once."

He took a wallet from his coat pocket, and out of the wallet he took the same thick stack of greenbacks Loring had seen at the hotel in Greensville.

There fell a pause. All eyes considered that thick heap, so closely compressed, like the pages of a book. The girl, Maruja, coming out through the kitchen door, glided on noiseless feet into the dull outer circle of the lamplight and stared down at the treasure also. Slowly she began to nod, unseen by anyone.

"That is a great deal of money," said Don José. "Yes, you could pay for all the cattle now. Why not?"

"Yes. Why not?" asked the boy very cheerfully.

"I'll tell you why not!" said a voice, so harsh and

strained that everyone started, because it was not recognized as coming from any of that company. But it was Jeems Loring. "Here's the reason. I made a bargain. Did I make the bargain for you, Dale?" he asked.

"Why, yes," said Rancie Dale, turning with innocent surprise and interest to his employee.

"And the bargain was payment when the cows were drove up the north bank of the Rio Grande, safe and sound. It ain't in the bargain to make even a half payment this far south of the river. But let that go. You can make the half payment, all right. But not a penny more. It ain't business. That's what it ain't!"

"And why not?" asked Don José, in the softest of soft voices.

"I guess you know why it ain't business," said Jeems tartly. "If the police or the border guard or a patch of Texas Rangers or the *rurales* got wind of this and started to...."

"Why," exclaimed Rancie Dale, "and what has this deal to do with the police, if you please? What is there about it that would interest them?"

"Look here," broke in Jeems Loring. "D'you think that you can buy cows for ten dollars a scalp when the regular price is...?"

The hand of Don José, unseen beneath the table, laid upon the arm of the speaker a grip of iron. Jeems Loring fell silent.

"Ten dollars," said Dale, "seems to me wonderfully cheap, of course. Is there anything wrong with the cattle, Loring?"

Loring, breathing hard, bent his head and looked fixedly down at the table. Then he said slowly: "No, there ain't anything wrong with the cattle. You seen 'em. They got plenty of life to 'em."

113

"Then I don't understand why the police...?" began the boy.

"No, you're new to the country, and you're green to the country," said the other. "I guess you wouldn't understand. It's only the way that we've got of doing business down here. What I said for the bargain is what I'd stick to. There ain't any two ways about it."

Dale rose with a laugh. "You argue with my friend," he said to the two Mexicans. "I'm no businessman. I'll walk out in the garden, because I can see a moon beyond that window. Let me know when you've come to an agreement, and tell me what I'm to do."

VIII
"CARDS"

HE HAD NO SOONER LEFT THE ROOM FOR THE GARDEN than the host, Flandes, stood up. He was a fine figure of a man with this peculiar feature—his hair and eyes were distinctly black, but his eyebrows were somewhat reddish in hue, and, since he was not very closely shaved, the skin of his face was slightly tinged with red.

"My friends," he said, "it appears that there is business between you concerning *Señor* Dale. I hope that he will not be injured in whatever you may decide."

Then he left the room. It was an odd speech, the sort that one would never expect from a hotelkeeper, even though the host were a gentleman born, as was *Señor* Flandes. When he had departed, the three rogues who remained looked grimly at one another.

"He thinks that we're gonna frame this kid," said Jeems Loring at last, thrusting out his long, lower jaw.

"And that," said Don José pleasantly, "is just what we are going to do." He turned to his henchman, the famous

114

Llano. "How much money was in that sheaf?" he asked.

"Of course, that depends," said Llano. "If there's nothing less than a hundred-dollar bill in the stack, then there's, why, there may be a hundred and twenty or thirty thousand dollars in that pile."

He said this impressively, but his chief looked grimly at him and answered: "I saw a thousand, three up from the bottom of the stack. There are a few thousand-dollar bills in that stack, I take it." He looked across at Jeems. "What do you think, Jeems?" he asked.

Jeems Loring was still hesitating. At last he spoke his mind frankly: "It's this way. I got this bird framed. I got him planted, and he's all mine. Then I lead him up and give you a chance to knife him. Why should I do that? Look a-here, José. You're gonna clean up big on your slice out of the cattle deal. You got those cows at not more'n five dollars apiece. You'll sell 'em for ten. That fool of a brat, he don't realize that they're stolen goods. He wants to make his clean-up honest. Why ain't you contented with your cut on the cows?"

Don José leaned his chin upon his left hand, and he smiled, deliberately and slowly, into the eyes of Loring. Then he said, "Jeems, dear friend!"

Jeems Loring stirred a little in his chair. "Don't be a pig, José," he suggested.

"Jeems, dear friend," repeated Don José. And still he smiled.

Jeems Loring grew flushed with passion. "I frame the whole thing, and I work it up," he said, "and then you want to knife in like you had joined from the first and helped make the plant. You wouldn't even know how much coin there was in the deal, if the kid hadn't been such a fool as to flash his roll. I never seen such a fool in my life!" he ended viciously.

"Ah, my dear Jeems, a kind fate that watches over good thieves," said Don José, "only sends to the world once in a long time a great deal of easy money from one loose pocket. *Señor* Dale is such a gift from heaven to us. Do you think that Providence intends that all of this loot should pass into one pair of hands? Do you really think that you are the only one who should be allowed to dip into the pot?"

Loring answered him savagely: "Whacha mean by that? I got a gang of thugs that'll drain me dry before I'm through with 'em. I got a dozen of the hardest-fighting boys north of the river, and you know it. They'll want money, and they'll want big money."

"For two or three days' work, they will not want more than two or three thousand apiece," said Don José. "I also have used some of those very same men, my friend. I know their prices. They are too innocent to think of the sums of money that can be made from simple people like *Señor* Dale."

Jeems Loring gritted his teeth. Then, suddenly, he threw up his hands. "It ain't my fault," he complained. "I was gonna make the play close to my chest. I wasn't gonna make any fool moves. You never would've known that you was next to a gold mine, but that rat-headed brat, he had to flash his whole roll…his *whole* roll." He ended with a groan.

"He should not be burdened," said Don José.

"We will help him to do without the money," said Llano, nodding his head.

Jeems Loring sat forward, rested his elbows on the table, and nodded his head in turn. "After the beans are spilled, there ain't any use crying," he said. "You know the low-down. And now I'll play with you. We split it all around. I'll need twenty thousand to square my gang, maybe. Count that out, and then we'll cut the rest in three lumps."

Don José allowed his gentle smile once more to play over his lips. "I also have retainers," he said.

Loring cursed violently, but softly, so that there was a hissing between his teeth. He answered finally, choking on the words. "This is a plain hold-up, but you have me cornered. I might've known that I'd be cornered when I come to this joint. We'll cut the whole lump in three chunks then, you robbers."

"Very hard words, very hard words," said Don José, and he laughed, looking at Llano.

The latter merely grinned, and his grin was exceedingly brief.

"Now then," said Jeems Loring, "since we've got the case all framed up, what's the best idea?"

"Send out word to run the cattle toward the river. It's late enough now," said Don José.

"All right. That's going to get the rest of the boys off my hands."

"True," said Don José, pinching his lips hard on the words. "They'll be gone north. After the money is split, if you ride south, you might never meet any of them, and you might never have to pay out hard cash to any of them."

He looked hard and straight at Jeems Loring, but the latter did not notice. He began to nod over his own thoughts. "Yeah, better march 'em on toward the north," he said.

Loring went to the door and called to Flandes to send a messenger to the head cowmen, controlling the herd, with orders to start them north at once toward the river.

"Is the river clear?" asked Llano, as the other turned and came back.

"I don't know, and I don't give a god damn," said Jeems Loring. "It ain't the cows that I'm interested in. It was simply getting that fool of a tenderfoot handy on the spot, with all of his hard cash in his pockets. He was telling me that there's a fortune in cattle. Sure there is, if they're worked the way that the three of us are gonna work 'em." He settled down in his chair, poured out a glass of the thick red wine, then changed his mind, and pushed the glass away. "I gotta have a clear head," he murmured.

"How do we begin?" asked Llano. "Do we simply use a knife or a gun, and then cover up the body?"

"Not here," said Don José hastily.

"Great heavens, no," said Llano, jumping up in reaction against his own suggestion. "I had forgotten Maruja. She would not like such a thing."

"Wouldn't she?" said Jeems. "She'd like any man that had a third of that money in his pocket, though."

"Suppose," said Don José, "that she may be out in the garden now, persuading young *Señor* Dale that the best plan for him is to ride quickly away and forget all about a herd of seven thousand cows?"

"Would she do that?" asked Jeems Loring.

"She would do anything," said Don José calmly. "She is not fond of thieves."

"She don't know what we're up to," said Loring. "She couldn't know."

"She has an instinct that warns her of danger when it is still far away," said the great Don José. "I understand her...a very little."

"She's a straight girl, is she?" asked Loring, interested. "Look here, brother, she's too pretty to be straight, and this far south."

Don José rested his glance upon Loring meditatively.

Llano, when he understood the implied insult, rose savagely to his feet, but with the mere motion of his hand Don José forced the other to sit down again.

"Do you know what you are saying, Jeems?" he asked.

"Me?" said Loring. "Oh, I see what you mean. No, I ain't reflecting on Mexican girls, José. No, women ain't anything to me. I'm too old for 'em. And they're too young for me. Too young altogether."

"So," said Llano, relaxing suddenly in his chair.

"Yeah, and exactly so," said Loring, scowling at the mustached Mexican.

"Quietly, quietly, my friend. There is only one thing to do," said Don José, "and that is to extract as painlessly as possible from young *Señor* Dale, that very young gentleman, the money that is now in his pocket."

"Aw, all right," said Jeems Loring. "I dunno that I care much what happens, so long as we get our mitts on the coin."

"It shall be done," said Don José.

"You bet it'll be done," said Loring.

"And why not the butt end of a gun?" asked Llano, thrusting out his chin in such a way that his beard bristled and thrust forward.

"Hush," said his chief, raising a slender hand, an expression of pain on his face. "Maruja would never forgive us, and her forgiveness means a great deal to you, my friend."

Llano settled back from his eagerness and squared his shoulders against the back of his chair.

"Cards, then," he said.

"Exactly," agreed Don José, "and you could win the longest feathers out of the wings of the angel, Gabriel, at poker or dice. You are the man."

IX
"IN THE GARDEN"

IN THE MEANTIME, YOUNG RANCIE DALE WAS strolling through the garden in the moonlight, and he had not gone far before Maruja Flandes came out to him, bringing his coffee in her hand. He looked at her with admiration that chiefly dwelt on her long, free, easily swinging step, the straight carriage of her shoulders, and the way her head was placed upon them, lending dignity to her whole figure.

She told him that he had forgotten the coffee, and dinner was not dinner without it. It was her father's chief secret. He made it so well that she, Maruja, had often advised him to go to the Mexico City, and there open a coffee shop. They would do very well at it, to be sure.

Rancie Dale took the coffee cup, and the girl waited for him to finish sipping it so that she could take it back. He was glad to hold her there in this way, with the mist of moonshine about her, making a close, intimate halo in the red-gold of her hair. It was odd to see her in such a light, she was such a vigorous, noon-day personality and figure.

"Would you like that better…to be in Mexico City?" he asked.

"In Mexico City?" she repeated, rather vaguely.

"Yes, you'd like that better," he said, venturing to put in the answer as well as the question. "I can imagine that things are pretty dull out here in the desert. In a big town, you could have a good deal more fun."

"Could I?" she answered. "I could settle down as a shopkeeper's wife. What fun would that be?"

"But think of all the parties and all the young people?"

"Making a lot of noise is not my idea of a party," she answered. "I've been in Mexico City. I'd rather go into a tomb."

"Really!" he exclaimed in cheerful surprise.

"Yes, I'd a thousand times rather live out here."

"I'll try to believe that," said Rancie Dale. "Will you tell me what happens out here in the *fonda?*"

"I could tell you for hours and hours," she replied. "I don't sit at home like a silly baby. I ride and shoot and rope almost as well as a man. So I do what the young men do. I go hunting. I can work as an extra hand at a roundup, if there's need of me. I've...I've bulldogged a yearling!" She brought this out as an exclamation that seemed as much of defiance and shame as of triumph.

"Bulldogged a yearling!" he repeated. "Why, I don't think that I could do that."

"It's a knack," she said. "I wouldn't want to try it again, I don't think. But I stuck at the game long enough to learn how to do it." She began to laugh.

"You've had your fun like a boy," he suggested.

"Well, more or less," she agreed.

"You could ride, or shoot, or run, or climb like a man?"

"No, not just the same. I'm pretty good with a rifle...I'm nothing with a revolver," she admitted. "I can hit something only once in a while, I mean. I can run. I can climb pretty well, but a woman hasn't the same driving muscles and sinews that a man has. I can swim, though, better than most men. I can ride as well as a lot of 'em, too." She added up those accomplishments gravely, without boasting, and went on: "You see, I can do enough to enjoy the country. Father and I have our good times in the mountains back there. It's a fifty-mile ride to get into 'em, into the good hunting districts. Sometimes we ride there one night, hunt two days, and ride back at night again. When you say Mexico City to me, I wonder what I would do there but wear a *mantilla* and sit still and talk small talk. I'd rather...," she ended, with some emotion, "I'd rather live out here in the desert with no more than a single hawk in the sky than be back there in the big city with half a million people around!"

He still lingered over the coffee, so that he could watch her more closely. "I can understand what you mean in part," he said. "For the same reasons, I should like to live somewhere in the West...in my own country, of course."

She nodded, but she said: "You have to learn how to live out here, you know. It isn't what it seems at the first glance. Before you can get along very well, you have to be toughened. D'you think that you're tanned enough to stand Western life?"

"Tanned? Do you mean colored by the sun?"

"Yes, prepared for hard use, like leather."

"I think that I could be hardened. I have the size, to begin with."

There was a stone bench at the edge of the pool of water lilies. She sat down on it and pointed to a place beside her. "I want to talk to you," she said.

He obediently took the place, turning toward her, holding the coffee cup rather high, perhaps to keep her from seeing that there was hardly a drop of the black liquid left.

"Do you know those three men in the house?" she asked.

"Loring and Don José and Llano?"

"Yes."

"Why, I have known Loring pretty well for several days. He was pointed out to me as one of the best men in the country."

"Best with a gun," she answered.

"How?"

"Best with a gun. A good many dead ghosts know how good he is with a gun."

"He's a fighting man, is he?" said the boy. "I guessed that much. There's a careless way about him that brave men have, as I've noticed before."

"He's killed a dozen men, at least." She waited, sitting a little straighter.

"As many as that?" exclaimed the boy with enthusiasm. "What a man! All of them fighting people, of course?"

"Oh, they were fighting people, of course. Couple of sheriffs on the list, I think."

"Really?" he asked. Then he laughed a little. "He's one of the Robin Hoods, is he?" suggested Rancie Dale. "I could almost have guessed that."

"Robin Hood? Well, other people call him by different names. The other two, Don José and Llano, they're the same kind."

"Robin Hoods?"

"At least, they're not working men," she commented, and again she waited, as if to let him take the hint that lay behind her words. He merely shrugged his shoulders.

"Some people are drudges," he said. "And some are fighting men who don't like work. They use their brains and their hands in different ways. Some of the most glorious people in the world are of that sort. I've met a few of 'em, here and there."

She paused again and, putting her chin on one strong fist, she stared at the silver glimmer of the moon spread over the face of the water and the big pads. On one of those pads a frog appeared and began to croak with a dull, booming note.

"How old are you, *Señor* Dale?" she asked.

"Twenty-four."

"As much as that?"

"Yes. Why?"

"But you haven't lived your twenty-four years out here, have you?"

"No, of course not."

"Well, all I can say is that, if I were you, I'd spend a few more years in the land before I made up my mind about the characters of the men who are in it."

"And what do you mean by that?" he queried.

"I can't say much more. You ought to be able to guess something from what I've said already."

"Guess?" he queried. "Guess at what, if you please?"

She stood up suddenly, held out her hand, and he meekly surrendered the coffee cup. He stood in turn, a big, stalwart form before her.

"I've said more than I should have," she answered. "I only hope one thing."

"And what is that?"

"That you come to no great harm."

"Harm?" he echoed. Then he added: "I understand. You think that I don't know enough to get along in the cattle business. Of course not, but you see that I'm taking in the best sort of experienced men to teach me what to do. There's my friend, Jeems Loring, for instance. He seems to know all about cattle. And I'll always have men like him around me."

"Will you?" said the girl more or less dryly.

"Certainly. When you think of it, it's a grand world where a man can find so much honesty and truth, kindness, and willingness to help others."

A faint murmur parted her lips. That was all.

"Even if the cattle business turns out a failure," he explained with his usual optimistic cheerfulness, "there is always the lesson learned, which is something gained." He lifted his head as he said this and smiled down at her with such tremendous faith in existence, as it seemed, that she actually moved a short step back from him.

Then, suddenly, she came straight up to him and said, looking up into his face: "Do you know something? I half believe that you don't mean what you're saying, and that you see through this situation and all of these people as clear as daylight."

"See through them? See through them?" he repeated. "Why, I see through them as they are, of course...free-swinging, honest, open-hearted, genuine Westerners, the sort of men I want to know, the sort of men I want for friends. That's how I see them, and how else could I see them?"

Slowly she said: "You great, foolish baby!" Then she turned and went swiftly toward the house. At that instant the door opened upon the garden and the voice of Llano called: "*Señor* Dale, will you come in?"

X
"SOMETHING GOES WRONG"

MARUJA WENT BACK INTO THE HOUSE, DROPPED THE coffee cup on a table, regardless of whether or not it shattered, and asked a startled *mozo* where she could find her father. He was in his own room, so she went straight up to him and found him lying on a couch that was covered with a pair of great sheepskins, reading by lamplight out of a book with a time-yellowed paper cover. Maruja sat in the casement with the moonlight streaming over her shoulders.

"Father," she said, "what is going to happen?"

"To the *gringo?*" he asked.

"Whatever he is," said the girl, "he has sat at your table and eaten your food."

"Food that is bought is not food that is given," said Flandes, with a slight shrug of his shoulders.

"You sat at a table with him," she insisted. "Was that right?"

"I sat where I had to sit," he answered. "You saw who was there, giving me orders."

"I saw three murderers."

He raised a quick hand to stop her.

"Murderers," she repeated. "You know that they're nothing else. Nothing but murderers."

"Nonsense!" he responded. "Whatever they are, you know my rule. Through no fault of mine or my father, or his father before him, we have been stripped of everything until we have only this house left. We have done what we could, honestly. We have only the house left. Now, whatever happens, so long as I have no hand in any rascality, I close my eyes."

"That is a weak religion," she stated.

"It is not a religion, but a necessity," he answered. "I've argued it out with you before."

"Nothing must happen to this *gringo*."

"Do you like his blue eyes so much, Maruja?" asked the innkeeper, looking calmly at her.

"I like him well enough," she said. "He is big, and I like bigness. He is handsome, and I like that, too. Besides, there is something else about him."

"His foolishness?" he suggested.

"He may be a fool. I really don't know."

"Think of an idiot willing to trust to José and Llano

126

and Jeems Loring, that cunning fox," he said, laughing a little.

"I don't want to talk as though I could read minds."

"Go ahead," he suggested.

"But," she continued, "while I was talking to him, a moment ago, suddenly it seemed to me that there was something behind his smile and behind his eyes, as though he were seeing through the whole situation and understanding it perfectly."

The man sat suddenly upright. "What nonsense is this, Maruja?" he asked.

"It may be nonsense," she said. "But all at once I was afraid of him. I'm not afraid usually, you know that."

"Well, I understand now. It's sentimentality," he said. "He's turned your head. A woman is always a little afraid of a man who's turning her head."

He waited for a denial, but, instead, she answered: "Perhaps that's it. I don't know, but I don't think so. I've had my head turned before, but it wasn't like this."

"Who turned your head before?" he demanded, sitting straighter than ever.

"Arturo Llano."

"He? A cutthroat! What was there about him that turned your head, if you please?"

"Several things. His scars," she answered, "his fame, his dead men, and the fact that he really seems to love me."

"Seems?" cried the father, leaping to his feet. "What do you mean?"

"He wants to marry me."

"I'll strike him dead," began the innkeeper, and then he checked himself.

"You'd strike him dead before you'd let me marry him?" asked the girl curiously. "No, you wouldn't quite

127

do that. Besides, he may still be seriously interested, but I'm not."

"Who else turned your head?" snapped Flandes.

"Don José, of course."

The innkeeper smiled. "Ah, Don José, of course!"

Maruja leaned her head a little to one side and studied her father, and all men in him.

"That would be different?" she asked.

"Why, Don José…of course. Don José would be different."

"The law will get him before it gets Llano," she said.

Her father waved this suggestion aside. "Don José is a prince among men," he declared.

"Among man-killers and thieves," corrected the girl.

"My dear Maruja, there is a sense of proportion in all things. Don José is known through the entire country. He is a prince of his kind."

"Well," said Maruja, "he turned my head for a while, but not for a great time. And I tell you that what I felt about Llano and about Don José was very different from what I feel about *Señor* Dale."

"Every woman has something in her that makes her pity a fool and makes her wish to mother him and shield him from the world."

"It may be that," answered the girl, with her usual frankness. "But a woman is not afraid of a fool."

"Are you really afraid of this *gringo?*" asked her father.

"In a way, yes."

"Stuff!" said Flandes.

He walked up to her and laid a hand on her shoulder. "Tell me the truth," he said.

"I always tell you the whole truth," she answered. "This big man, with his foolish, frank way, I'm not so sure that he is so entirely open and frank. That's all."

"What could be behind it? He's in the lion's den. Do you think that he put himself in with the lions on purpose?"

She lifted a forefinger. "That," she said, "is exactly what I have been thinking. Only an idea, just a dark shadow of an idea. If he came here on purpose, knowing all of the danger, then he is such a man as that I have never even dreamed. Not even a José Oñate would dare to do such a thing." She stood up from the casement, her face alight.

"On purpose?" exclaimed Flandes. "Came here on purpose knowing what Jeems Loring and José Oñate and Arturo Llano really are? No man would dare do such a thing. You are a foolish girl, Maruja. Go to bed and get these silly thoughts out of your head."

She kissed him good night and left the room without another word, but she did not go to bed. Instead, she went to that upper room to which Don José and Jeems Loring had retired to drink more red wine and tell tales, each man, out of his crowded past.

When she tapped at the door, Oñate opened it to her and would have bowed her in, but she remained in the dusky gloom of the hall, hardly touched by the lamplight from the room.

"José," she said, "you are going to take the money from the *gringo*, is that not true?"

"Of course, it is true, Maruja," he said instantly. "It is a dangerous thing to allow such a man to wander about through the world, carrying such a burden. He might fall into rough hands, and then what would happen to him?"

"Very well, I understand," she stated. "I don't care about the money. But his life, José?"

"Do you care about his life?" asked José.

"He is such a great, young fool," said the girl.

José leaned in the doorway, laughing. The metal braid of his jacket gleamed and trembled. "He is a fool," he said.

"And now about his life?"

"Why," said José, "the money will be taken away from him so painlessly that he will hardly know how it left him."

"Will you pick his pocket?" she asked.

"No, not even that. Llano is even now taking the greenbacks by means of stacked cards or loaded dice, or both. I can't tell which. However, you can be sure that young *Señor* Dale is rapidly approaching poverty at this very moment. And, in the morning, his heart may be rather heavy, but he will be reproaching his bad luck, and not his bad enemies."

He laughed again. The girl laughed a little, too.

"It would be strange if Llano failed," she said, and turned away.

Ⓥ Ⓥ Ⓥ Ⓥ Ⓥ

In the lower room where Arturo Llano and young Dale were together, at this very moment, Llano was shaking a box of dice. There was a faint smile under his beard, and there was a flash in his eyes as he rattled the dice. He had before him a great stack of bills. Before Dale, at the opposite side of the table, there was a similar heap.

To make up the sum of the last bet, it appeared that Don Arturo had not possessed quite enough hard cash, and now he had laid upon the greenbacks no less than four rings, set with four great jewels. His golden spurs were there, also, together with a number of other trinkets, that Dale had admitted as wagers at two or

130

three times their real value.

"Now!" cried Arturo, with a ringing voice, and rolled the dice out on the table.

An exclamation of dismay burst from his lips. He had expected—he had really *known*—that three sixes would lie there, looking up at him from their black eyes. Instead, he saw a five, a tray, and an ace.

"Bad luck," said Dale, raking in the money carelessly. "Perhaps your friends will give you another gambling stake, Llano. Or, if you wish, we'll play now for your horse and saddle."

XI
"COUNCIL OF WAR"

ARTURO DID NOT ANSWER AT ONCE. HE STARED AT THE spot that his pile of money had occupied, and then he looked gloomily toward the pile the boy was arranging.

"We could make the bets smaller, if you wish," said young Rancie Dale. "I'm sorry that you've had the bad luck."

"Luck?" said the gambler. "Luck?" He made a gesture. "I have no more money. Perhaps I can get some, though. Will you wait here?"

"Certainly," said Randal Dale. "Take all the time you wish."

He settled down into a chair by the window and seemed to lose himself at once in the contemplation of the moonlight that drifted over the garden wall beyond, and spilled in silver across the garden itself. Far away in the center of the plot, the face of the waterlily lake glistened like polished silver with the dark design of the pads stretched across it.

Arturo Llano retreated hastily from the room, still

dazed by what had happened, and it showed in his face when he reached that upper room where Don José and Jeems Loring were sitting.

On the way, Arturo passed the girl, coming down, and she said to him: "How was the game, Arturo?"

No other woman in the world could have won a single syllable from him at that moment, but to Maruja he turned grimly and said: "I have lost three thousand dollars in American money, my rings, my spurs, and a few other things. The evil one was against me."

"You lost!" she exclaimed. "But you never lose, Arturo, except when you're playing against old friends. Is there a demon in this *gringo?*"

"Demon?" repeated the Mexican. "No, no! It was only chance, and because my fingers suddenly became foolish. That's all. Simply because my fingers grew clumsy and began to stumble. I played like an old fool." He gritted his teeth. "Dice, too," he said. "As though I could fail to throw correctly with loaded dice, Maruja!"

"Loaded dice, and yet you lost?" she asked.

"Not one six in three loaded dice," he complained and hurried on up the stairs, saying over his shoulder: "But I'll get more money and go back and win every penny in that wallet of his, or else my name is not my own."

He hurried on, and the girl, looking after him, murmured, "If you get more money, you'll have simply more to lose. I was right. I was right. There is something to this Randal Dale. There is more to him than the eye sees in one quick glance. Oh, Jeems and Arturo and Don José, is something going to happen to all three of you?"

She began to laugh, in an odd way, as she went back downstairs. As she stepped into the garden, she saw the head and shoulders of Randal Dale silhouetted against the window. Softly, softer than a cloud shadow stealing over a meadow, as silently as this, she drifted near and nearer, until she was very close. Stepping on a low mound, she was enabled to look in and down toward Randal Dale.

He was looking away from her, into the garden, and his face was blankly and innocently contented in its expression. There was no triumph in his look, such as a youngster might betray after putting several thousand dollars into his pockets in cash and fine jewels. There was only the calm and gentle absorption of one dreaming over the poetic beauty of the night.

The girl, seeing this, staring hard at him, finally shook her head in surrender. Then she stepped back from the mound. There was a black bush behind her, making a background against which she must have been totally, or almost totally, invisible. Yet, although in her backward step she made no sound whatever, the man in the window leaped suddenly to his feet and whirled about. A Colt revolver was in his hand, leveled at her in so straight a line that she could have sworn that she was seen. She almost cried out in alarm, then she saw the figure in the window shrug his shoulders, and the revolver disappeared, with one deft movement, inside his coat.

Randal Dale, leaning against the window, stared toward her for a moment, and then turned about and resumed his chair, but only after he had dragged it out of sight within the room.

She had seen quite enough. The first gesture announces the celebrated actor; the first note tells the audience the capacities of the great singer; the first blow struck is the sign and index of the fighter. And now the cat-like speed with which big, young Randal Dale had moved, the deftness with which the gun had been conjured into view and made to vanish again, told the girl all that she wanted to know. Besides, she was no mean judge of such things. She had seen experts working many a time before this, but never had she seen a speed and surety of gesture to compare with this tigerish silhouette at the window.

She had dropped to her knees when he first stirred. She remained there for a moment, getting her breath back, covering her eyes, while her brain whirled. *The helpless tenderfoot, whom the others were planning to rob, was very patently a consummately clever rascal who knew all about how to take care of himself. He was playing a part, the rôle of an innocent, and before he finished acting, who else would be left on the stage?* What ought she to do—hurry to her father and tell him what she had discovered, or go directly to Don José and the others and let them know?

Something in her revolted against this. She had no love for the *Americanos*. On the other hand, the thought of warning three celebrated fighters that another man was also a warrior seemed suddenly too absurd, too grotesquely unfair. Besides, they were acting the parts of spiders, and they were enticing the stranger into their trap. Well, let all the ropes and the beams of that trap be strong as steel and cunningly devised, or else the intended victim would escape.

So she did nothing at all, except to remain there on her knees for a moment, turning the whole matter about in her mind, such excitement rising in her breast it became almost impossible to breathe. *What was to happen? The consummate gambler, the great Llano, was already turned back, but he remained a fighting unit. The other two, would they guess that Llano had been defeated by something more than luck and the vagaries of loaded dice?*

That same Arturo Llano now stood before Don José and Jeems Loring, saying to them: "I've heard of luck before, but never of luck that will best loaded dice. Now, mind you, he did not know enough to roll the dice, at first, without spinning one of them off the table...or else he piled them out in a stack, one on top of the other. But, in spite of having to learn how even to throw the dice, he beat me and my loaded set." He threw up both his hands. "Think of it, friends!"

"Yeah, I'm thinkin' of it," said Jeems Loring, "and it's god-damned funny. I've seen you make water come out of wallets that wouldn't bleed two dollars a year. I've seen you bring out the hard cash in a flood. But you couldn't tap that tenderfoot?"

"Suppose," suggested Don José, "that he's no tenderfoot at all? What about that?"

"Yes, what about that?" said Llano, grasping at the idea. "But no, he could not have manipulated the dice box. I was watching him every moment. Every single moment!"

"That's all right," said Jeems Loring. "Don't you gents get excited. I've seen a lot more of the kid than you have, and there's nothing to get startled about. There ain't any real trouble in him, mind you. Not a god-damned bit."

"Is he really a tenderfoot, as he seems?" queried Don José, frowning a little.

"Why, he's so green that a forest fire wouldn't even singe his top branches," Jeems Loring said confidently. "Only, it's kind of funny that loaded dice should go wrong in a throw."

"They're loaded to go right," said Don José. "What about it, Arturo?"

"They will go wrong, one of them once in three or four times. Two of them once in a hundred times. Three of them once in a million times, maybe. *¡Hai!* That I should have lost when I already had two or three thousand of his money...then to raise the stakes, as if to favor him in winning back, and then to have him win. Think of it, *amigos!*"

"Beginners always have luck," said Jeems Loring. "But this streak of luck ain't going to last."

"It won't last," agreed Llano. "Give me a thousand or two, and I'll go back and win every penny that he has, because now he is excited, and he says that dice is an amusing game. Hah!" He snorted.

"Yeah. I'll stake you," said Jeems Loring, reaching for his wallet.

Don José held up his hand. "That won't do," he said. "Never put your money twice on the same horse, unless it wins the first race. You can't make a horse run faster by betting higher on him. No, no, Arturo, your hand is out tonight. Let's try another way with our friend, *Señor* Randal Dale."

"All right," said Jeems Loring. "I don't mind taking him over and opening him up."

"How?" asked Don José.

"With a gun."

"That is a cruel and blunt way of action, *amigo* Jeems," said Don José.

"Aw," said Jeems Loring, "I just change into other clothes, speak a Mexican lingo, and change my voice like nobody would know me, with a black hood over my head. Then I step through the door and take the coin away from him. It's simple, it's quick, and it gets the cash."

XII
"THE LITTLE JOKE"

EVERY GOOD PLAN IS SIMPLE. THAT IS AN OLD TRUTH. Now it was not difficult for Jeems Loring to gain the approval of the others for his plan. The clothes were readily got from the innkeeper, and a few moments later Loring, equipped with fresh trousers and shirt and a black sack to cover his head, with eyeholes cut in it, went down to the room where young Rancie Dale was still waiting for the expected return of his late friend, Arturo Llano.

The door was cast open, and Jeems entered with a gun held before him, a little more than hip high, and these words growling from his throat in a deepened, husky voice: "Get up your hands, brother, and get 'em up quick, will you?"

Randal Dale hoisted his hands above his head instantly. He rose from his chair at the same time and seemed to be stretching up to the utmost of his power in order, perhaps, to touch the beamed ceiling of the room.

Behind his shadowy mask, Jeems Loring grinned.

It was, after all, even simpler than he had expected to find it. He looked at the strained face and strained eyes of the boy and felt a touch of compassion for him.

"Turn around!" he commanded, not with words, but with a swinging gesture of his left hand.

Terror seemed to have laid hold of the boy, for he wheeled at once and presented his back to the intruder. At the same time, he said: "I don't know who you are, but I warn you, if you take a penny from me, you're going to curse the day that you were born. I have friends in this place."

"What friends have you got?" demanded the other.

"Arturo Llano and José Oñate. More than that, one of the best men in Texas is my partner. If you rob me, Jeems Loring will never rest till he's run you down."

At this, laughter well nigh throttled Jeems Loring. Yet, he was touched with pity, also. Trust always moves us, even in our worst moments. Still, what tenderfoot has a right to so much money as this lad was carrying with him into no man's land?

He laid the muzzle of his revolver against the small of the boy's back.

"Don't shoot!" cried Randal Dale.

"Budge a muscle and I'll shoot," said Loring.

Reaching around the body of Dale, he dipped a hand into the inside coat pocket and brought it forth again, carrying that same sleek, heavy, thickly wadded wallet.

A little sigh came from the lips of Loring, as he grasped that wallet. It meant the consummation of all that he desired. A brighter and a better life he saw extending before him. To be sure, he had just finished agreeing with José and Llano, that he would split the profits with them, but why should he be bound by that obligation when, just outside the window, lay the wide security of the night and so many fast horses fit to carry him into it?

"Now, stand fast," he said, "and don't you stir an inch or…." He began to back away, as he said this, and he naturally tilted up the muzzle of the heavy revolver a little as he moved away, bringing it into firing position.

As he finished saying: "Keep your face shut and your feet still and maybe no harm'll come to you," just, in fact, as he uttered the last of these words, the body of tall, young Randal Dale twitched slightly around, his head jerked about so that he could look over his shoulder, and the long, right arm that had been straining

138

so high into the air dropped like a bar of lead. The balled fist struck across the right forearm of Loring, and the gun exploded and fell to the floor.

Jeems Loring cursed. But he was not a fellow to venture to close quarters armed with a single gun. Neither did a disabled right hand make him helpless. Beautiful and smooth and swift was the grace with which he slipped out the revolver with his left hand, ready for a shot that would smash its way straight through the foolish heart of Randal Dale, but, before his forefinger curled affectionately around that trigger, a great misfortune happened to the expert Jeems Loring.

It took the form of a large, bony fist, that, as Randal Dale kept on turning round, moved in what is known as a left hook, up, across, and then sharply down, with a whiplash jerk at the end, when the big knuckles of the fist found a lodging place on the rim of Mr. Loring's jaw, just beside the point.

He fell neither forward nor backward. He simply collapsed in a heap. When he got the red flame and whirling darkness out of his eyes, he saw Randal Dale seated on the edge of a table, holding in his hands both of his guns. The sight helped to clear the staggered brain of Jeems Loring at once. He was quite capable of hearing the words that ordered him to rise, and rise he did and stood with empty hands before the boy.

"Take off that mask," said Dale.

Jeems Loring plucked it off, and, as his bare face appeared before Randal Dale, a random sense of shame came to him, something that he had not felt for many years and made his skin flame hot. But he was amazed to hear no reproofs, no outburst of honest indignation whatever.

"Why," cried Randal Dale, amidst choking laughter, "it's my old friend, Loring! It's Jeems Loring! Man,

man, it's a good joke. If I'd guessed that you were only playing me a practical joke, I never would have hit you. I'm sorry. I'm mighty sorry. There's a big, red lump rising all along your jaw now. I'm terribly sorry, Loring. Forgive me."

It was difficult, even for the swift brain of Jeems Loring, to understand which way the cat had jumped. At last, he made it out. According to the idiotic understanding of this lad, there had not been any real attack at all. There had simply been a practical joke that had hung fire a little.

Loring cleared his voice and said grumblingly: "You might have known me by my voice, Rancie. No need to break a man's jaw for a little joke between friends?"

"I know it," complained Dale. "I'm terribly sorry. It was the thought of losing all of that coin, d'you see? It was that put me off balance. I saw black...I was so excited, partner."

"You saw a way home to my jaw," said Jeems Loring. "You could see that far, clear enough. What you wearing on the back of your hand, a horseshoe or brass knuckles, Rancie?"

"Here?" asked Dale. "Why, nothing, of course. What do you mean?"

"Never mind," said Jeems, caressing his face tenderly, "but I'm gonna have a lopsided jaw the rest of my life, I reckon. I thought the old, gray mule had off and kicked me again, is what I thought."

"Here are your guns," suggested the boy. "I'm sorry. Just saying it, doesn't tell you how sorry I am." He handed back the guns, then, turning and stooping, his face quite away from Loring, he picked up the fallen wallet from the floor. *Why did not Loring cover him again, at that moment, and take the wallet?*

140

It was something that he himself never would be able to explain in after times. But there was a rediscovered sense of shame, perhaps, controlling him. The thing he had failed to do, when he was wearing a mask, he could hardly attempt now that his face was bare. Perhaps, too, the ringing of a bell in his brain had a little to do with the matter. It was still as if a bullet had passed through the base of his skull. What a punch that boy, Rancie Dale, carried up his sleeve. So, perfectly still, he watched Dale pocket the desired wallet, so sleek, so thick, so filled with fortune.

Then he said: "I'm gonna go and douse my head in cold water. I'm still seeing stars, Dale."

Dale accompanied him to the door of the room, a hand half affectionate and half apologetic resting on his shoulder.

"You're not going to hold it against me, partner, are you?" asked the boy. "You realize that it was just an accident, don't you?"

"Accident?" repeated Loring, raising a hand to his aching jaw and passing the same hand back across the base of his skull. "Yeah, you can call it an accident. But I'd call it a left hook."

"I suppose that's what it was," said the boy. "You see, Briguez was a great boxer, too, and he used to teach me a good deal about using my fists. A left hook was his favorite punch, and he taught me and taught me until I knew it by heart. I must have used it on you, without thinking."

"Yeah, you know it by heart," said Loring. "What a sock!" He turned toward the door again.

"No hard feelings, Jeems?" pleaded Rancie Dale.

"Aw, now. No hard feelings," said Loring. "Only, when a joke gets turned around, it ain't so funny, either. I was just gonna raise a laugh, and instead of that I got a bump raised along the side of my jaw. That ain't so funny, either." He opened the door. "Wait till I get my head soused," he said, "and then I'll be coming back. So long for a minute, partner, and I'll be right back. We gotta get the business polished off, don't we?"

"Of course," said the boy.

"And we'll get it polished pretty *pronto*," said Jeems Loring, in a mutter, as he passed through the door and shut it behind him. Then, in the darkness of the hall, his hand still upon the knob of the door, he paused for a moment, conjuring up a more complete darkness by shutting his eyes, so that his thinking might be the clearer. *Could it be, or were his eyes playing a trick upon him, that at the last moment there was a slight twinkling in the eyes of young Randal Dale?* He opened his eyes again with the question still unanswered. Then he began to climb the stairs slowly, fumbling with his hand for the balustrade, and with his feet for the steps. His mind was still half at sea from the effects of the strong punch.

XIII
"DISCOVERED"

WHEN THE GREAT JEEMS LORING WAS HALFWAY UP THE stairs, he encountered Maruja, again coming down them.

"Are you ill, *amigo?*" she asked.

"I'm dizzy, Maruja," he told her. Putting a hand on her shoulder, he let her assist him up the rest of the way.

"What's happened?"

He heard a gasp and a flurry of excitement in her voice, but he could not place the source of it. As a matter of fact, his wits were not operating to the full of their capacity.

142

So, when they came up to the room where Don José and Arturo Llano were continuing their consultations, she opened the door before them and literally handed him into the chamber.

Arturo Llano stood up and raised a lamp; it was only that he wished to look more closely into the face of his companion.

"So," he said, "what witch told me that Jeems Loring would come back to us like this?"

He lowered the lamp again. Loring was standing beside a chair, and the girl remained near him, as one anxious to do whatever she could to be of help.

Don José had not risen. He merely said: "What's happened, Don Jeems?"

"Bad luck, that's all," said Jeems Loring. He lowered himself into his chair.

"Hello," said Maruja gently. "Was it bad luck that gave you the swollen jaw, Jeems Loring?"

He looked up at her—and sighed. "Are you laughin' at me, Maruja?" he asked.

"Laughing?" she said. "Laughing, Jeems?"

He wagged his head from side to side. "I got him cold," he said to the men. "I stuck him up and had him flat-footed. I could've salted him away. I had him right under my gun, and his hands stickin' up into the air over his head. That was the way of it."

"Great heavens," said Maruja, "and still he was able to do this to you?" She pointed toward the swollen jaw as she spoke.

"Maruja," said Don José, "you'd better go and leave us alone here."

"Certainly," she said.

He followed her suddenly to the door, with his wonderfully swift and silent cat's step. There he held

143

her for a moment with his eyes, while she turned about and faced him, letting her glance fall to the floor.

"Look up at me, Maruja," he said.

She looked up.

"You are laughing," he said.

"Never!"

"Maruja," he persisted, "I see the laughter in your eyes."

"Don José, you are looking too closely."

He laughed softly. "I never guessed that there was so much deviltry in you," said José Oñate, much pleased. "Will you answer me one thing?"

"Perhaps," she said.

"This fellow, this American, what do you think of him?"

She merely laughed.

"I thought that you might be a little too interested in him," said Don José.

"But why should I be interested?" she asked.

"Because he's alone here, surrounded by danger, with the odds against him...because, I don't know exactly how, he's managed to slip through the fingers of Loring and even Llano."

She laughed again, outright but softly, at this. "Let me tell you the truth," she said.

"Of course. That's what I want to hear."

"Well, then, I was never interested in more than one American, more than one *gringo*, in my entire life."

"Is that true?"

"Yes."

"Who was that lucky fellow?"

"Ah, Don José, you've had the truth, but now you want names."

He nodded. "Well, Maruja, tell me one thing more,

144

and this won't be prying. Tell me if you think that this *gringo* may be more than he seems on the surface."

"I couldn't guess what he is," she said, choosing her words with the utmost care. "He seemed to me, when he came in, the simplest fellow in the world."

"When he came in?" pressed Don José. "And what has he managed to seem, since then?"

"You know," she said, in answer, "that I've hardly seen him at all since he came in."

Don José grunted. Then he said: "Maruja, you've grown up so much that I no longer know what's going on in your mind."

"Nonsense, José. A great man like you...of course, you see through everything."

He grinned at her, not a smile, but a twisting grin. "Later on, Maruja," he told her. "Later on, I'll have to try to know you better."

She, with a shrug of the shoulders, turned away, and then looked back, smiling, over her shoulder, before she left the room.

Don José rested his hand on the knob of the door, very much as though he were minded to pursue her. But he seemed to think better of this, and presently turned slowly back toward the others in the room.

"What's wrong with Maruja?" asked Jeems Loring.

"Do you think that there's something wrong with her?" asked Don José.

"No. Only she's a little different. What deviltry's got into her tonight?" asked Loring.

"I don't know. I was trying to find out from her, and I failed," answered Oñate. "Go on and try to tell me what was in your mind. How is she different?"

"How's a man different," asked Loring, "after he's fallen into a million?"

"So, so," muttered Oñate. "I thought the same thing. As though suddenly she had become rich and cared for nothing that she had cared for before."

"Exactly," said Loring. "But let her go. What's to be done with that fool of a Randal Dale and his money?"

"The last I heard," said Don José, "you had him under the muzzle of your gun and his hands were in the air. Now it seems that all you've brought away is a swollen jaw and no money."

Loring nodded, with the air of a man who has been too much tried to care about appearances or what others think of him. He simply said: "I had him covered and turned around with his back to me. I reached about and got the wallet out of his coat. He was shaking...he was so scared...the poor tenderfoot. He was begging me not to shoot, as I backed away, and then suddenly he turned and slammed me. You know how it is. You get a rat cornered, and it'll fight when you don't expect it. He's big, and he's fast. He turned around and slammed me. It wasn't no baby trick, either. He knows how to use his hands, I'm telling you." He caressed his jaw as he said this. Tenderly he touched and stroked it. An absent light was in his eye.

"I went down in a heap," he continued, "and, when I got up, he was sitting on the edge of a table, swinging one foot, and he had in his hands my two guns. I tell you, he slammed me for fair, and he used only a left hook. He used a hook that skunk of a Briguez had taught him."

"Briguez?" exclaimed Don José.

"Yeah, Briguez. What of it?"

"Briguez!" exclaimed Don José again.

"What's the use of sayin' the name over and over again?" asked Jeems Loring. "I never liked it much."

146

Don José broke out: "Do you hear, Llano?"

"I hear the name of Briguez. What of that?" asked Llano.

"Briguez was not a man who could teach anyone to use his hands like a prize fighter. Briguez."

Suddenly, Oñate laughed.

"You laugh, do you?" said Jeems Loring, snarling and sitting up straight.

"I laugh," said Oñate, suiting the action to the word, "because I knew Briguez well enough to say that he was lost and helpless unless he had some weapon in those terrible hands of his. Briguez? Why, that murderer could carve out a heart at twenty yards with a knife. But he couldn't use his hands to hurt a baby that was put into them. Briguez taught this *gringo* to fight? The *gringo* lies, and, if he tells one lie like that, he is all a lie! All a lie, do you hear?" He struck his hands together in excitement.

"Whacha mean, all a lie?" asked Jeems Loring.

"I mean that, and only that!" cried Don José. Still he laughed. He seemed to be rejoiced by his discovery. Then he said: "All a lie, from top to bottom. He is no tenderfoot. He is one of us! He is one of us! I thought that he sat his saddle like a man who had been there before. Tenderfoot? Hah, hah, hah!" He fairly roared at this point.

"You mean…?" began Jeems Loring, and then paused, while a very ugly look spread over his face.

"I mean that," said Don José. "And for such a man, why, *amigos*, there is only one thing that I can do for him."

"And what's that?" asked Llano.

At one stroke, all of the laughter, all of the good humor departed from the face of the Mexican. He said

147

grimly: "You'll see, or at least you'll hear, what I do to him. Come down behind me and guard the door of the room. I'm going in to talk to him. Do you realize that by this time the first cattle of the drive are sniffing at the waters of the Rio Grande, and we, my friends, have not had one single dollar in pay?"

XIV
"STEPS ON THE STAIRS"

NOW, WHEN MARUJA HAD AT LAST GONE DOWN THE stairs, stopping to laugh to herself now and then on the way, she paused and tapped at the door of the room where the inn's American guest was staying.

He called out, and she entered. There was still laughter in her eyes, but her face was grave enough. So were the words she spoke. "*Señor*, you have done very bravely and well. But now it is time for you to go."

"Time for me to go?" said Rancie Dale. "But why should it be time for me to go, *señorita*, when I have not yet completed the business of the sale, and when…?"

Cheerfully, she smiled at him. "I understand," she said. "I think that I understand a great deal more than you suppose."

"Such as what?"

"That you never intend to pay one penny for the cattle."

"I?" he cried, touching a forefinger against his breast.

"No," she answered, "not even a penny."

"Ah, Maruja," he said reproachfully.

"I think," she went on, "that is the truth. You don't intend to pay one penny for them. Will you confess that, *Señor* Dale?"

"A terrible thing, Maruja, if you are calling me a

thief."

In fact, he looked as though his large, blue eyes would start out of his head in sheer terror.

"You have told them only one true thing," she declared.

"Only one?"

"Yes, only one."

"What is that?"

"That Briguez is your friend."

"Ah, Maruja, only lies...all the rest that I have said?"

"Well, there are lies and lies," said the girl. She leaned back against the door and regarded him with obvious approval in her eyes. "You reckless scamp of a man," she stated.

"Reckless? Scamp?" said young Randal Dale. "Maruja, what are you saying to me? Who has been talking about me to you? Because that would anger me."

"My own wits have been talking to myself," she assured him. "That is all. No one else guesses, I hope, though they may soon. You've made complete fools of two of them. They may have begun to guess by this time. Only, I hope not. But I, Don Rancie, was outside the window a little while ago, when you heard a whisper in the dark."

She paused. Randal Dale, in a single instant, lost the look of innocence and made a long, feline stride toward her, his head drooping a little forward, his shoulders sloping also. He checked himself at once and straightened again. His right hand made a gesture toward the bosom of his coat. "You were out there, when I made a fool of myself? You saw?" he asked her.

"I saw," she said. "I saw it all. I have watched the best of them handle their guns, but no one more skillfully than you, Don Rancie."

Suddenly, he shrugged his shoulders. "Why should not one friend know another?" he asked her.

She waited, making no answer to this, but with her eyes fixed very straight upon him.

"It was the sound in the dark, or almost something less than a sound," he explained. "It startled me. I turned around, hardly knowing what I was doing."

"As if you were out in the hills," she suggested, "with many men hunting you, and suddenly a sound outside the rim of the light of your campfire...."

"Many men hunting me?" he quoted, with a frown.

"Why should not one friend know another?" she demanded quickly.

He smiled at her. "You are a bright girl, Maruja," said. "But it is foolish to talk of some things, is it not?"

She made a small gesture. "As you please," she said, her face growing colder.

At that, he went up to her and took both of her hands in a sweeping gesture into one of his.

"Suppose that it is true, then," he said. "Suppose that I, also, am a man that the law wants. What would you think, Maruja?"

"I would think that partly for the sake of Briguez, you have attempted a terrible thing for any one man to do."

"Coming here?" he questioned.

"Yes, coming here. Partly because you wanted to make some money...partly because you wanted to harm these people for the sake of Briguez."

"Briguez?"

"Yes. You are the sort of a man who would never stop trying to avenge a friend."

She, watching him very closely, saw his nostrils quiver, and there was a faint gleam of perspiration across his forehead.

150

He merely said: "You have good eyes and a mighty clever mind, Maruja."

"That is all I have," she answered.

She felt a pressure that prevented her from withdrawing her hands.

"Am I to take you into my whole confidence?" he asked.

"I haven't requested that," she said.

"You wish it, though."

"Yes. I wish it. Is that beast, that Briguez, really a friend to you?"

"Yes, really a friend," he said.

She sighed. Her eyes, this time, opened, and she stared at him. "Briguez," she murmured.

"They cheated and robbed him when he was helpless," said the tall American. "They betrayed him, and the government caught him. There is only one way that I know of to get him out of danger."

"Money?"

"Yes," he said.

"But your pocket is filled with money."

"One or two bills on top are honest, and three or four on the bottom," he explained.

"Ah, ah, ah! Wicked fellow." In spite of her words, she laughed and clapped her hands together. She was fairly dancing, her body as well as her eyes, as she looked up to him. "*Señor* Dale," she said, "you have come here with counterfeit money, and you are making thieves try to murder you for the sake of it. Why?"

"Because there has to be time for the cattle to be driven through the river. Once they are on the north bank, I may manage to handle them."

"And the men who are still with them?" she asked.

He made a quick gesture with his hand that was free.

"There must be a chance taken," he answered.

"So you have put yourself into the trap, and you are the bait?" she suggested. "You are the bait that they can worry, while the cattle are driven north of the river into your country? Ah, *señor*. That is a terrible madness. Because you have dealt with the other two, but you have not dealt with that Don José."

"No, he's left for the last," replied Dale. "I know that. And it's the way I would have it. What does poor Briguez care about the other pair? Why, nothing at all. It's only because of Don José that he's eating his heart out...that beautiful, lying hound of a man. Tell me, Maruja, how it comes about that you are able to resist such a face and such a pair of eyes and such great fame?"

She shook her head. "I have been waiting," she said, and she looked into the eyes of the American in such a way that he started a little.

Then he bowed over her hands and kissed them. "Maruja," he said, with his eyes still fixed low on her hands, "I'm a worthless thief of a man, a gambler, and all the rest. I'm not worthy of a glance from you, really. But tonight...." He paused.

And she answered: "But tonight you could use my help. Is that not true?"

"That's true."

"For instance," she said, "if I were to put together the best horses in the stable, and saddle a pair of them...?"

He pressed her hands again. "Would you really do that, Maruja?"

"See if I read your mind correctly."

"Very well, then, but I think that I hear someone coming down the stairs."

"That will be Don José. *Señor* Dale...."

152

"Yes, Maruja?"

She went rapidly toward the window, and he followed her, as though compelled by her strength. She was whispering: "If I saddle the gray horse and the black horse, then take two more of the best on the lead, turn loose the rest from the barn the instant that I hear…a noise from the house?" She gasped.

"Then Maruja, you and I will ride around the world and laugh at other people, laugh at 'em, d'you hear?"

She closed her eyes. The color flooded up into her face.

"But you, *señor*, you have faced enough danger for one night. If you go now, there will be time to fly away from them. I'll show you."

The steps on the stairs came nearer, and, now, in answer, Randal Dale lifted a finger toward her.

Maruja understood. There was nothing that she could do or say at this last moment sufficient to convince or to persuade him. With a sigh that was half a moan, she slipped suddenly through the window and was gone silently into the moonlit gloom of the garden.

XV
"THE GUN FIGHT"

WHEN DON JOSÉ RAPPED AGAINST THE DOOR, YOUNG Randal Dale called out at once in answer, and Oñate entered to find the *gringo* seated by the table, near the lamp, reading a time-yellowed newspaper printed in Spanish.

José, entering, closed the door softly behind him. When he saw that intent figure, he was on the verge of snatching a revolver on the spot, but something restrained him.

153

He said: "You have found a long bit of news, *amigo?*"

"News," said the other, "that you wouldn't believe, except that one sees it in print and on paper. And print doesn't lie very often, I suppose, Don José?"

"Not lie?" said the other, smiling. "Oh, well, that may be so, but I have found lies enough in newspapers."

"But such a thing as this, and about you, Don José?"

"Hah! About me?"

"Yes."

"What is it?"

"Slander, I say."

"Slander, eh?" said José. He brushed his knuckles across his chin and smiled a little grimly. He knew that newspaper. He had read it two weeks before thoroughly, down to the advertisements, as a bored man will do. There was in it not a single word about José Oñate.

"Yes, horrible slander," said the boy, putting down the newspaper and looking up, with a sigh and a shake of his head, toward the Mexican. "I never read such a thing."

"And what is it about, Don Randal?" asked the robber.

"Why, about you and about Briguez. It connects you with poor Briguez in a terrible way."

"In what way?" asked Don José sternly.

Dale made a sign for silence and stole to the door. He slid the bolt of it home, still with his fingers to his lips.

José watched like a cat, and once, twice, his right hand flickered down toward a revolver, and each time came away. He seemed to be thinking to the bottom of this situation, and finding a great deal in it that was worth pondering.

Now Randal Dale stood again beside the table. He sat

154

down upon it, swinging one leg and shaking his head as he looked at Don José.

"Of course, there's nothing in it," he said.

"I hope not," said Don José. He added: "Then, what's the story?"

"Why, the story's a thing to burn up the heart of any man," said Randal Dale. "You see, it says that at one time you were the friend of my old friend, Briguez."

"If the newspaper says so, the newspaper must be right," said Don José dryly.

"And then it says," continued the boy, "that you were with him for a long time, that you learned a great deal from that old master of knives and guns."

"A master of fists, too, eh?" asked Oñate.

For a moment the glance of the boy steadied upon him, but Randal Dale returned no direct answer to the last remark. He simply went on: "The account says that after you had learned all you wanted to get from Briguez, you found yourself short of money, and it was then that you remembered, very strangely, that there was a price of twenty thousand *pesos* upon the head of poor Briguez, dead or alive. Is it true?"

"There was a price on his head. Go on," murmured the Mexican.

"Therefore," said the boy, "you sent advices to the *rurales*. And they came in the night. They came while you were supposed to be on guard, watching the camp. They surprised Briguez, and captured him before his eyes were open. It was not until their hands were on him that you opened fire and shot your bullets into the air. You ran, and they pretended to chase you, but in due time, at the appointed place, you got your reward, half the blood money that was on the head of Briguez."

He paused. All the sham was abandoned now. His

155

blue eyes flared with wild fire as they stared at th[e] outlaw. Yet Don José endured that glance steadfastly.

"That stuff," he said, "is fit to be written in [a] newspaper. But it is not fit to be repeated by a man wh[o] is about to die, *Señor* Dale."

"Am I about to die?" asked Randal Dale, smiling coldly.

"You are about to die," said José Oñate.

"I am glad to know it. It gives me time to say a few quiet prayers for the repose of my soul," said Dale.

"You sneer, *señor*," replied Oñate. "However, I'll tel[l] you one other thing. Briguez was once my friend...it i[s] true that he is my friend no longer...but it is false that [I] betrayed him. Not one penny of blood money has ever come into my hand. I, José Oñate, tell you this thing."

"You, José Oñate," said Dale, "are a bloodsucker, [a] sneak, and a cur. I, Randal Dale, tell you so. Now fil[l] your hand, you rat."

He said it through his teeth, but the other merely smiled.

"When the time comes, I shall kill you, *señor*," said Oñate. "Be sure of that. I am not a Llano or a Loring."

"And I shall work on you with something other than loaded dice, or my fist," said the boy.

"How did you manage Llano?" asked José.

"It was simple enough to palm his dice and put in my own. My own were honest. That was the difference."

"Ah, then you were taking chances."

"I believe in chance taking, *señor*," said the boy.

"You are more the fool," replied Oñate. "You were taking chances today, also, when you tried to play with the three of us, like three mice in the paws of a cat. Now I am to show you how great a fool you were."

"I wait for you, Oñate. Afterward, I'll have the

pleasure of meeting your two friends. They shoot straight, I understand."

"They shoot straight," agreed Oñate, "but not as I shoot."

"My own bullet is for your head, Oñate," said the boy. "Briguez, he'll die happy if he knows that you've gone before him."

"If he needs that to make him happy, then he'll die miserably. Tell me, how does it happen that they keep him alive so long?"

"Oh, a little matter of torture, *amigo*," said the boy, his voice careless, but his eyes filled with fury. "Of course, you didn't dream of that. You thought they would order out the firing squad for him at once. It would cut you to the bone to know that they preferred to torment him first, in the hope of extracting useful information from him. That would be a cruel thing for you to learn, Don José, eh?" His teeth snapped upon the last word.

"I learn it now, and it is wine to me," said Oñate. "Is that all that you have to say?"

"I'm finished."

"I've finished also," said the Mexican. "Only I cannot help reminding you what a fool you were to bring a fortune in hard cash south of the river and into my hands. It was kind of you, but a little foolish, *señor*."

"Fortune?" said the American, smiling. "You don't understand, poor Oñate, that it is all counterfeit? Fifty cents' worth of counterfeit. Hardly that, hardly worthy of being called more than stage money."

Strangely enough, the insults that had preceded had not moved Oñate, but the sting of this remark caused the blood to rush to his face and turn purple in his cheeks.

"You lie," he said.

157

"In the meantime," said the boy, "the cattle belonging to the poor, foolish tenderfoot have crossed the river and are running north, where I shall pick them up. They are all running safely north of the river." He laughed.

"You will never reach them," said the Mexican.

"As soon as you are dead, I ride." He held up his hand. "Listen," he said, "the horses are being turned out of the stable, now."

In fact, they could hear through the open window the snorting of horses, then the rattling of hoofs, speeding away toward the horizon.

"By heaven," murmured Oñate. "You have brought up helpers, eh? You are not the hero I thought, after all."

"I brought no helpers, but I found one here," said Dale. "The lady you were raising under your own eye the loveliest girl south of the Rio Grande, or north of it for that matter. She has turned the horses loose, and she is saddling now, the best of them all for herself and me."

"You lie! You lie!" screamed Oñate, and he leaped at Dale, tearing out a gun as he sprang.

It was a stupid move. If he had not been bedeviled almost to the point of madness, he would never have dreamed of springing in like a blind bull at his enemy instead of standing firm and making the draw.

Swift was that gun flash nevertheless, but Don José saw before him, forever imprinted on his very soul, the calm smile of the other and the glint of the jumping revolver that sprang into his hand. He saw that, but, even as he thumbed the hammer of his own gun, he heard a thundering report in his very face and was knocked flat backward into darkness.

Instant pandemonium broke out in the hall beyond the door.

"José! José!" shouted his two friends.

Regardless of the hands that beat on the door, Randal Dale stooped over the fallen man and examined a long, ragged wound that ran down one side of Oñate's skull. He shook his head as he straightened again. "A miss, only a graze," said Randal Dale. "Who will believe it, at such a distance? Will poor Briguez believe it? Damn my luck. I can't shoot a helpless man."

XVI
"GOING NORTH"

WHEN LLANO AND JEEMS LORING BROKE DOWN THE door and rushed in, they found their friend lying with eyes wide, but with the faculty of sight only gradually returning to them.

"Maruja," said the wounded man. "The black demon has stolen Maruja from us. Get horses, ride, ride with wings, tear the souls out of the mustangs, but get Maruja back from him."

Llano howled like a wild beast when he heard these tidings and fairly flung himself out of the house and toward the stable, but, when he came to it, there was only one horse to be seen, and that was a lame, old, gray mare, hobbling about near the front door of the barn. On her bare back, Llano flung himself and fastened his spurs in her flanks, but only at a hobbling lope could she go over the plain, and it was only the frantic yelling of the rider, and not Arturo Llano, that overtook that thievish master of men and women, Randal Dale, as he galloped smoothly along on the tall, black stallion the girl had saddled for him.

He looked back over his shoulder, murmuring: "They have started, Maruja, but you see they're already falling back."

"José!" she cried. "Did you kill him? Is he dead Randal?"

"José? No, there's only a glancing surface wound down one side of his head."

"Oh, I'm glad of that."

"Glad that rascal is alive?"

"If he were dead, there would be blood on my hands," she said. "And he was always kind to me. How did you manage to do it? How did you overcome him? And no one scratch on you, not one."

"It was a matter of talking, Maruja," he said. "Talking will bring guns out of the holster before their time, and talking will dim the eyes and make them see more red than light. He came at me with the best intention in the world of killing me. He came at me so fast I almost missed the easiest shot that I've ever tried in my life…like a snipe flying against the wind, and I barely grazed him. Maruja, if only I had Briguez out of prison, I would make him start at the beginning and teach me all over again how to shoot."

"Was it true that he taught you?" asked the girl.

"Every word, or almost every word. I left out that, when he went to Mexico on the boat, I went along with him."

"With Briguez?"

"Yes, with Briguez. I wish I had remained with him. There would have been no dog of a José Oñate to betray him, then."

"Oñate betrayed him?" cried the girl. "Oñate hated him, but he was so far from betraying him that…why, Randal, he killed that traitor with his own hands, when the dog came sneaking, to hunt for a reward."

"¡Hai!" cried the boy. "Is Oñate such a man?"

"He's a hero," said Maruja. "There is nothing mean

160

and small about him. Oh, I know him like a book."

"A little too well, Maruja, to make me entirely happy."

They rode on, stirrup to stirrup, over the undulation of the desert, and now there was a sting of alkali dust in their nostrils, a sudden, far-off promise of coolness in the air, and they knew that they were drawing near to the river valley. Through the night and into the first gray of the morning, that turned the moon into little more than a luminous wisp of cloud, they still rode on and found, at last, the widely trampled bank of the river where the great herd had gone down, and the beaten, broad way on the farther side where it had climbed onto the territory of the United States.

They were quickly over the ford and straight on into the rose of the morning before they found the cattle. They had traveled all through the night as fast as wild horses would travel, not at all as heavy-sided cattle might be expected to amble along. Now, in the morning, while a few riders on the points kept the herd spreading peacefully over a wide, grassy hollow, the rest were gathered about a small campfire to boil coffee and drink it down, scalding hot.

Toward them galloped a single rider. Maruja kept far in the rear, and Randal Dale, as he galloped, was shouting: "Help! Help! Saddle and ride! Don José, Jeems Loring, Llano!"

A dozen guns were out, covering him, when he came up. But they recognized no real danger from a single horseman on a foaming horse. From them all, he picked out the lean, ashen face of the albino, Ricardo Girones, and flung down at his feet a revolver.

"It is from Don José!" shouted Dale, waving his arms frantically. "He sent me off when the danger came. He

161

gave me this gun to hand to you, as proof I was from him. Danger at the inn. At the *fonda* of Bartolom Flandes. They...."

The lean hands of Girones fastened in the throat of Dale. "Fool!" he shouted. "Tell us the truth, did Flandes betray them and did...?"

"No, no, but the *rurales* have come. They have besieged the place. A dozen *rurales*, I think. They are shooting, and it is terrible. They are shooting with rifles. They are shooting to kill. And Loring and Llano are in there with Flandes to keep them off. I don't know how long they can manage it. Go, go! Ride in the name of Don José. He's already wounded. I saw his blood. Look! This is his blood, drying on my hand." He held out his hand, and the flickering light of the fire showed the stain clearly enough.

It is said that there is always a certain honor among thieves. At least, it is true of Western thieves, be they Mexican or American. There was one general shout of rage, one general imprecation against the *rurales* of all times, one vow to wipe this band from the face of the earth. Then the brave riders who followed Don José and the men of Jeems Loring—that hand-picked twelve—mounted their horses and rode, whooping like Indians, across the plain, back to that land of sunshine and knives.

Randal Dale waited for Maruja to ride up. Together they sat down to a pot of hot coffee, and sipped it at their ease.

TWO SIXES

"Two Sixes" *under the byline George Owen Baxter first appeared in Street & Smith's* **Western Story Magazine** *in the issue dated 3/17/23 and has not been reprinted since anywhere. Because Frederick Faust's Western stories are driven by their characters, and the circumstances in which they find themselves, the drama unfolds necessarily, not according to any plot convention, but according to the power of human emotion and the unpredictability of fate. Although Jack Maynard is presented with a second chance, his dilemma is whether or not he will accept it.*

I
"VIA THE WINDOW"

HABITUALLY MAYNARD TRAVELED LIGHT. FIFTEEN minutes after the letter came to him, he was packed and had paid his bill at the desk of the hotel. A quarter of an hour before, if he had been asked what could have stopped him in his journey south, he would have sworn that nothing under heaven was strong enough to check him. But when he paid his bill and turned from the desk, he found himself at the very gate of opportunity. Beyond him, only a step, was the Land of Promise. For he saw before him that golden dream that haunts all professional gamblers, the million-dollar table, with himself the dispensing power. Yonder was Andy Capp, his wallet heavy with a fortune in copper newly dug from the earth. Talking to Andy was Charley Raymond who had struck it rich at last, after thirty years of labor,

163

and he was now rolling on a tide of money that poured out of a gold mine in Nevada. And yonder was Sim Harper, whose plunging in cattle in the past six months had quadrupled a fortune already big. Three millionaires, and all three of them so intoxicated by recent profits that they would bet and lose a thousand with as much nonchalance as another would bet and lose a dollar. Surely this was, indeed, the Promised Land.

There was only one fly in the ointment, and that was Bud Clune, gambler extraordinary, who was now talking with Raymond. But even Bud would be a slight encumbrance at a poker table if Jack Maynard decided to get going. There they were, all the elements that go to the make-up of a rollicking game. And this at the moment, of all others, when Maynard wished to be off and away. It was a trick of fate that stung him to the quick.

He paused to consider it, frowning, as he rolled a cigarette. The contents of the letter from Collins in his pocket rushed across his mind once more.

Dear Jack,

You haven't heard from me for a long time because everything has been quiet down here. But in the past three days trouble has begun to pop. Roll your blankets and start home, old son, if you expect to get here in time to have a welcome from Louise. What I mean is that she hasn't batted an eye at any of the boys in town since you left. But the other day a young gent named Sandy Lorrimer blew into town, and he knocked Louise right off her feet. What's more, he's going to give you a fight for her that will make your hair stand on end. In the first place, he's only twenty-five, about three years older then Lou. And that means he has a pull of ten years over you. In the second place, you've been away so long that I guess Lou has almost forgot what you look like. In the third place, I think some talk has been going around and has been buzzed in the ear of Lou that the way you make money is not grubstaking prospectors, but by gambling. Not that Lou believes all she hears, but I think she's heard enough to start her thinking. And you know that she <u>can</u> think when she tries.

Now along comes this Sandy Lorrimer. He's got pale-yellow hair and pale-blue eyes full of deviltry. He goes around smiling all day long, with a handshake and a good word for everybody and a voice smooth as a calf's ear. That's Sandy. He can sit down at a piano and bat out any tune he hears. And what's more, old son, he can sing like a bird. When it comes to dancing, he's an authority on all the new steps. When the other boys try to do what Sandy does, they just make themselves look foolish. There was a dance over to Riccon Friday night. That was when Sandy showed up for the first time. He had all the girls corralled and tied in half an hour. All he had to do was to take his pick. But the one he picked was the one that held off, and that was Lou, of course. But all the rest of the evening he sort of floated around in the lee of her. Pretty soon they started dancing together, and they sure looked fine. I could see that Lou was getting excited. When she come around past where I was standing, I seen her heart beating in her throat, and her eyes were bright, and she was smiling all to herself.

Well, it didn't look good to me, Jack. I waited for a chance and found Sandy outside, smoking a cigarette, after the next dance started. I drifted him right into talk about Louise. Pretty soon I let him know that Louise is your girl.

"You mean she's engaged to Jack Maynard?" he

said.

"Sure she is," I said.

He doesn't say nothing for a while, but he starts in smoking so fast there's half an inch of red-hot coal on his cigarette.

"Who's this Maynard?" he asked.

"Born and growed up in this here town," I explained.

"That don't mean nothing to me," said Sandy.

"I dunno how you'd place him," I said, working to throw a scare into him, "but did you ever hear of Hal Dugan?"

"The gunfighter? Sure, I've heard of him," said Sandy.

"Jack is the man that killed Dugan," I said.

"Ah," said Sandy, "is that so?"

And then he goes right back and makes a beeline for Lou. Might have thought I'd told him you were a cripple living in Russia, the way he acted with Lou the rest of the evening. Didn't pay no attention to nobody else. Sure made himself conspicuous. Louise tried to head him off for a while, but he was just so dog-gone good-natured and handsome and such a fine dancer and good talker that she began to weaken. Before the night was over everybody was wondering how long it would take you to get back to town, and what sort of flowers they'd send for Sandy's funeral.

But I waited a couple of days to see if Lou wouldn't come to her senses. I didn't write to you, and I wish that I had. Because for these two days Sandy has been hanging around pretty close. And if Lou ain't weakening, then you can put me down as blind! She's making a fight to stay true to you, but she sure is having a hard job, and all I got to say is: Come quick!

That was the letter that had started Jack Maynard

packing, and still the words ran through his mind. In the cloud of cigarette smoke he blew forth, the face of Lou was shadowed, smiling, with her head raised and turned a little, just as she smiled in that picture he wore inside his watch. His dream was shattered by the hand of big Sim Harper that now fell on his shoulder.

"What about a little game?" asked Sim. "We've got four, but we need five for a real poker game, and there ain't anybody in the Southwest like you for speeding up a game. What you say, Jack, old boy?"

It was manifest destiny, decided Maynard. If fate had not intended this thing, it certainly would not have moved Sim to play with fire. Now that Maynard was swept away toward another point in the compass, Sim Harper was standing there before him, urging him to sit down to a game. It was the tale of Tantalus retold. It was like having a fortune in gold dangled within his reach at a time when he was fleeing for his life and dared not add a single pound to his burden. But, with a sort of inward groan, Maynard made his decision. Long as he had waited for this opportunity, long as he had dreamed of his million-dollar poker table, he loved Louise Martin more than money.

"I've got to be traveling," he said. "Sorry I can't sit in with you, Sim…sorry as the devil."

"Ain't that hell!" exclaimed Sim, turning away. "Maynard can't sit in with us."

The announcement brought exclamations of dismay from the others, but from Bud Clune it brought a low-pitched snarl of anger—a bare whisper—but Maynard heard it. Clune came straight to him.

"Maynard," he said, "it won't work."

"What won't work?" asked Maynard.

"This quitting…this sitting out on me. You've had

your whirl at me, and I get my whirl at you, or I'll know the reason why."

"What's wrong with you, Bud?"

"Three thousand dollars is wrong with me, Jack. Ain't much, is it? But it's three thousand that you've got out of me, and I'm going to have a chance to get it back, understand? I'm talking business, not fun. I don't care what you got on hand, you're going to give me another whirl at you. That's final. Yonder is the table that we're going to sit at."

His words were strong enough. His manner was even stronger. He was a terrier type, this Clune, built meagerly, with a long, narrow face and a long, narrow jaw. Now, as he spoke, he shivered, as though he were sick. Maynard knew that tremor well enough. It meant that every fighting nerve in the man's body was jumping with eagerness to be at the throat of the enemy. He knew the meaning of the nervous twitching of the fingers that rested on the right hip of Clune. In another instant they would dart down and jerk out the heavy Colt that weighed down the holster along his thigh.

Maynard considered. He was daunted, of course. Only old fools and young heroes see a gunfighter ready to work without feeling fear. Nevertheless, he was reasonably confident that, if it came to the last pinch, he could handle Clune well enough. He had met more formidable men than Clune in his day. Little incidents of palmed cards and strange deals had occurred at the gambling table, and at the gambling table men do not protest with words, but with guns. Such, at least, had been the code according to which Jack had lived. He was known as a gambler through most of the Southwest, but most of the Southwest also knew him as "Honest" Jack Maynard. He himself knew that his reputation for

168

integrity had been based on a speed of hand and a sureness of eye that enabled him to beat possible detractors to the draw. Three men had died on the opposite side of the table from Honest Jack, and half a dozen more, when they recovered from their wounds, had decided that it was better to be discreet and live, than to tell what they knew or suspected of Honest Jack's methods with the cards. Yes, there was not much doubt in his mind that he was a better man in a fight than Bud Clune, but a fight was what he least wanted in all the world. He wanted to get back to Louise, and he wanted to get there at once. He turned the matter swiftly in his mind. There were very few in this section of Texas who knew him at all. There were none, he was sure, who knew the small village he called home; and in fifteen minutes the train would pull out. All of these things had passed through his mind and had been weighed within half of a second. At the end of that time he was smiling in the face of Bud Clune.

"All right, Bud," he said, "I'll sit in with you. There's some extra fancy pickings loose tonight at that. I've checked out. Wait till I get my room back and dump my bag in it, then I'll be down. You boys get the table...."

"A good thing," muttered the ominous Clune, and turned away.

Maynard picked up his bag again, hurried to the desk, and, in a few seconds, was on his way to his former room. The bellboy opened the door for him, took the liberal tip with a grin of welcome, and then closed the door on this free-handed guest.

As for Maynard, he paused only long enough to lay on the bureau a five-dollar bill that would recompense the hotel for his room and leave something in his favor. Then he went straight to the open window and looked

169

down. It was exactly as he had recalled it. There was a broad ledge six feet below the window, and below that there was a twelve-foot drop to the ground. It might have made an average man hesitate, but Maynard was in no sense of the word, average. He had grown fat, as a matter of fact, through his ability to top the ways and the thoughts of the average man by a liberal margin. Through the window he dropped the bag to the ground and heard it land with a crunching noise. Then he hurried after it, gained the ledge, slipped from it, and yet managed to land on his feet, as lightly as a cat, on the ground below.

He scooped up the bag and was off. The train had whistled. Already it was slowing up, and Maynard sprinted at full speed through the back yard, vaulted a fence, and cut away for the station. He swung onto the rear steps of the train, just as it gathered speed leaving the station, and on the back platform he remained, as he watched the lights of the town spread out behind him, contracting gradually to a point that finally went out, as the night and the darkness closed across the desert.

There was no doubt that Bud Clune would follow. But in the meantime there would be a day or two to establish himself with Lou Martin again. A day or two, he flattered himself, would be enough.

II
"MAYNARD MEETS THE SHERIFF"

IT WAS LATE MORNING OF THE NEXT DAY BEFORE HE left the train. It was late that afternoon before he stepped down from the stage, stretched the kinks out of his muscles, and looked about him upon home. It was the same sunburned town. He had approached it with the same wonder that those monotonous miles of desert could harbor any life whatever. No matter that he knew there was wealth even in the desert, and that the few cows he saw scattered here and there at great intervals, plucking busily at the dried bunch grass, grew, when one counted them over sections of a hundred square miles at a jump, into enormous herds. He could think back to many a roundup and the multitudes of wiry, fierce-eyed cattle that were brought up out of the sands of the dead country.

Yes, there was wealth in that region, but the eye would never tell of it to a stranger. The heat was so terrible that the stage horses were dripping from every pore before they had gone a mile. The air was so dry that they had hardly stood ten minutes before the black sweat turned to an encrustation of white salt. It was a bitter country, but Maynard delighted in it. To be sure, he had no use for the labor of a cowpuncher's life. He had no desire to take those terrible gambling chances that are part of the cattle raiser's life. But he was delighted to come into the desert again, for everything that prospered here was just one thing more for him to prey on. He looked upon a dust-grayed cowpuncher, loping his horse past the stage, as the eagle on high looks down upon the kingfisher, an industrious servant who must pay the liege lord and master heavy toll, sooner or later. For can an eagle fish? Neither could Maynard work. But the more the number of hard workers increased in his desert world, the more his chances of obtaining a fat income at their expense increased. The more cowpunchers were grinding away at their forty dollars a month, the more he would encounter after pay day, when the 'punchers were recklessly bent on throwing away their meager paychecks as fast as possible. Such were the fish that Honest Jack Maynard drew from the stream of life.

Not that he was ordinarily cruel or selfish in the common affairs of life. Indeed, no man was more open-handed. No man was more indulgent of others. But when he sat down at a card table, business was strictly business. He no more minded breaking a poor, rough-handed cowpuncher than Napoleon minded annihilating a regiment of honest fellows who happened to be fighting for the enemy. There was no feeling of animosity. It was simply a necessary deed that must be accomplished. To the same fellow, the very next day, Honest Jack Maynard might loan half of what he had won from him the night before. But at the gambling table itself he was merciless and without morals. Two hours a day he sat down with his cards and his dice. Two hours a day he suppled his fingers until there was a separate intelligence living in the sensitive tip of each. Two hours a day he practiced the rudimentary tricks of his profession, just as the most brilliant pianist must labor over his scales.

So it was that Maynard looked upon the men of the desert with a peculiar awe and wonder. A single day of their ordinary labor would have been a horror to him. They accomplished work that was beyond his imagining. They accepted with a shrug day after day, under a withering sun, the very thought of which made him shiver and pass his hand over the delicate white skin of his face. They lived in white light. He lived in sheltering shadows. And yet, for all their strength, his strength was still greater. They dared the desert that he dreaded and shunned with a peculiar fear. Yet he possessed strength far greater than theirs—the agility that made him master of the card pack, made him also master of the gun play that struck down his enemies, as a bolt of lightning from the sky, an unavoidable power.

He looked around him, up and down the single street. Nothing had changed. A year had passed since he was last here, but he knew the face of every man and the face of every building. A very ugly street, no doubt, but it was home to Maynard, and Honest Jack looked about him with a strange, half-sad pleasure. In his wild boyhood, he had celebrated every corner of that street with some fight or other escapade. There arose the steeple of the church, to the top of which he and some of his mates had hoisted the buggy of the minister on one joyous Halloween night. There were the long, broad steps of the courthouse, down which he and Sammy Young had wrestled and rolled to the bottom.

Stepping out from the awning, he blinked, as the glare of the sun beat into his face. Almost immediately he was seen. It was old Bill Dunn, not less wrinkled than of old. It seemed to Honest Jack Maynard that Bill Dunn had never changed in appearance as far as he could remember. There had always been the same upright, spare figure, the same spare and withered face, the same eyes grown dull from squinting into the sun. Now the skinny hand of Bill was raised in greeting, and Jack went to meet him. Two sets of slender fingers met— those of Honest Jack soft, delicately tapered, white, with all the strength of that grip concealed, and the fingers of the old man, that were like the dried and trailing roots of the mesquite, hard as iron and brown as the skin of an Indian. There was still a young man's strength in that grip, however, and there was still the clearness of a youth in the steady eyes of Bill Dunn. There was just the same amount of boldness in his speech.

"Well, Jack," he asked, "you come back to get

married?"

It startled Jack Maynard. He was not accustomed to having his thoughts read, whether at the card table or elsewhere.

"Married?" he echoed. "Who's been talking about marriage, so far as I'm concerned?"

"Nobody," answered Bill. "I just been putting my thoughts together."

Maynard was on fire to find out what was in the head of Bill Dunn, but he knew that direct questions would gain nothing. He forced himself to be patient.

"How's everybody at the ranch?" he asked.

"They're getting on."

"Mamie's boy must be a whale of a fellow by now."

"He's a-rarin' and a-tearin'," said the old rancher with a faint smile. "He needs a tamin', but I never was no hand to break a colt too young."

"A wild colt makes a good hoss," declared Honest Jack with much sympathy.

"You ought to be one of the best then, Jack," said Bill Dunn, and laughed entirely to one side, on account of the balance of tobacco in his mouth.

In that laughter Honest Jack joined, and he felt that he had come considerably closer to old Bill.

"And Mamie's girl, Nell?" he asked.

"She's hooking up with the Chesterton boy next month."

"You don't say, Bill? Well, I'm damned!"

"Are you?" said Bill, looking up again in his mild way.

"I didn't know she was as old as that."

"Well, I dunno...she's too young to get married, by my way of thinkin', but she's too old to keep quiet. Might as well be upsettin' the Chesterton house as mine,

174

eh?"

Honest Jack smiled. "Which brings me around to Lou," he said. "How come you to play detective, Bill?"

"About what?"

"What makes you think that I've come down to marry Lou?"

"Well, ain't you been engaged to her?"

"That's right enough."

"What's been holding you off, except lack of the coin? Or maybe you been trying to find a nicer girl, eh?"

"I ain't a fool, Bill."

"No, I'd say that quick if anybody was to ask me. Now that I see you got plenty of coin, I know that you'll be marrying Lou."

"How d'you know I've got the coin?"

"By the hungry look in your eyes, Jack. A gent will go along plumb docile, but, give him some money, and he gets an appetite quick. Like the first drink for a gent that's got a taste for red-eye. Nothing gives a gent that hungry look except a pile of coin, or a fight in sight."

He placed the slightest emphasis upon the last words, and at the same time his mild eyes sharpened a bit, as though he were peering far off across the desert. Yet he was only looking deep into the face of Honest Jack Maynard.

"I don't get your drift," said Jack slowly, and all the time his brain was working hard to get at a solution of the last remark.

Bill Dunn chose a rather oblique manner of answering. "Suppose a gent was to strike pay dirt and file a claim…?"

"Well, Bill, what of that?"

"Suppose he was to come back from filing that claim

175

and was to find another gent with a set of tools hanging right around his claim?"

"Well?"

Bill Dunn kicked a white quartz pebble in the dust and paused a moment to admire the colors in the stone. "Nothing," he said at last. "Only I been getting decorated all up since I seen you last, Jack." He took his vest by the lapel and turned it out. To the astonished eyes of Jack Maynard he exposed the broad and glittering surface of a star.

"What the devil, Bill!" exclaimed Jack.

"Ain't it the devil, though," rejoined Bill, "when they got to pick out an old-timer all stiffened up with neuralgia and rheumatism and such like to be sheriff?" With sad eyes he looked up appealingly to Jack.

"You can't fool me, Bill," said Honest Jack. "I've seen you handle a gun, and I know what you can do. Well, here's shaking on that new job. The town never had a better sheriff than you'll be."

"Thanks, Jack," said the old rancher. "But times have been mighty dull lately. There ain't been any breaking of the peace."

"I'll bet there ain't...not when they knew that you and your Colt were on the job."

The sheriff laughed modestly, then frowned with deep anxiety and pain, as he saw that this time he had overshot the mark.

"And I'll be glad to have somebody like you in town, Jack," he said. "You'll be a good one to have to depend on if there *should* be any trouble. Need good men for the posse these days."

"I see," said Jack slowly. "The boys got a regular posse all fixed up?"

"Regular is right," said the sheriff. "You see, about

six months back there was a lot of shooting around this here town. Got so a body couldn't do no sleeping without having one ear cocked open to hear the shots. No sooner would you get to sleep than you'd hear a big gun go, *bang!* You'd sit up in bed. 'There goes Joe and Riley having it out,' you'd say. 'I wonder who gets buried tomorrow?' Just as you get to sleep again, there would come another *bang!* 'There goes Joe's brother calling on Riley,' you'd say. Got no idea how tiresome it was, Jack. So the boys got together and started to put an end to the trouble. You know how it used to be.

"A gent would sink a pound of lead into somebody he had a grudge against, then he'd fade away into the hills for a couple of months and wait till things quieted down. Then he'd come in, give himself up, and get acquitted on self-defense. But it riled the folks to see the undertaker getting so blamed prosperous. So they got together a posse, all pledged to start riding hard the minute there was a shooting scrape. First come Dodge Bennett. He dropped Sinclair one night, and we got on his trail mighty *pronto*. We landed him before the next night. He was tried right away, while folks was heated up, and he didn't have much of a chance. They hung poor old Dodge up by the neck and let him kick till he was through. You got no idea how unpopular shooting has been in this here town ever since. Couple of times strangers have blowed in and tried their hands with their guns, but both times they were caught. One of 'em got off pretty easy, though. He only got ten years. Still and all, I'm mighty glad to have a gent like you to back me up, Jack…in case there should be a fracas while you're in town."

"Thanks," said Jack, and bit his lip.

"Not at all," smiled the sheriff. "Give my love to Lou. I'm sure fond of that girl, Jack. So long."

It was all very clear to Jack, as he went down the street. Bill Dunn knew—and, therefore, the rest of the town would know—why he had come back so quickly. It was to meet this Sandy Lorrimer and back him into a corner and pick a fight, then he would finish him with a well-planted bullet and lament to the town next day that he had been forced to fight in self-defense. That had been the simple and effective plan Jack had had in mind. Now it seemed that all was not so well. It was no laughing matter to draw upon one's head the power of a wild-riding gang of gunfighting cowpunchers. He remembered when he was a boy how such a crowd had swept out of town on the trail of a murderer five minutes after the killing. He remembered, also, how that crowd had come back at the end of the day, with weary horses blackened with sweat, and the jaws of the riders set grimly. They had no prisoner with them, but far away in the hills under a cottonwood tree there was a newly dug grave.

The picture was newly painted in the mind of Honest Jack. The words of the sheriff had called it back in color as fresh as day. If it was not to be with a bullet, then, that he was to brush his rival from his path, it must be with a longer process—maneuvering for an advantage. As he walked down the street, a new idea sprang suddenly into his head, an idea that pleased him even better than a gun play.

III
"LOUISE MARTIN SPEAKS"

STRAIGHT FOR THE MARTIN HOUSE HE HEADED, AND every step he took assured him that he was right. If ever a woman had been born with a high soul of honor implanted in her to control her actions, Louise Martin was she. Suppose that he met her cheerfully, joyfully, as though never the shadow of a rumor had come to his ears concerning Sandy, the piano player? Suppose that he told her in the first joyous outburst that he had his stake at last, and that they would be married the next day? To be sure, he had only five thousand, but, once married, he would find means to increase that sum and make it twenty-five thousand. With Lou to make happy, he could make money grow out of the hard boards of gambling tables, he knew. Necessity would inspire him. There would be another million-dollar group such as he had left behind him the night before. If he came to Lou in such a fashion, what could she do? She could not plead that she wanted time to make up her mind. They had been engaged for three years. No, the thing to do was to take her by storm in this fashion, and very shame would keep her true to her engagement. And so he would sweep out of the life of Sandy, the nimble-fingered, with Lou in his arms.

So deep were his thoughts that he found he had walked past the Martin house. As he turned, the door of the house opened. He heard the high, sweet voice of Lou herself. The door closed, and down the steps came a slender youth. It was Sandy. He was easily identified by the pale, reddish hair that gave him his name. One could see at a glance that this handsome, smiling face, these bright and eager eyes were created by nature to pluck the heart of a girl out of her bosom.

Here was a foeman worthy of the steel of even Honest Jack Maynard. Indeed, for an instant even, his cool nerves failed him, and panic began to grow up in his brain. For the very walk of the other, light and rising on the toes, was the walk of a conqueror newly come from the scene of the conquest. To look upon that alert face and think of failure was impossible. The two ideas could not live together. More than that, he was no soft-handed stripling. Many an honest wind and many a stinging sun had burned his face as brown as a berry. The swing of his shoulders revealed a little ripple and play of lithe muscles under the thin cloth of his coat. No, if he was half dandy, he was also half hero. Which was the predominant half, Honest Jack could only guess at, and hope for the best.

Sandy turned up the street, and, as he passed the gambler, their eyes met. It was only a passing glance, but in it Jack Maynard felt that he had been probed and weighed to the last scruple. By such a glance he would have recognized a formidable foeman on the other side of a card table. By the same token he knew that luck must help him if he were to win Lou from this careless fellow. A man with such a smile would still be smiling as he fought, and a smiling fighter is only less terrible than one who prays, as he goes into action.

Here was the familiar gate. It creaked in the well-remembered way upon the rusted hinges, as he swung it open. Now the gravel crunched noisily under his feet. He felt a growing excitement, and there was a falling of the heart, a giddy sickness in his head. It was very like the first day at a new school. He dreaded, with a great dread, that meeting with Lou Martin. Now he was climbing the steps. He knocked at the door. Presently he heard a footfall hurrying toward him, the light and rapid tapping that was certain to be a girl running. *Was it not odd that her light feet fell in perfect rhythm with the hammering of his heart?*

The door opened, and there was Lou. Oh, how delightful she was—more so than he had remembered. She had been a little too slender, a little thin before.

Now she was as willowy as a whip stalk still, but there was a greater fullness. And there was a difference in her bearing. There was a softer effect about her eyes. So that all he could say to himself was: *When I left her, she was a girl, and now I come back and find that in a single year she has become a woman! Had the passage of a single year been enough to work such a change in her? Or was it not the effect of this wild fellow, this young conqueror, Sandy?*

All of these things passed through the wretched heart of Jack Maynard, as he stood at the door. It seemed to him that at sight of him Lou drew back with eyes that were widened by dismay. But if that were so, it was only the hesitation of a moment. Then she had dashed the door open and had thrown her arms around his neck. In a flurry he was brought into the house. His hat was taken from him, and he was seated in the big chair. There with the same shaft of the sunlight streaming over him and over the girl, as she stood laughing before him. He looked up into her face and wondered how he could ever have doubted her for a single instant. Be faithless to him? There was no power in heaven that could make her be false.

"Oh, Jack," she was crying, "such a happy surprise!"

"Do you guess why I've come, Lou?"

"To see me, I hope. Is that it?"

"And something more."

"More?"

"I've made my stake at last…twenty thousand, honey. We'll be married tomorrow and then away. What d'you say?"

He had risen as he spoke. He had made a gesture to take her in his arms, as though he would carry her away with the tide of his exultant thought. He could feel that his hand was at the very door of victory. Then, suddenly, he saw that she had withdrawn and was leaning against the wall, with her hands behind her back, shaking her head, while she looked out at him sadly.

"What's wrong, Lou?" he asked in dismay.

She still shook her head. "Not marriage, Jack. Oh, I'm sorry...I'm a thousand times sorry...but not marriage."

He wanted to bluster her down. He wanted to sweep her still before the great tide of his love. But he felt himself grow sick and white. He tried to raise a storm of words, but only a few and feeble ones came.

"Lou, what's wrong? D'you love me no more?"

It brought her from the wall with a rush, but, alas, he could see that it was pity that moved her.

"Sit down again, Jack. Let me sit here beside you. Oh, I'm so sorry that it has had to come so quickly. I...I thought that some of the others would write to you and prepare you for a change. I wasn't honest enough, or brave enough, to write to you myself."

"What change?" he asked hoarsely. Then he strove to retrace his steps. "But I don't want to talk about changes. I want to talk about you. There's no change in you, Lou. You're the same pure gold. There's the same ring to you. When I come back to you, do you know how I feel? Like a miser who's been around the world in hard luck and then comes back to his treasure and takes it up in handfuls, do you see? In handfuls, Lou."

And he made a gesture toward her, as though to touch her, as though to rest his glance upon her merely was a rich reward for labor. He found that she was watching him with a fixed and painful intensity, as though she were seeing a new man. And, indeed, he had never talked with her like this before. It was a new vocabulary. He was saying things he had never rehearsed before. But his heart was speaking for itself and telling him that he must have her—that there was no happiness in the world except happiness with her. Yet, as he talked, he could see that he was simply saddening her.

"Jack," she said suddenly, "do you remember when we were engaged?"

"Do you think I could ever forget that?" he asked her.

"How long ago was it?"

"Three years, almost to the day."

"How many days have you spent with me in these past three years?"

He was stunned. "I don't know, Lou," he said slowly. "Not very many, I suppose."

"Not more than a dozen," she answered.

There was a sad and solemn pause.

"What are you driving at?" he asked huskily at last.

"I think you've guessed, Jack."

He moistened his white lips. "There's another man, Lou?"

She nodded. "I didn't want to say it so coldly and badly," she said. "I had a whole speech made up, but speeches are no good. I might as well tell you the truth and have it over with…there *is* another man, Jack."

She had been so dazzlingly close to him that now this sudden removal seemed to whirl her away to a great distance. It left him sick and stunned.

"If you love him so much…."

"I haven't said that I loved him."

"What do you mean?" cried Jack Maynard, catching wildly at a new hope.

"I simply mean that, since I've known him, I no longer care for you as I used to, Jack. Do you see?"

"He's rubbed me out of your mind...is that it? But he hasn't written himself into the vacant place. Lou, is that what's happened?"

"Just that. I've fought against it...I've tried to keep true to you...but, in spite of myself...." She paused miserably.

Suddenly he began to laugh: "But now there's a fighting chance for me still! I thought I was lost, that there was no hope left. And now, Lou, I'll win out still. I've wanted nothing really, that I haven't won sooner or later. But first tell me...you haven't bound yourself to him, Lou?"

"Not a bit!"

"And our engagement? Does that have to be broken?"

She turned slightly away to the window. A cowpuncher was swinging down the street on his pony, the wind of the gallop jerking the brim of his sombrero up and down.

"I don't know what to say, Jack."

"Then say nothing at all. That's what I want to hear. I'm going now, but you'll see a good deal of me in the next few days."

"And with you and him...there'll be no trouble, Jack?"

He looked down closely at her, but he could make out in her face no special anxiety for his rival. That concern he saw might be as much for him as for Sandy Lorrimer. It was not her request of which he thought next. It was of the warning of the sheriff and of that old picture in his mind of that returning posse from the desert—the sweating horses and the grim-faced men.

"No," he said heartily, "there'll be no trouble between me and Sandy Lorrimer...not if I can help it."

"Dear old Jack," she exclaimed. "They've been

saying horrible things about you, but I've always told them that I knew you."

"Horrible things! What things?" he asked sharply.

"You know that I haven't believed them, but they've said that you made a gambling table into a gold mine, Jack."

"What hound dared tell you that?"

"I won't give you names. And they said you were a professional gunfighter, but I knew that you weren't."

"I'm coming back this evening."

"Not *this* evening, please."

"No? Busy?"

"Yes."

"It's Sandy Lorrimer, I suppose."

"I couldn't guess that you were coming today, Jack."

"Of course not. Good bye, Lou."

And he hurried out of the house.

IV
"SULPHUR AND SANDY"

HE WENT DOWN THE STREET WITH A BLACK BROW, indeed. It was far worse than he could have guessed. When a girl comes to such a point that she confesses freely what is going on inside her mind, it means that she is very greatly disturbed, he decided. And if she were disturbed by the conflict between her duty to her old fiancé and her affection for her new lover, the gambler had not the slightest doubt that the new affection would win out. He was in town to fight a losing battle, he felt. Yet fight he must, even though his hands were tied behind him. If he followed instinct and reached for his gun to settle the debate, he would have a whole posse on his trail in a thrice. He must work deftly

185

with his wits. That was the solution.

Passing down that winding main street of the town, he was halted by a scuffling and shouting in the middle of the street. There were half a hundred men and boys gathered in a close knot, and from the center of the knot came a deep-throated, terribly muffled snarling that told a dog fight was underway—a planned dog fight. Jack Maynard hurried to join the spectators and see the fun. It had been one of the chief amusements of his boyhood, baiting dogs until they flew at the throats of one another. He grinned now in anticipatory enjoyment.

He wormed his way in toward the core of the group. There twisted the struggling dogs in the dust, but the battle was almost over. A chunky, little bull terrier, his small eyes squinted almost shut with satisfaction, had clamped his long jaw over the throat of a great, long-legged wolfhound. The hound was almost dead. Swift enough to run down the biggest lobo, strong enough to give a lobo, single-handed, the fight of its life, it had slashed and punished the terrier terribly. The white body of the smaller dog was now pink with blood, but the terrier, fast as thought and wicked as an evil spirit, had finally closed and got his grip, just where the throat narrows toward the jaws. There he fastened his teeth, and, in a moment, the great hound would be a limp wreck. Already its eyes were bulging, its purple tongue lolled far out, and froth formed in its gullet from its frantic efforts to breathe. It could no longer fight back. It could only weakly struggle to bring one breath of the life-giving oxygen into its lungs.

It was easy to find the two owners of the dogs. There was one fellow built very much like the terrier. He had a short, broad, heavily muscled body. His jaws were set with a savage satisfaction. His nostrils spread, and his

186

eyes squinted with a grim content. Opposite him there was a giant of a man, now turning into a raging fury. He was leaning over the two dogs, shaking his fist in the face of the wolfhound, roaring out a torrent of abuse. Once Maynard saw the poor beast turn its eyes up toward its master, and, at the same time, the tail of the hound was lifted, as though even in its death agony the abusive voice of the master was dear to it.

It was all over in a moment, but not before a figure slipped through the dense bank of spectators. Sandy Lorrimer plunged out of the mass, saw the dogs, watched the faint struggle of the wolfhound, and saw the steady working of the terrier's jaws, as he worried toward a deeper grip.

"Great God!" said Sandy Lorrimer. "This ain't a fight...it's a murder. Call off the dogs!"

"I'll call off Terry...ready and willin'," said the chunky man. "All I want is for Jud to admit that his dog is licked. I ain't wanting to kill the hound."

But the big man flew into a new passion at the thought of surrender. "I'll see the skunk turned into buzzard food sooner!" he roared. "Let him die! This is costing me enough!"

But Jack Maynard paid no heed to the convulsed face of big Jud. He was watching Sandy Lorrimer eagerly, and he saw the other pass one quick glance from the big man to the owner of Terry. Then he acted.

Whipping out a bunch of sulphur matches, Sandy scraped them across the sole of his foot. Instantly the yellow heads turned into a fuming mass of blue sulphur fumes. Then he dropped to his knees and thrust the fumes squarely against the snout of Terry. The dog winced, shuddered, and then gave back, releasing his death grip and coughing out the foul gases it had drawn into its lungs. It hesitated only an instant, however, and flew back to the attack. That assault was not aimed at the prostrate and now motionless wolfhound, however. It drove straight at the new enemy and leaped at the throat of Sandy. What followed was to Jack Maynard a revelation of swift work with foot and hand and eye. Sandy swerved, while the dog was in mid-air. With both hands he caught the terrier by the throat, just under the jaw, and brought forty pounds of bone and muscle crashing into the dust of the street. He looked up at the heavy-set man.

"Call off your dog!" he exclaimed. "Take this pup, will you?"

Without a word the other stooped and swept his little warrior into his arms. There the terrier whined and struggled, but the muttered words of its master kept it from breaking away. Sandy stood up, dusted the dirt from his knees, and leaned over the wolfhound.

"Poor devil," he said. "He's almost done, but he'll come through yet."

As he spoke, the hound, coughing and gasping, reared itself upon trembling legs. They gave way under its weight, and it sank back into the dust again.

"Who'd ever have thought it," groaned big Jud. "Three weeks ago I seen that same dog run down a loafer wolf and kill it. And here that mite of a dog licks the yaller-livered...."

"If you knew anything about terriers," said Sandy Lorrimer, "you'd never have made the bet. That big fellow of yours is cut out for fighting big things...he ain't calculated to stand off a lightning streak."

"And what d'you aim to know about dogs?" cried Jud. He turned on Sandy with a growing anger. "And what d'you mean by coming in between them dogs?

Who knows now which dog won?"

"What?" cried the owner of the terrier. "Wasn't your hound within a wink of dying? Couldn't everybody see that? Ain't I right, boys?"

Appealingly he turned from one to another of the spectators, but there was a general silence. The bystanders exchanged glances and then looked furtively to Jud. But apparently the latter was a known man, and what they knew of him kept them from talking too freely against his interests. The result was a blank silence.

"You see?" challenged Jud triumphantly. "They agree with me. And ain't it known to everybody, that ain't a fool, that a dog fight ain't lost or won until one of the dogs is dead, or till the owner of one of the dogs hollers quits?"

The short man turned gloomily to Sandy Lorrimer.

"Here's what comes of you butting in, kid. I lose five hundred by this, and I'll have it, or take it out on your hide!"

It was apparent that he had no care to mingle with big Jud in a fight. It was equally apparent that he had no fear of Sandy Lorrimer. Yet Jack Maynard, looking the scene over with a critical eye, would for his own part have sooner faced five Juds than one Sandy.

"You ain't going to lose," Sandy was assuring the owner of Terry. "You think that Jud is going to beg off...but he won't. You don't know him. He's talking sort of free and large just now, but I aim to state that he ain't got it in his head that he can dodge paying the money that he's just now lost on his hound. Am I right, Jud?"

It was very innocently spoken. There was even a faint smile on his lips, as he turned to big Jud. To the

189

astonishment of Jack Maynard, the red anger grew dim in the face of Jud. He frowned down into the dust, hesitated, and then answered mildly enough: "Oh, I guess there ain't any doubt but that my dog lost. But you'd ought to keep your hands off when there's a fight on that ain't any of your business, son."

"Sure," said Sandy meekly, "that's good advice."

As he turned back from facing Jud, Maynard saw in his eyes a faint gleam of battle anger, rapidly fading. But it was not hard to guess that Jud had seen the full flare of the same thing, that Jud had noticed, also, the uneasy and nervous twitching of the fingers of Sandy's right hand. It was fear of sudden and inescapable death that had constrained Jud.

V
"CLUNE CALLS"

THE OTHERS STAYED TO ENJOY THE AFTERMATH OF BIG Jud's humiliation. They paused to see the money exchange hands, but Jack Maynard went slowly on up the street. On the way he encountered the sheriff, headed for the group, but he paused and accosted Jack.

"I hear there's some trouble up yonder?" he queried.

"Not much," said Jack. "I guess that the worst of it's over."

"I'm glad of that," sighed Bill Dunn. "I sure hate trouble worse'n a sore tooth. I wasted a lot of time hoping that things would be cleared up before I arrived."

"Not a very active sheriff, eh?" smiled Jack Maynard.

"Sure I ain't," said Bill naïvely. "Active sheriffs cause a pile more harm than they can cure. The sight of a sheriff turns more'n one argument into a gun fight.

Looks like the boys all want to prove that they ain't going to back down…not for ten sheriffs, standing around waiting to run 'em in! So I aim to steer clear of trouble. It only takes one chunk of lead in a gent's vitals to keep him quiet for a tolerable long spell. And I ain't ready to die, Jack. I got a lot of talk left in me, and I ain't collected enough good yet to feel easy. But what's Sandy been doing?"

For the group was breaking up, and several men were clustering around Sandy, as the latter walked away.

"Mixed in between a gent named Jud and another fellow," reported Jack gruffly. "Jud took water as smooth as you please, and Sandy got away with his talk. Things ain't the way they used to be, Bill. Big talk sure counts for a lot more around the old town than it used to."

"You think so?" said Bill Dunn with the same quiet interest. "Tell you what, Jack, none of the boys like Sandy's medicine. Folks will buck up to any of these here badmen that come along with a chip on his shoulder trying to *make* trouble, but Sandy don't make no trouble at all. Just the same, when trouble seems headed his way, he pricks up his ears like a pup that seen raw meat. He looks so plumb pleased and happy at the sight of a fight that it sort of takes the heart out of the boys. But, between you and me, Jud is likely to make it hot for Sandy later on if he gets a chance. Jud is one of them sure-thing bettors. When he's sure he's got a man licked, he's a terrible hard fighter."

The faded smile of the sheriff followed the form of big Jud, as the latter trailed off down the street with the down-headed wolfhound, following slowly at his heels. Maynard went on toward the hotel.

He registered for his room in a haze. He could not

recall even the face of the proprietor when he finally found himself in his private room. So he stripped off his coat and threw himself into a chair. But the chair was covered with new varnish, softened to stickiness by the heat, and the view he faced out the window was a prospect of roofs over which played a mist of heat waves. It was blindingly hot. The air was a faintly pink haze, through which the eye could travel many miles, but always with that sense of suspended particles dancing in the oven-like atmosphere.

Presently he threw himself on the bed. Now that his eyes were taken from the picture, it was better. But what of the men who were not actually looking at the desert, but rode in the full pressure of the sun with no covering, saving the wretched tent of a sombrero? He shuddered at that thought. He raised his long, pale hand. The back of it was covered with little beads of perspiration, and he could feel the neckband of his shirt growing wet. Yes, it was a very hot day. It put a heavy, thumping pulse in the back of his head, and with his puffed lips he muttered a word of pity for those who were exposed to the desert sun. What a curse that he had been destined to live in such a country.

If it were cool weather now, he would be able to plan and scheme in such a fashion that he could circumvent this dashing youngster, Sandy Lorrimer. In half an hour he would have a plan that would be enough to paralyze Sandy, thrust him out of the picture, and bring Jack back into his own again. But this heat numbed the brain. He had turned impatiently on the bed when there was a knock at the door, and then the lock turned.

"Who's there?" asked Jack.

"Bill Gregory," answered a man from the hall.

"Bill Gregory!" shouted Maynard and leaped from

the bed.

For Bill Gregory of all men was the one nearest to his heart. Often he told himself that he had no real friends, but, if there were any man who could qualify for the part, Bill was the man for it. For it was from Bill that he had learned all the endless finesse that goes with rolling the dice—trained or untrained dice. It was Bill who had taught him the single-handed deal in blackjack—the consummate one-handed manipulation that allowed him to show the bottom card, and yet to bury cards under it at his will. These and many another thing he had learned from the old reprobate. And, as a result, he felt that all of his fortune had been based upon the wisdom of Gregory. And his heart for a moment beat high with a joyous expectation. But, with his hand upon the key, in the very act of turning, he realized that he had been wrong.

It was not Bill Gregory. It was a voice low and husky like Bill's, but still there was a difference. He closed his eyes in the intensity of his effort to recall what Bill's voice had really been. The more he thought, the surer he was that it was not his old friend who stood in the hall. If not a friend, then an enemy come under a disguise.

Maynard turned the key, and, as the lock clicked, he took a long stride to the side, flattened himself against the wall, and leveled his revolver.

"Come in," he called. "Come in, Bill, old man."

A boot struck heavily against the door. It flew open, and into the doorway, face pale and jaw set, a naked Colt long and glimmering in his hand, was Clune. Too late he saw his enemy at the side. He started with a convulsive motion, then he saw that he was beaten hopelessly, and dropped the gun to his side.

Savagely he glared at Jack Maynard until footfalls

sounded down the hall. Then he kicked the door shut and dropped his gun back in its holster.

"Not so easy, eh?" asked Maynard, feeling his own tension relax.

"Never mind," said Clune. "I'll get you yet, you yaller skunk."

Insults were nothing to Maynard. He had been called every name in the book in his gambler's life, and he had come to care for nothing except action. And, even when the time for action came, he waited until he had been driven into a corner before he struck. It was easy enough to kill, he had discovered, but it was another thing to get rid of the effects of a killing.

"Sit down," he said quietly to Clune.

"I'll stand," answered Clune, as he loosened the bandanna that was knotted around his throat.

Professional gambler and indoors man that he was, he was, nevertheless, as brown as any cowpuncher. He was a man of the desert, who loved it for its own sake, and, accordingly, Maynard looked upon him with a peculiar wonder and awe. For his own part, he would not have worked himself into such a dripping perspiration, as that which poured from Clune and turned his clothes to wet rags, for a thousand dollars.

"Stand up, then," said Maynard. "Have a smoke?"

He dropped his revolver back into its holster. For, good man though Clune was on the draw, Jack Maynard knew himself to be better. He knew that Clune understood the same thing. It was for that reason Clune had attempted to gain an advantage by that cowardly trick of the assumed name. As he spoke, Maynard tossed papers and tobacco to the other, but Clune beat them aside with a savage hand.

"I ain't going to be soft-soaped out of this," he

declared.

"Out of what?" said Maynard, and he leaned to pick the makings from the floor.

It was a very nervy thing to do. He saw the hand of Clune fly to the butt of his gun, but the hand came harmlessly away again. The very boldness of Maynard had paralyzed Clune, and Maynard straightened again with the papers and the tobacco in his hand. He was so plainly the master of the situation now. If he had spoken a single, rough word, there would have been a fight that would have forced him into a killing, and a killing would have brought onto his heels that terrible posse with the wily, old sheriff at its head. He had been twice warned since his arrival in the town, and he could take it for granted that, if he were concerned in a gun fight, there would be no questions asked. They would turn out to hunt him down as a professional gunfighter, and that would be an early end to the flourishing career of Jack Maynard.

"You're not going to be soft-soaped out of what?" he asked.

"Maynard," said Clune, biting his lip with his hatred, "sometimes I figure you to be almost the greatest man in the world."

"And other times?"

"*All* the time I know that you ain't a real man at all, but just a chunk of the devil wrapped up in a man's skin."

"Thanks," said Jack Maynard, "but this ain't the stage. You ain't getting paid for fancy speeches, Clune. Let me have some facts, will you? What's been biting you all this time? Is it that three thousand I touched you for? Are you such a poor loser as all that? Are you still whining because you had a run of bad luck at the cards?"

"Bad luck?" said Clune savagely. "You call it luck when you run up the pack and put a double crimp in it?"

"I asked you if you wanted another man to deal at our table," said Maynard. "You said you didn't. I wasn' pretending to play straight with you, and you weren' trying to play straight with me. Why, Clune, do you think that I was blind? I saw you try to switch packs on me, and that was why I called for the new deck that time."

"*Bah!*" sneered Clune, after the fashion of one consumed with passion but rather unsure of what he can safely vent his rage on.

"There's something else behind it all," went on Maynard. "What is it, Clune? Why do you hate me so?"

Clune moistened his lips, hesitated, and then shook his head. He made an ugly spectacle, as he stood in the center of the floor, with his legs spread and his head dropped forward between his shoulders, and his big hands clenched. He had little, pale-blue eyes crowded close together on either side of a stub nose, and his great unshapen mouth was only partially hidden behind a loose growth of mustache.

"Besides," he broke out suddenly, "you lied to her about me."

"Lied to her?"

"You can't cover it up. After she talked to you that day, she hadn't an eye for me any more. You double-crossed me there."

Maynard remembered with dull wonder. It was so rare for him to be innocent when he was accused, that he could hardly believe his ears. He could recall the girl Clune loved very vividly. She was tall, with rather large, black eyes in a sallow face, and an air of sickly gloom,

196

that Clune, it seemed, considered to be an interesting melancholy. And he was accused of having intrigued with this poor girl in order to win her affection from Clune? Maynard was swept by an almost irresistible desire to laugh, but he fought that desire down and conquered it. Such a burst of laughter would have meant sudden death for one of them, he knew well.

"Clune," he said, "I swear to you upon my solemn word of honor that I never so much as said five words to her when you were not nearby."

Suppressed mirth made his voice tremble, and the tremor was taken by Clune as a passion of sincerity. He wavered in the intensity of his hatred, though he still kept the murderous scowl upon his face.

"Maybe there's something in what you say," he admitted. "But I ain't satisfied yet. I'm going to watch you close, Maynard. I know that you're a tricky one. And I tell you plain that, if I thought you was aiming at her, I'd kill you, Maynard, as sure as there's a devil."

"You'd have enough good reason to do it. But now sit down and have a smoke, Clune. I'll tell you, man to man, much as you hate me, you'll find that I'm a square-shooter. As for you, I don't blame you for being peeved. Thinking what you thought about me, how *could* you be blamed?"

His manner was full of deferential courtesy. His voice was even more charged with the same quality. Clune, in spite of himself, was flattered. He began to feel that, after all, he must be a more important man that he had ever suspected. If Maynard were so filled with courtesy, there must be a reason for it. That reason came out at once.

Hardly had Clune rolled a cigarette from the makings that were thrown to him by Maynard, hardly had the first cloud of smoke been blown forth, than Maynard sank back in a chair and mopped away the perspiration that had been running down his face in rivulets.

"Hotter than a fire, eh?" he gasped.

Clune, though his thick eyebrows were drenched with perspiration ready to roll down into his eyes, merely shrugged his shoulders.

"Ain't much of a day," he declared. "Sitting inside, a gent always feels it more, you know. Get out, stirring around in the sun...."

"I'd as soon stir around in a fire," gasped Maynard. "Wonder it don't rip the skin off a man's face and neck."

"You get used to it," said Clune, "unless a gent lives pretty soft the way you do...always in the shade."

"But why in the name of the devil don't they plant trees around the hotel?"

"Costs water and money and work to make trees grow down here. You'd ought to know that. You can't balance looks and a mite more comfort again' hard cash, can you?"

Maynard sighed. He returned to the scheme that had grown up in his mind, a scheme that, take it all in all, he felt to be the most brilliant he had ever conceived. For it united two essentials—it was effective, and it was simple. What could be more effective than to remove two enemies? What could be more simple than to remove them by sending them at the throats of one another? Indeed, it was brilliant, a perfect inspiration. He could barely keep himself from smiling, as the whole beauty of the scheme presented itself to his imagination.

"I'm glad that trouble with her is off the slate," Clune was saying. "That leaves nothing between you and me but the three thousand that you cleaned me out of and the fact that you ran off before I got a chance to get even with you. But now that I see you're square, we can fix that up, Maynard, eh?"

There was only one thing, thought Maynard, that was displeasing in the scheme, and that was that he must destroy such a man as young Sandy Lorrimer through the use of such a reptile as Clune. But all was fair, he told himself, in love and in war.

VI
"SALLY GETS AN INVITATION"

SPEAKING OF WHAT YOU'VE LOST, CLUNE," HE BEGAN in his most conciliatory manner.

"And what about that?" cried Clune.

"Nothing, except that I think I see how you can get it back a couple of times over."

Clune sat up and blinked his little eyes at the other. His tremendous greed had been the thing that ruined him as a gambler, for it was impossible to disguise his excitement when he felt himself approaching a climax with a chance for a killing not far away.

"Get it back a couple of times over?" he breathed. "Clean up six thousand? Say, Maynard...."

"After all, it's simple enough."

"Go on! Go on!"

"I'd do it myself, but they're waiting for me."

"How's that?"

"I'll put it to you in a nutshell, Clune. For the past six months they've had old Billy Dunn in this town for sheriff, and Billy is a nacheral gunfighter. He's cleaned out the crooks, and, what's more, he's cleaned out the gamblers, Clune."

"Well?" said Clune.

"But I've worked out a scheme where a gambler can make a cleaning."

Clune nodded. He was hanging, breathless, upon every word.

"You know the old gag of starting in plumb innocent by losing a little and having a bum streak of luck?"

"Do I know my own name?" laughed Clune.

"When you string 'em along that way for a while and let *them* have a bit of luck, they're willing to keep in the game, while *you* clean up."

"Nothing truer than that," said Clune. "I've had the poor fools wait a whole day for their luck to turn. Had one man wait till he'd used up the price of his farm. I cleaned him out, right down to his shoestrings."

He laughed uproariously, while Maynard bit his lip to keep his sneer from showing.

"Well," said Maynard, continuing, "I'll tell you frankly, Clune, that a professional gambler wouldn't last a day in this town. First of all, you've got to establish yourself as an amateur and a bad amateur at that. You understand?"

"How can I do that?"

"How much coin have you got?"

"About fifty dollars," said Clune, flushing heavily.

"Not much to start for a clean-up, eh?"

"You wiped me out," said Clune, "and I've had no luck since I grounded on you."

Maynard took out a wallet, and from its capacious depths he counted out five hundred dollars.

"Look here, Clune," he said, "a fool could lose five hundred dollars and make it look like nothing. But a wise player can string out five hundred and make it last so's it looks like he's losing five thousand. You understand?"

"I dunno that I get your drift," muttered Clune, scowling up at the other.

"I mean this way...you start out free and easy, like you had a million dollars tucked away in lumber in Montana, or something like that, understand? There ain't nobody from Montana in this here town. You act like winning or losing at the cards didn't make no difference to you. Suppose you're playing poker. You start in talking about other things...you crack a joke, if you can, here and there."

All that was righteous in Clune rose in revolt.

"Crack a joke during a *poker* game?" he shouted.

"Don't yell," snarled Maynard. "There ain't no need to let the whole town in on what we're talking about."

"Right you are...go on...go on," panted Clune.

"Well, you act like winning wasn't in your mind. It's just the fun of the game that you want...understand?"

"I've tried that before," groaned Clune, "and it never worked."

"Because you looked like a starved dog the minute you got a good run of cards, and somebody started betting against you. But this time it's going to be different. Understand? I'm going to be behind you in this here game, Clune. If you go broke, I'm going to supply you with a little more coin. But if you work it right, you can stay ahead with that five hundred. There are ways. You make a little winning on the last hand of the first game you play in. The next time you sit down to the table with some of the boys, bet a couple of hundred on two or three bad hands, and, when you lose, tell them that's all the money you have with you...you're broke till you wire for more coin. Understand? That will put you in right. The news will get all over the town that you're a good loser, and that money means nothing to you. But not unless you can laugh when you leave the table. Can you do that?"

Clune groaned. "I can try," he said.

"You can pretend to get a fresh batch of money in the morning," went on Maynard, "and in the afternoon you can start playing again, win a little, and close off the game with a couple of big losses. If you work it right, you can be right in the evening to make your clean-up. Everybody in the town will be talking about you and saying that it's easy to make money at your expense. You ought to have a hundred dollars left, and that's enough. If you start winning, nobody will dream that you're winning by crooking the cards."

"I get your drift," said Clune eagerly.

"And tomorrow evening," went on Maynard, "I'll steer the prize goat to your table. Young gent by the name of Sandy Lorrimer. He's got a pocketful of cash, understand? You can sink a prong into him and get away with a pile of money, Clune."

"The only thing I don't make out," said Clune, "is why you don't make this clean-up yourself?"

"Two good reasons. First place, they know me in this here town, and they know that I'm a gambler. They wouldn't sit in with me if the stakes begun to climb and get big. In the second place, if I made a clean-up, my name would be mud around here ever after."

Clune nodded. The reasons were clear enough. Five minutes later he had left the room and was on his way to hunt for a party with which to begin his first play.

In Maynard he left a feeling of approaching triumph. There was still much to be done, but Maynard was gaining confidence. It would be the hardest sort of hard luck if he could not manage to bring Sandy Lorrimer together with Clune, and it would be strange, indeed, if, once together, there were not an explosion. If they fought at close range, one of them was sure to die. It did not greatly matter which one. For the other would be hounded out of town by Bill Dunn's posse, and, with either Clune or Lorrimer, there was far more apt to be a killing at the end of the posse's trail than a mere capture.

So far, then, all was well, and, with Sandy Lorrimer out of the way, it would not be too difficult to win back Lou Martin. Indeed, she had not been wholly captured by Sandy Lorrimer even while Maynard was away, and now that he was back, the power of old times would fight strongly on his behalf. There would be the strength of pity to help him also—Maynard was not above counting upon that emotion—and, if all went well, their wedding would take place within a month after Clune and Lorrimer were dead.

He felt as he did after he had succeeded in marking all the cards in a deck and was master of the game. There was nothing the others could do to shake him; it only needed that he should be able to steer Lorrimer to the game with Clune at the proper time. To do that required that he become the friend of Lorrimer. But even this was not a task beyond his powers.

He made his preparations for the first step at once. No matter what it cost him in pride, he would attend that same dance to which Louise Martin was going with Lorrimer. There he would choose his opportunity to talk with Sandy. There he would manage to smooth things over between them.

Full of that thought he went downstairs again. From the room behind the bar, he heard a burst of voices. He stepped back to the door and found that Clune was already at work. There was a table with five poker players sitting in. There was a little crowd of a dozen or more gathered to watch. And, even as Maynard stood in the door, he saw Clune push in a stack of chips to call a hand, saw the chips swept away from him, and heard Clune say, laughing: "There goes a month's profit. Ain't that luck, boys."

"Poor fool bucked that up on two pair," Maynard heard one of the bystanders mutter to another. He went on toward the front of the hotel. As a matter of fact, he had not dreamed that Clune would make so good an actor. The man's laughter had rung as true as any good coin of mirth.

From the verandah of the little hotel Maynard looked up and down the street. The fierceness of the late-afternoon heat had abated. The evening was now coming on swiftly. The intense, reddish, desert sunlight of the midday was now softening to yellows. It was the hour when people were beginning to venture forth from their houses. For who would be under roof when the wonder of the desert night began to descend? Not one step of its approach could be missed. The blacksmith yonder paused in spite of his haste to finish the last job of the day and came to the sooty door of his shop through a cloud of smoke to enjoy the changed air. Children were already at play, raising clouds of dust to the fury of the people who had come out on the porches. Girls and men were walking here and there with laughter and many greetings. In spite of all the noise the street seemed silent to Maynard, for the silence of the great desert night was rolling in toward it.

His mind was taken from that half-gloomy and half-mysterious thought by the shrill music of a girl's laughter nearby. She came, running like the wind, a blue-eyed, red-haired, brown-skinned girl. She checked her flight by grasping the post of the hotel verandah near Maynard's chair, and there she looked back, laughing, toward her pursuer, but the latter was already retiring.

"Oh," cried Maynard suddenly, "you're Sally Hopkins!"

The blue eyes flashed up at him. "Yes, I am," she said.

They laughed together, and then they shook hands.

"How long has it been since I saw you, Sally?"

"Since the night you came to your window and hollered...'Stop making that infernal noise out in the street, you kids! I want to sleep!' "

"I never called that to you."

"You did, though."

"But Sally playing in the street, and Sally grown up, aren't the same person."

"How come?" asked Sally.

"If you won't take my word for it, look in the mirror."

Her eyes softened, and she flushed a little. "What do you mean by that, Jack?"

"I'd need a pile of time to explain, Sally."

"I got nothing but time on my hands."

"Are you going to the dance tonight?"

"With my brother," said Sally.

"Dodge him and come with me! Will you do it?"

"I'll tell a man," cried Sally with the frankest delight. "I'd like to see 'em stop me!"

"Then I'll call at eight."

"Now I'll start home."

"What's the hurry? We ought to get acquainted, Sally."

"I need every minute I can crowd in," she assured him. "If I'm growed up, I'm going to look the part, or bust!"

And, laughing again, she went off down the street. Maynard looked up and found the quizzical eyes of Bill Dunn fixed upon him.

"I been waiting for six months for the boys around town to wake up about Sally," he declared. "You've started a stampede, Jack!"

VII
"LIKE A SLAP IN THE FACE"

AT EIGHT O'CLOCK MAYNARD STOOD AT THE DOOR OF Sally's house, and, when he was admitted, he found Sally the central figure in an admiring family group before which she turned slowly that they might admire. From the grinning father to the ecstatic mother, it was plain that they were seeing Sally for the first time in all her glory. And glorious she was, with a pale-green frock, that clung to her slender, young body, and her red hair coiled in flaming light and coppery shadows high on her head. A violent alteration had given that frock a low neck, and although powder could not quite cover the sharp line where the sunburned neck met the pearl skin of the bosom, yet one could not pause to examine such minute details when looking at Sally. She was not a classic for regularity of features, but youth and joyous color and laughter, bubbling just at the surface of her heart, made amends for all else. Maynard gazed upon her in a mute wonder. He had not dreamed that there could be such a transformation. She had been touched with a fairy wand. Yet, as he stared at her, he saw behind her the picture of Louise, made even more enchanting by the contrast. Others might see more in this newly risen sun, but for his part she recalled him only the more strongly to Louise.

206

"And do I *look* grown up?" she cried, dancing over to him.

"You look like a million dollars," he said, smiling.

"I don't care...I want to look twenty-five. Do I look that?"

"Better than that."

"You're the nicest old thing," cried Sally, "in the whole wide world!"

While her mother gasped and her father protested and her younger brothers and sisters crowed with excitement, she threw her arms around the neck of Jack Maynard and kissed him.

"Sally!" cried her mother, as the girl danced back again, her color flaming, but her eyes shining defiantly.

"Cut it, Sally!" exclaimed Mr. Hopkins.

As for Honest Jack, there was only one thing that saved his equilibrium, and that was the haunting memory of Lou which would not go away from him.

"D'you know what'll happen if you do that to some youngster a shade nearer your own age, Sally?" he asked her.

"I don't care," she sang at him.

"You'll wake up the next day all married and settled down for life. And you know, when a girl marries, the good times are ended, eh, Missus Hopkins?"

"Hey, Maynard, what are you driving at?" roared Hopkins, but he joined in the laughter.

In another moment they were seated in the buggy Honest Jack had rented and were rolling away for the dance. "But what am I to do tonight?" she asked, as they swept out of town in a cloud of dust.

"Make me happy," he said.

"Oh, it's not that," she answered with an instinctive wisdom. "There's something else behind it all. You have a reason, Jack. Can't you tell me? Is it..."—she hesitated—"is it to make Lou Martin feel that she's not the only person in the world you're interested in?"

He looked sharply down at her. She had struck so close to the truth that he was amazed. The last he remembered of Sally she had been a ragged urchin, kicking up a great dust in the street and making more trouble for the town than any three boys. And here she was, a woman of women, and reading his mind with an uncanny accuracy. Suddenly he decided to be as frank with her as she had been with him.

"Suppose I say it's partly that?" he suggested.

"Why, then," said Sally, "it won't work. Lou...there's nobody like her, you know."

He smiled to himself in the darkness. "You'll find a pile of people disagreeing with you about that when you get to the dance," he said.

She made no answer to this for a time, doubtless because she did not entirely understand him. For his own part, he decided that a girl who was wise enough to understand the value of silence was also wise enough to take care of herself.

If he had any doubts, they were removed when they reached the dance. The old schoolhouse was crammed with lights and music. For a Western dance begins early and ends late. It begins before the dusk of the summer day has hardly thickened to night, and it ends not until the sun is rolling close to the horizon, and the sky is filled with the chill of the first sunlight. There was a mighty gathering of rigs and saddle horses in the sheds near the school yard and at the racks, and others were tethered under the trees. They entered the little cloakroom—where Jack had so often left his wet slicker on rainy, winter days—in the midst of a dance, but there

208

were a half a dozen new arrivals in the crowded little room, and there was a quick centering of eyes upon Sally as she came in. Maynard watched her closely, and he saw her head go up, while her color heightened ever so slightly.

Instantly she was surrounded. Half a dozen hands reached to help her out of her coat, and then she was with Jack again. They had stepped into the hall, with the rush and whisper of many feet on a floor that had been brought to a glassy polish by a liberal coat of wax, rubbed in by dragging a bale of hay around the room.

"That snob, Bill Vincent," she said, as they glided into the waltz, "he hasn't spoken to me for a year except to say...'Get out of the way, Sally. That off hoss of mine thinks you're pretty fresh and green. He's apt to take a chunk out of you.'"

"Look here, Sally," Maynard cautioned her. "You take my advice. Let bygones be bygones. The way gents treat a girl and the way they treat a woman is a pile different. Tonight, don't you forget, you're a *woman* for the first time. Don't you hold no hard feelings."

She danced away from him a little and looked searchingly up into his face.

"You *do* know a lot," she commented.

"Thanks," chuckled Jack, and he began to search for Lou in the crowd.

He found her almost at once. For, as always, she danced with her partner in a little cleared space. There was not a young fellow in the county who did not want to see Lou in her glory, and there was not a girl who did not want to study her style of dancing. So a path would always appear for her, as if by magic, through the thick of the press. She was not dancing with Sandy Lorrimer on this occasion, but it made no difference. She seemed to the gambler to float along in a cloud of glory. He was barely aware that Sally was growing anxious and nervous. So the dance ended, he hardly knew how, and still his eyes were wandering off over the heads of the crowd toward Louise.

The hand of Sally touched his arm. "Do your best, Jack," she was saying. "Don't pay any attention to me. You go find her and win her back, Jack. Oh, I wish you all sorts of luck."

He was amazed and ashamed. "I'm here with you, Sally," he said. "The rest of the world can go hang."

She shook her head and laughed a little. "Don't you trouble about me," she whispered suddenly. "Besides, I guess I'm going to have company enough."

As they strolled across the floor, hunting for a pleasantly situated chair, Maynard discovered that half a dozen youths who had been without partners in the preceding dance, or who had got rid of their dancing mates with uncanny expedition, were now moving in a direction of which he and Sally were the vortex. In another moment they were surrounded, and he abandoned Sally willingly enough. He needed to get outdoors again to draw a few deep breaths of the open air.

He looked back from the entrance to the hall. Sally was deeply packed in with a swirling circle of young fellows who were grinning and nodding, as though their lives depended upon their amiability. There was no question at all that he had launched her social craft with glorious success. He stepped on through the door, and there he found a group of men and girls gathered around Sandy Lorrimer. That young worthy was doing a juggling feat worthy of the stage. In the flat palm of his left hand he had balanced a short section of inch board, and with his right hand he spun high in the air an opened jack knife with a great blade, polished to dazzling brightness and keen as a razor. That swiftly falling streak of light he caught on the edge of the inch board, although the slightest unsurety would have caused the knife to miss that target and drive straight down through the palm of the juggler's hand. He was not only performing this daredevil feat, but he was laughing joyously as he did it, and his eyes seemed far more centered on the faces of the crowd around him than upon his hazardous work. Presently there was a sharp interruption.

"Sandy, you wild man!" cried a voice beside Jack. Maynard turned to see Lou whip past him, as oblivious of his presence as though he had been a dissolving cloud. Down the steps she flew, darted through the circling spectators, and stood panting before the entertainer.

"Don't you know that knife is bound to miss sooner or later?" she cried.

"Not tonight, Lou," said Sandy.

It irritated Maynard, for some reason, to hear this fellow call her by her nickname. For that matter, she was Lou to the whole town, but the town had a right, he felt, the other did not have. In the meantime, she had taken Sandy under wing. They went back up the steps, and the others followed, laughing and talking and pointing most significantly. Maynard gritted his teeth. This open demonstration of anxiety for Sandy under the very eyes of her former lover was like a slap in his face. If there had been any milk of human kindness in the veins of Jack the moment before, it was dried up now and left only a cold resolution.

VIII
"AFTER THE DANCE"

THERE HAD BEEN NO LACK OF WARNINGS FOR SANDY Lorrimer that evening. A dozen men had told him to beware of Jack Maynard. A dozen men had described with minute detail the battles in which Jack had engaged in the past and out of which he had always come victorious. So that, for all his juggling tricks, for all his carelessness and laughter, Sandy went like a man in a hostile country. There were no guns worn at the dance, of course, at least in open view, but Sandy knew well enough that every other man had a weapon of one sort or another tucked away in his clothes. He himself carried a gun, and it was a long, formidable Colt. He had learned long before how to stow away such a bulky weapon as this, so that it showed by not so much as a wrinkle in his clothes. And while he had it with him, he was quite prepared to meet the danger of Jack Maynard.

Not that he underestimated that danger. He had watched with a fierce eagerness. In the first place, he had not expected that Maynard would come to the dance. When he came, and with such an armful of fresh and girlish beauty as Sally Hopkins, Sandy had observed him as a new and strange star.

He recognized him at once as the tall and white-faced man whom he had passed near the house of Louise Martin earlier that day. The more he stared now, the more he felt his heart sink. It was impossible that Lou could look twice at him, when this magnificent and stately man was near her. No matter that Honest Jack was a gambler. In fact, that would probably appeal to her romantic soul and make him twice as attractive to Lou. He had been on the peak of confidence a little before. He was suddenly in the depths of gloom.

As was his way, the more his heart fell, the more profoundly he was convinced that he must keep a high manner, and never had he been so gay. The juggling was only a small episode. All evening he maintained his spirits. He was the life of whatever group he found himself in. But always from the corner of his eye he was watching Lou and Maynard.

It was a full hour before they danced together, and then a little whisper of admiration ran around the room, and Sandy found himself murmuring in sympathy. For they made a wonderful couple, tall and graceful, and dancing perfectly. He could see that Jack Maynard was whiter than ever with excitement. He could see that Lou, also, was taking fire. It seemed to him that she had never smiled for him as she smiled for Jack Maynard now. A thousand miserable suspicions grew up in his mind. She had been only playing with him from the first, perhaps. She had been using him as the decoy through which she should draw Jack home to her again. The more he thought of it, the more confident he became that this must be the truth. And yet all he knew of Lou told him that she could not be underhanded. But every woman was a mystery; there were things about every woman no man could be expected to decipher.

After that dance he found Lou suddenly before him.

"I've got to go home," she said to him in a whisper. "I can't stay, Sandy. Will you take me home?"

"What's wrong?" he asked.

Now she was trembling, and her color was coming and going.

"I don't know…nothing's wrong," she gasped. "Only take me home at once…please, Sandy."

He took her outside, and a little later they were started

for her home. He tried to find something to say on the short way in, but his lips were locked. He could only steal wretched side glances at her from time to time. When he did speak, it was to say the last thing in the world that he should have said.

"What do you want me to do about it, Lou?" he asked.

"About what?"

"I'll go if you want. If my staying here makes you unhappy, I'll say good bye to the town and never come back."

"Why do you ask me that?" she cried. "Are you trying to make it harder for me, Sandy?"

He bit his lip. "I'm only trying to do the square thing," he answered.

"And so am I. I'm trying with all my might to do the square thing...and God help me to do it. There's no one in the world so unhappy as I am, Sandy."

He dared not speak again until they stood at her door. Then his misery tortured him into speech again.

"Lou," he said, "you love him. I saw it in your face, while you were dancing with him. I'm only waiting for you to tell me the whole truth. Then I'll stop bothering you."

"If I only knew." She added faintly: "Sandy, I've been so happy playing around with you...you've been like a brother and a friend rolled into one."

"I've hoped to be something more," he murmured slowly.

"And you were!" she cried. "But now...oh, Sandy, how can I talk to you about him? But if I don't talk to you, *whom* can I talk to? If I leave him, I've ruined his life."

He shut his teeth hard against the retort that rolled up to them.

214

"He talked to me tonight," she ran on in the same hurried and half-broken whisper. "He talked to me tonight as I've never heard anyone talk…while we were dancing. And…."

"When a man begins to beg…," began Sandy bitterly.

"You don't understand. He doesn't beg."

"Simply says he'll die unless he has you?"

"Sandy!"

He saw that he had gone much too far, and he bowed his gloomy head.

"Don't you see?" she went on. "I've always known that there was great good and great evil in him. He's capable of doing fine things and terrible things, and I think it all hangs on me. If I marry him, he'll become a good man, Sandy…if I don't marry him, he'll become a perfect wolf of a man."

"I got no answer," said Sandy. "Seems to me, Lou, that nobody could love you as I love you. The thought of you runs in me like music." He stopped short. He had always despised high-flown eloquence, and now he checked his flight. "But, whether you marry me or not, I won't go to the dogs, Lou. If you give yourself to me, you ain't giving yourself to any charity." He had not meant to end his sentence so bluntly. That excess of honesty, which made him underrate all that was fine in him, had forced him on until he offended her. And how seriously he had offended her he could begin to guess, as she drew back from him. It was only a short half step that she drew back, but, as she straightened and lifted her head, he could see that there was a great gulf between them.

"I was sick for the want of somebody to talk to," she said. "But I see that I was wrong to talk to you. Good night, Sandy."

"Lou!" he cried in desperation.

She had opened the front door, and the light from the hall lamp struck faintly across at her. It glowed in her hair; it glinted delicately across the outline of her face; it brought a highlight upon her throat; it changed the color of her dress to something to be dreamed of, but never named.

"Well?" she asked coldly.

He could not answer. A sort of holy awe had fallen upon him. She seemed so pure, so removed from earthly things, so infinitely above him, that something akin to worship poured up in his heart and locked his tongue.

"Good night," she said again, and the door closed upon him.

He would have torn the door open again and uttered in a flood all the things that were crowding to his tongue. But, as he stretched his hand to the knob, he heard the lock turned and felt that he was that instant cut from her life.

Weak of body and dizzy of brain, he went back to the street. Such great and terrible things had happened to him, and so suddenly, that he felt he had come to the end of his rope. There was no refuge left for him. He reached the hotel in the same numb condition of brain, but hardly had he come to it when he saw a sight that set him instantly tingling. It was big Honest Jack Maynard coming back from the dance and singing softly as he strode along. Truly he was a magnificent figure of a man. *If a bullet were planted in the middle of his body, might he not crumble like any other mortal? And was not that the shortest way out of the difficulty—to fight it out?*

He thought another thought—it was of Lou Martin, as she had stood with lifted head at the door of her house. *No one but a fool would dream that she could be fought for like an ordinary woman!*

IX
"FALSE FRIENDLINESS"

SANDY WAS ONLY A STEP BEHIND MAYNARD, AS THE latter gained the level of the verandah, and with his soul in his eyes he watched the gambler. There was no shadow of a doubt that Jack Maynard was a formidable man. For all his bulk he carried himself lightly. He walked with an easy grace, and Sandy Lorrimer was careful to note that the footfall of the big man was as soft as the padding of a cat's paw.

His own approach had been noiseless enough, but, just before Maynard passed through the door of the hotel, he swung about and faced Lorrimer. There was a lion-like dignity, thought Sandy, about this man. And for his part he felt like a small-souled sneak who had invaded the rights of the king during the king's absence. It was the first time they had actually encountered, though plainly each had seen and heard the other's name at the dance. Sandy held himself tinglingly ready to fight, if fight he must. But the hand of Maynard shot out to him, and the smile of Maynard brightened above him.

"Hello, Lorrimer," said the big man. "I'm mighty glad to have a chance to shake hands with you at last. I've heard a mighty lot about you…a lot too much, some folks would say."

Maynard laughed with a frank cordiality that seemed marvelous to Sandy. But, of course, he decided, as he shook hands with Maynard, the latter had fought and won his battle this night, and Honest Jack was smiling because he could afford to smile. The next words of Maynard's staggered that thought.

"People are looking for trouble, a regular explosion, when we meet, Sandy. But I guess we'll have to

217

disappoint 'em some, eh? I'm not looking for a fight. Revenge of that sort ain't going to do *me* any good!"

Happy Jack smiled in a wry fashion that seemed to point to the fact that he very well understood the joke was on him. Sandy, listening, was amazed. What he himself would have done in similar circumstances he could only guess, but he judged that he would fly into a passion. His first words would be a challenge; his first gesture would be toward his gun. The equable voice and the gentle manner of Honest Jack were almost beyond his comprehension.

"I don't quite foller you, Maynard," he said feebly, as their hands fell apart.

"I don't mind talking frank," said Maynard, still smiling. "What I mean is that I don't bear you any grudge, Sandy. I think that the best thing I ever done was to win a smile from Lou...and now that you've done the same thing, I figure that you ought to be at least as good a man as I am."

Sandy crimsoned to the eyes. He was for the moment blinded and amazed by such startling nobility. It was quite beyond his own reach, as he freely confessed to himself.

"You're talking mighty white!" he managed to say to Maynard. "And it makes me feel a pile more like a skunk than ever about the way I've acted to you...and...and to Lou, Maynard."

It seemed to him that Honest Jack blanched a little, though whether the pallor came from pain or rage or shame, he could not guess. And, indeed, it was such a passing change that the smile of Honest Jack the next moment wiped out all thought of what had gone before.

"You've done nothing," he said heartily. "Great guns, a man ain't to be blamed if he falls in love with the

218

finest girl that ever stepped, is he? What would I have done if I'd come along and found Lou wrapped up in some other gent? One of two things…tried to move him out of the way, or get Lou away from him some other way." He smiled and nodded again. "Of course, I've had my bad time about this, Sandy," he went on. "When I first heard about it, I wanted to tear your liver out and feed it to coyotes. But I'm over that. I see that there ain't anything to blame you about except that I should have stayed down here on the job, unless I wanted somebody else to steal my thunder. Besides, Sandy, I like to have the folks in town see us together. The sheriff has been standing around like a crane on one leg, waiting for us to come to the surface, fighting."

In another moment they had entered the hotel together. It seemed to Sandy that this must be happening in a dream, and, in spite of himself, a warm admiration for the gambler filled his heart. He looked up to the actions of Honest Jack as the child in the gallery leans out and stares at the matinée idol in all his grace and glory on the stage. *How almost more than mortal are his actions. How irresistible by man or by woman.*

There was no one in the office of the hotel, but there was a murmur of voices from a back room, and Maynard suggested that they see what was happening. In another moment they reached the door of the room where the poker session was in progress. There were four playing, and Maynard saw at a glance that Clune had not obeyed instructions. He had been playing hard and playing to win. With what success, the pile of chips before him attested. And the other three whom he had been pillaging were watching his motions closely, suspiciously. Perhaps he had gained five or six hundred dollars, but now the three were playing

219

cautiously, very cautiously, and their wagers were small. They refused to bet unless their hands were very strong, and even strong hands they laid down without a struggle when Clune raised the bets too rapidly. There was no doubt that by this time Clune had marked every card in the deck.

Maynard looked down to the face of Sandy Lorrimer. It was too bad that such a fine fellow as Sandy must be sacrificed, but it was no time for tenderness of heart. Something must be accomplished and accomplished at once. He had seen and heard enough that night to make sure that Louise Martin had drifted so far from him and so far toward Sandy that nothing but death could remove Sandy from her life. And here was Clune, too, a bulldog on the trail of Maynard. It would be a perfect thing to remove the one by the other. Whoever fell, it would be a gain.

"Look at that," said Jack Maynard to Sandy. "Look at that highway robbery!"

"Robbery?" asked Sandy.

"That's what I said. There sit all three of them with no more chance of beating Clune than a dog has of calling the moon out of the sky. He's got every card marked, I guess, by this time."

"Marked cards?" growled Sandy with a peculiar change of voice.

"Clune is an old hand," said Honest Jack. "I play a good deal myself, and everyone knows about Clune…except in this section of the country."

"Then why haven't you warned people about the hound?"

"I'd warn a friend, of course, but it's a pretty serious thing to spread around word that a man is a cheat, Sandy."

The hand of Sandy fell upon his arm. "You're a fine fellow, Jack" he said heartily. "But what does that skunk do? Pack a couple of crayons and smudge up the cards with 'em?"

"That's it. Every ace has a little smudge near one corner...blue smudge if the back of the card is blue, and red smudge if the back of the card is red...understand? It ain't hard for the crooks to do. They just carry a red and a blue crayon in their vest pocket, and they got a moist handkerchief in their coat. They get a finger tip wet and touch it on the crayon...then they make the blur on the back of the card. Mind you, it has to be done with a pretty sharp eye. An amateur makes a big blotch that every man in the game can see, but a professional makes a little blur so dim that he can hardly see it himself, even when he knows what to look for. You understand?"

"But suppose a man keeps his cards covered with his hand? And every one at that table is doing it?"

"That would stop an ordinary crook, but it won't phase Clune. He's a shark. He can read the backs of those cards, while they're still in the air, you might say. Before a gent has clapped his hand over the back of his card, Clune has spotted it. Then all he has to do is to watch the discard."

"And he remembers what's in every hand?"

"Of course."

"The dirty dog!"

"He's all of that."

"Maynard, why don't you show him up?"

"I'm a gambler myself," sighed Maynard. "I suppose you've heard that, but I hope you've heard, too, that I'm a square one."

"I don't need to be told that," exclaimed Sandy

heartily. "You're the most aboveboard man I've ever met, Maynard."

"Anyway, I can't sit in a game and talk about another player being crooked. They'd say I was crooked, just because I knew what to look for."

"Well," murmured Sandy, "they can't say that about me. *I'll* sit in that game!"

"Don't go it," cautioned Maynard, though it was the very thing toward which he had steered the other.

"Why not?"

"It ain't safe to show up a gent like Clune. He's a gunfighter, Sandy."

A shade of suspicion made the eyes of Sandy hard as he looked into the face of Jack. Then he shrugged his shoulders, as though banishing an impossibility from his mind.

"If it's gun fighting, I'll be ready for him," he declared. "I'm going to sit in at that game."

"Better not, Sandy."

Sandy was already halfway across the room. "Got a place for number five?" he asked. "Need any new blood in this game?"

"Sit down," said Clune. "Glad to have you."

There was a brief round of introductions. In half a minute Sandy was sitting behind the little stack of chips he had bought, and Maynard turned down the hall away from the room.

It was done now, he felt, this work of his. He had brought the wolf and the bulldog together. Which one would win? For he knew beyond the shadow of a doubt that within five minutes there would be an explosion, and an explosion meant guns, and guns meant death for one of those two cool-headed fighters. As for the other, Bill Dunn's efficient posse would attend to him. So the

222

field of battle would be left cleared for Jack Maynard, and Lou Martin would be his without an effort. For he was certain that she did not love Sandy too well to forget him.

X
"A DOZEN HORSEMEN"

UP AND DOWN THE HALL HE WALKED SOFTLY, ROLLING a cigarette, lighting it, smoking it almost to a butt—and still nothing had happened. Yet it could not be that those two could be in the room together, after what he had told Sandy, without a fight. Maynard waited breathlessly. How perfect it was that, in case of trouble, his hands were so completely washed of the fight that he was not even in the room. Though, perhaps, he might be of use in shooting down the fugitive. At that thought his upper lip curled back from his teeth, and he smiled savagely in the dimness of the hall. There was only one smoky lamp burning. But that was enough to send a highlight down the polished barrel of his revolver. It would go hard, indeed, if he did not kill his man with the first shot in such a shooting gallery as this. He touched the outline of the gun under his clothes. Then he shifted it a little to make it readier for a sudden draw.

Now it came, shrieking and sudden, in spite of the fact that he was waiting for it. There was a sharp voice raised, the brutal voice of Clune that always soared to a scream when a crisis came, though it was a heavy bass ordinarily.

"What the devil do you mean by that? You…!"

Through the stream of abuse came the voice of Sandy, and Maynard knew suddenly that he was a terrible fighter. His voice was as calm as though he were bidding Clune good day, and yet there was force in that quietness to overwhelm the staccato yell of the gambler.

"I say that these cards are marked."

"You lie!"

"Clune, d'you mean that?"

"I say…!"

"Boys, look at the backs of those cards. If you find some little smudges of red and blue, then we'll ask Clune if we may have a look through his pockets to find crayons."

"Look here, Lorrimer, you can't insult me like this and get away with it."

"If I'm insulting you, I'll apologize when this is cleared up."

"You think I'll submit to being searched?"

"I hope so."

"I'll see you in hell first…you…!"

There followed a curse that admitted of only one answer, and that answer came. It crashed against the raw nerves of Maynard, waiting—the heavy roar of two long-barreled Colts. He seized his own gun and prepared for a snap shot at the fugitive, whether it should be Clune or Lorrimer. But no one dashed through the door. Instead, there was a tingling crash of window glass.

He gritted his teeth. He had been a fool not to think of that possible way of an exit. He rushed into the room, his gun in his hand. It was Clune who had fallen. He lay on his back with his arms outspread. The shattered window told where Lorrimer had made his exit. The others in the room were in the wildest confusion, running here and there. It was Maynard who dropped to his knees. It was Maynard who tore open the shirt at the breast of Clune. And there he saw, with inward rage, that this first part of his plan had completely failed. Clune had fallen from the force of the blow, when the bullet struck his body. It had landed on his chest, but his body must have been half turned, for it had glanced along the ribs and had come out again under the shoulder. It was simply a nasty surface wound. And the striking of his head against the floor was doubtless what had stunned him and kept him motionless now.

The aftermath of this fight came clearly into the mind of Maynard. In the first place, as soon as Clune was known to be merely slightly injured, Sandy would go free. And as for Clune, he would soon learn how the suspicions of Sandy had been directed toward him. He, in turn, would tell Sandy how Maynard had been behind the game. There would be a sudden dénouement in which Maynard would be disgraced in his own town, and Lou would turn from him forever in sorrow and shame. In addition to all of these disasters, Clune and Sandy Lorrimer would both become his bitter enemies.

All of this ran through the mind of Maynard, as he knelt over the body of Clune. He looked up. There stood Sheriff Bill Dunn, wrath in his face and a curious hunger in his eyes, the hunger Maynard had seen before in the faces of men who love battle and the risks of daring death.

"What's this, Maynard?" asked Bill Dunn, and his thin voice seemed ludicrously childish and out of place in that room. "Have you had a hand in this?"

"It's Lorrimer," said Maynard. "It's that young fool, Lorrimer."

"How's this man, Clune…ain't that his name?" asked the sheriff, leaning above the body.

A sudden inspiration filled the brain of Maynard. Here was his chance to brush Sandy from his path. He

225

stumbled to his feet between the sheriff and the wounded man.

"Drilled clean through the heart," he said. "Yes, his name is Clune, and he'll never answer to that name again on earth."

"Good guns," groaned the sheriff, "I'd rather have had a boy of my own do this than have it come on a gent like Lorrimer, but"—and here his face grew stern—"business is business, and it ain't for me to play no favorites. Maynard, you ride with me tonight."

It was all Maynard had asked for. At the side of the sheriff he left the room. At the side of the sheriff he ran to the church, and there the sheriff opened the door to the building and in another moment was tugging at the rope that ran up into the belfry. Instantly the clangor of the big bell began.

"It'll be a warning to Lorrimer that we are coming after him," gasped the sheriff, as he pulled at the rope, "but it'll bring the boys together. This is their signal. Go get your hoss, Maynard. Over at the livery stable you can get a good one. Tell Jerry to give you his new roan. Hurry!"

To the livery stable fled Maynard, and on the way he passed through a street that was suddenly alive with people. From every house the inhabitants had poured forth. And half a dozen mounted men were already fleeing for the church at full speed. Certainly the sheriff's standing posse was well disciplined. At the livery stable he found Jerry, the owner, rubbing the sleep out of his eyes.

"Dunn sent me for your new roan," he called. "Get him for me quick, Jerry!"

"All right," groaned Jerry. "But I suppose this'll be a hard ride and…."

226

He ceased his murmurs to run to the back of the stable and drag a roan horse from a stall, a tall and well-made animal, with big, strong legs. The keen eye of Maynard was studying the horse quickly. He had only one thing in common with the cowpunchers of the desert—he knew horses. Indeed, following such a profession as his, it was above all things necessary that he should be expert in all such things as quick getaways. And, since horses were his means of travel, he knew horses as though he were reading them out of a book.

"Jerry!" he called.

"Well?"

"That ain't the roan I want!"

"What?"

"I say that ain't the hoss the sheriff sent me to get. I want *the* roan!"

"She's too small for you," began Jerry sadly.

"You lie! Get that mare quick!"

Jerry, with a sigh, submitted. He led the way to a little corral behind the stable, and there Maynard saw a small, rather long-bodied animal, but her small, compactly made head, her big, glistening eyes, her little pricking ears, spoke of breeding, and breeding was what told on a desert trail.

"That's the one," he said, and two minutes later he was in the saddle. Weight? The roan mare danced under him as though he were made of feathers instead of flesh and bone. Even by her prancing, he could guess at her speed.

"Treat her kind and gentle," said Jerry. "She's only four, and she's all heart and spirit. She'll kill herself running if she gets a chance."

"I'll take care of her, and I'll pay you her price, if anything happens to her."

"Money can't make up for what...."

The words died out of the hearing of Maynard, as he sent the mare at a wild and clattering gallop over the floor of the stable and out of the door into the street. He wove her through a cluster of running men who were answering the alarm. She answered the touch of the reins with the speed and the quick-footedness of a great cat. They reached the open street. Far down it a dust cloud was vanishing into the night. After it he flew, and the little roan flattened toward the earth, as she got into her stride. She flew over the ground, it seemed to Maynard. And that dash brought her up with the rearmost riders of the posse before the latter were well out of town.

On a less-frequented trail the cloud of dust died away, and Maynard could make out a dozen men, only a dozen, whereas the disturbance in the street had made him suspect fifty. Another glance at these men told him that the dozen meant more than fifty ordinary riders. They were all picked from a thousand—men and horses. There was no excitement, no vain shouting, no boasting, no threats. They were not running their horses, either, but had already drawn them back to the measured and easy lope cow ponies can keep up all day.

"Maynard!" called the thin voice of Bill Dunn.

He pressed forward to the head of the procession and to the side of the little sheriff.

"Maynard, you're the only man who saw the killing."

"I didn't see it. I was walking down the hall when I heard a couple of guns."

"That's all I wanted to know. Matter of fact, Jack, I was afraid that you might have had a hand in this game. I know you ain't got any call to be friendly to Lorrimer."

"Maybe it was Clune's fault...he's a gambler," said Maynard faintly.

"Gents have got to get over the habit of saying what they think of each other with slugs of lead. That's my business. If it wasn't Lorrimer's fault, why did he cut and run for it?"

Maynard was silent. It was all working out more smoothly than he had dared to hope.

XI
"MAYNARD FIRES"

THE DAYLIGHT BEGAN EARLY. THE SUN ITSELF PUSHED up at five in the morning, and it found the party twenty miles from the town and well into the desert, limitless miles of red sand, with sharp ridges of porphyry shaking their backs, here and there, like monsters about to rise from the sea. From one of those humps the eye traveled far off and plunged into the horizon. With a strong glass, such as every member of the party carried, it was possible to detect almost every moving object. Certainly it would be impossible for a horseman to escape them, if he were at all close. But Lorrimer was not to be seen.

Now they held a council of war, and there was a divided opinion, but little Bill Dunn was calmly assured that he was right.

"Lorrimer is one of them fast riders," he said, "and he's young. He'll aim for the first mountains, and the first mountains are west. He'll aim for the first pass in them mountains, and the first pass is Wilson Gap. We'll head for Wilson Gap, and we'll catch him."

They cooked breakfast, a hasty meal, and went on again. The day had barely begun, but it was already scathingly hot. The young sun threw a slant light behind them. It burned through the coat of Maynard. It seared the shoulders and the small of his back. It scorched his neck until he rearranged his bandanna. As the perspiration poured down his face, he looked at his companions. They seemed perfectly at ease. Neither the stinging dust, that puffed up each time a hoof was planted, seemed to bother them, nor the heat of the sun itself. And they held on at a steady pace, rolling and smoking innumerable cigarettes, talking a little, heading constantly after Bill Dunn, who kept the lead on a tireless, gray horse. They were at home, and Maynard was in the fires of torment.

The others moistened their mouths every twenty minutes from their canteens, but Maynard could only keep from choking with a swallow every ten minutes. By mid-morning they came in sight of Wilson Gap, and by the time they sighted it, Maynard was nearly spent.

Rough-headed mountains cut like the teeth of a saw into the western sky, with one deeper jag than the others—a place where a tooth had been broken off. That was Wilson Gap. It would be noon before they reached that crest, and beyond the crest lay more desert, and the sun, sloping down the western sky, would begin to sear their faces. The heart of Maynard failed in him.

"What if Lorrimer should decide to double back?" he called to Bill Dunn.

"Double back to where?"

"Back to town."

"Back to town to get hung?"

"No, but to see somebody. He might turn and come back behind that range of hills yonder."

To the south a long and muscular arm put out from the main range. It rippled toward the east. And the

230

thought of the shadows among those rocks was like a promised blessing to Maynard.

"We'll keep on the way we came," said Bill Dunn.

It was like a doom of death to Honest Jack. He pushed his horse to the side of the sheriff, and the little roan went eagerly, with high head, as though eager to be off and away.

"Bill," he said, "I'm done for. I can't stand the work. I'm burning up."

Dunn looked anxiously at him. "Damn me," he said, "if you don't look it. You're all sort of red and purple. I didn't know that you was as soft as that."

"Soft? No, but I simply can't live in an oven." He thrust his hand out into the sunlight and drew it back, as though from fire. "It's hell, Bill!"

"What you want to do?"

"I want to quit without having the boys call me a quitter. I want to head south to those hills and rest there in the shade until evening. When it cools off, I'll start back for town. I'm done. Bill, I can't keep up."

Bill gnawed his lip thoughtfully. "Jack," he said suddenly, raising his voice so that the others could hear, "I think you may be right. Lorrimer may head back behind those hills. You go down there and, if you see him, stop him. If he goes that way, you can't miss him…the ravine is pretty narrow. So long, Jack. And use your eyes."

It was very strange, thought Jack, as he headed south. It was almost incomprehensible that he should be giving up the trail that meant the death of Lorrimer. For, once Lorrimer was found, there was no doubt that he would fight, and, if he fought, these men would surely not fail to kill him. And once he was dead, Lou would be left to her old sweetheart. She was fond of

231

Lorrimer, beyond a doubt, but she had not yet come to love him.

Yet even the face of Lou was a dim thought. It was washed away; it danced to nothingness in the heat waves that tossed above the sands. Her memory was burned and blackened in his mind. There was one thing more important, and that was to escape from the desert, while the desert could still be left. He looked back. The posse was still plainly in sight, jogging steadily on. *What manner of men are they? They seem made of iron.*

In an hour he was among the hills. The sun hung steep in the sky, but he found a projecting rock that offered shade for him and yet left him open to whatever wind was stirring. There was a pint and a half of lukewarm water in his canteen. That would have to last him until mid-afternoon, and, when mid-afternoon came, he would ride down the ravine and return home. On the way, as he had heard one of the posse say when he left them, he would find a water hole—not three miles down the rock-bound valley. That would save him.

But, before he had waited an hour, while the sun was only barely at the meridian, he obeyed a blind impulse and down his aching throat he poured the last of the water. When he realized what he had done, a cold horror began to torture him.

He must start at once for the water hole. That was most apparent. The gallant mare would need it badly by that time. With a filled canteen he could retire again to a shadowy place among the rocks. Yet three miles under that wild sun was a small hell in contemplation.

Climbing into the saddle, he started the mare. The heat was furnace-like, the instant they left shelter, and it made the brain of Maynard reel. Yet he pushed across the ridge and into the ravine itself, a narrow-throated little gorge that would probably be oven-like compared with the open sweep of the sands, where some wind could move. He was on the verge of riding down the slope when he heard something very like the creaking of saddle leather. He rode his horse around the big boulder that cut off his view, and there, down the valley, he saw Lorrimer coming, trotting along on a tall bay that tossed its head and seemed as full of life as a freshly mounted racer in spite of all its long journey. Maynard's mind cleared. It was like giving up hope at the very moment one reached the wishing gate. He smiled savagely, rubbed his swollen and numbed lips, and grasped his revolver. But the shot was too long. He must still wait.

Again he smiled to himself. *What would the sheriff and the posse think when it turned out that his guess had been correct?* Nearer drew the fugitive, riding erect and lightly in the saddle. Now he was close—almost even with Maynard.

"Sandy!" shouted Honest Jack, and whipped out his gun.

Even so he was hardly in time. The draw of Sandy Lorrimer, taken by surprise as he was, was like the flash of a whiplash. The gun glittered in his hand and was swung up, but, before he could fire, Honest Jack had planted his shot.

At thirty paces he could not miss—hardly if his arm were jogged. He heard his bullet clang on metal. The revolver was dashed into the face of Lorrimer, and the shock flung him, stunned, from the saddle, while the tall, bay horse whirled with a squeal and dashed off up the valley, never stopping until he was over the next ridge and out of sight.

XII
"UNDER SUN-BLISTERED STONES"

WITH POISED REVOLVER MAYNARD WAITED, CURSING his fate. To take Lorrimer alive back to town was the height of folly. It would simply be shown, when they arrived, that Clune was not in the slightest danger of dying, and the eyewitnesses would doubtless be ready to swear that Clune had provoked the attack, or first reached for a gun. But Lorrimer, falling, had landed squarely on his head. It was not impossible that his neck had been broken. But Sandy stirred, groaned, rose, staggering, to his feet.

"Get your gun, you," yelled Maynard. "Here's where we shoot this out!"

To his amazement Sandy merely reeled and fumbled at the air. Maynard rode closer, and now he saw what had happened. The gun that had been dashed into the face of Sandy had struck him across the eyes. Blood streamed across one eye from a gash, and the other was already closed, a purpling mass. With bitterness in his soul Maynard decided that he could not murder a helpless man. He rode alongside Lorrimer.

"We're starting home," he said. "Take hold of this rope. It'll help you along and show you the way."

"Maynard," groaned Lorrimer. "Oh, Jack, I thought you were my friend."

"You rat," snarled Maynard. "I was only patting you on the back till I had a chance to knock you in the head. What, Lorrimer, do you really think I'd be a friend to a hound that stole my girl while I was away?"

Lorrimer held his hand across his eyes. The bleeding was stopping, but the heavy blow had so bruised the flesh that his eyes were closed. He could see no more than if it were night.

"Well," he said finally, "I see where I've been a fool again. Go on, Maynard. I'll walk behind you."

Only that. Where Maynard had expected a wild torrent of abuse, only these quiet words. It stung him with shame to the very heart. How would he himself have acted in a similar condition?

"I'm taking you down the cañon to a water hole," he said. "I'll leave you there and ride on to get help."

There was a little pause.

"Leave me there blinded...and in this sun?" asked Lorrimer at last. "Well, go on."

Maynard bit his lip, then started the roan mare ahead. It was a far cry down that cañon, as hot as an oven by this time. He could only walk the mare, with Lorrimer walking behind him, stumbling over every unevenness in the way. And in the silt-like sand the little mare plowed slowly ahead. It took them a full hour to cover the three miles, and before the hour was over the throat of Maynard was as hot and dry as the sands over which they were traveling.

When they reached the water hole, there was not a drop of water left in it. The deep bowl of blue mud was burned gray by the heat of the sun, and there were cracks three inches wide worked in a net across the surface. Maynard sat silently in the saddle, breathing heavily.

"Good Lord," gasped Lorrimer suddenly.

Maynard looked down into the blind, disfigured face and saw that it was white with realization of what the halt and the silence meant.

"It's dry!"

"Yes," said Maynard. He swallowed, and the effort was painful. An old story he had often heard flashed through his mind, of how a miner in the desert mountains had left his mine to cross the valley, of how he had run out of water, of how in the scant space of four hours he had almost died, struggling to get back to his mine, that was in full sight all the time, and, with life barely left to him, how he had reached the hole at last. It would be as sure a way of killing Lorrimer as a bullet.

"Lorrimer," he said, "I'm going to try to get help."

A horrible and derisive laughter came from the parched throat of Lorrimer.

"On my honor," cried Maynard, and, as he loosed the reins, the good mare struck off at a sharp trot.

After all, who could blame him when he reached town and told the true story? Lou Martin, perhaps, might hold it against him for a time, but time had cured deeper wounds than this. Besides, would it not be hard enough for him to reach town alive, even with the speed of the mare at his service? He checked her on the next rise of ground and looked back for the last time. There was Lorrimer coming steadily after him, with hands stretched before him, as though he were striving to guess the way, his head thrown back a little, regardless of that terrible sun. He stumbled, fell on his face, rose, and went on again. Maynard went cold. What other man could have kept from falling on his knees, shrieking for mercy, or begging for quick death to end the torment? But yonder was Lorrimer, struggling silently and hopelessly ahead. Wonder filled the heart of Maynard. Ah, well it was for him that he was not leaving Lorrimer in the lists to fight against him for the favor of the girl. This was horrible, but necessary. All was fair in love or war.

He turned to resume the journey, but something turned his head again. Still Lorrimer was struggling on, but he was slanting to the side now in his direction. Doubtless he would walk only in a blind circle. Maynard reached into his pocket. Aimlessly he drew out a pair of dice. Suppose that men were to gamble for such dreadful stakes as these? The thought took hold of him like a great hand. Suppose he were to throw the dice—honorably—with Lorrimer?

The imp of the perverse urged him on, but all the dead honor at the bottom of his soul rose up and thundered in his heart of hearts. He thought of Lou Martin at the dance, smiling, happy, aloof in beauty. He could never face her after this. And, after all, even if the dice went against him, could he not refuse to abide by their decision? But suppose he should win the cast—one chance out of two—what an endless balm to his conscience. He turned the mare and rode back.

"Lorrimer!" he called.

The other halted, but said not a word, and for some reason that silence seemed a gigantic proud, strong thing to Maynard. No bitter reproaches and no slavish appeals, only silence to greet him. He threw himself from the horse.

"Lorrimer," he said, and the voice that issued from his dry throat was hardly more than a whisper, "if you were on this mare, she'd take you safely home. She wouldn't miss the way back to her stall. Lorrimer, we're going to throw the dice to see who rides her home."

"Do you mean to do this fine thing?"

"Yes."

"One thing first. Is Clune dead?"

"No."

"Then I have a right to throw the dice."

"I throw first," said Maynard. "One roll and the high man wins."

"And God have mercy on the soul of him that loses," came the hoarse murmur of Lorrimer.

Down stooped Maynard. On the level, hard-packed surface of some gravel he made his throw and then threw up his hands to the heavens in exultation.

"A six and a five, Lorrimer," he said. "God help you, Sandy."

"Give me the dice," said the blinded man and reached vaguely for them. Maynard put them in his hand.

For another moment Sandy stood straight, juggling the dice in his hand, his jaw set. Then he stooped and rolled. Over and over the little cubes winked in the light and came to a rest. And the unwilling voice of Maynard gasped: "Two sixes! Great guns, two sixes!"

He looked to Lorrimer. The winner had hung his head. Now he reached out. Maynard took his hand.

"Jack," said Sandy, "I've heard of a pile of fine things that gents have done here and there. I ain't heard of anything to top this. Maybe I ought to refuse to take the mare, but I know that you wouldn't let me stay after I've won. I only hope that I come across somebody, while the hoss is taking me in. If I do, I'll send you help. I'll keep hitting straight for town, and if I can get help to you in three hours...."

Three hours! Three centuries! Already the throat of Maynard was on fire. What kept him then from leaping onto the back of the mare and riding off? He himself could not tell, but he was frozen to the spot where he stood. He saw Lorrimer fumblingly find the stirrup and mount. Vaguely he heard the last promise, and, still chained to his place, he saw the roan mare start away at the untiring lope. Then his wits returned. He started forward at a wild run. He strove to shriek after Lorrimer, but his throat closed. Only a faint whisper rushed out.

238

He stopped, swallowed with an agonizing effort, and then managed to call, but by that time the mare had swept Lorrimer out of earshot. He was left alone, and the white sun beat steadily down on him, a ceaseless rain of heat.

Ⓥ Ⓥ Ⓥ Ⓥ Ⓥ

They found him afterward in the same place. He had not stirred from it, or made an effort to save himself. He lay on his back with his arms thrown wide and the gun in his hand with which he had forestalled a wretched death by thirst. There it was, too, that they buried him and heaped a great mound of rocks over him to tell the story. And there, at Easter of every year, Mrs. Sandy Lorrimer journeys, and throws flowers over the sun-blistered stones.

ACKNOWLEDGMENTS

"Winking Lights" by John Frederick first appeared in Street & Smith's *Western Story Magazine* (1/6/23). Copyright © 1923 by Street & Smith Publications, Inc. Copyright © renewed 1950 by Dorothy Faust. Copyright © 1997 for restored material by Jane Faust Easton and Adriana Faust Bianchi. Acknowledgment is made to Condé Nast Publications, Inc., for their cooperation.

"The Best Bandit" by David Manning first appeared in Street & Smith's *Western Story Magazine* (3/5/32). Copyright © 1932 by Street & Smith Publications, Inc. Copyright © renewed 1959 by Dorothy Faust. Copyright © 1997 by Jane Faust Easton and Adriana Faust Bianchi for restored material. Acknowledgment is made to Condé Nast Publications, Inc., for their cooperation.

"Two Sixes" by George Owen Baxter first appeared in Street & Smith's *Western Story Magazine* (3/17/23). Copyright © 1923 by Street & Smith Publications, Inc. Copyright © renewed 1950 by Dorothy Faust. Copyright © 1997 by Jane Faust Easton and Adriana Faust Bianchi for restored material. Acknowledgment is made to Condé Nast Publications, Inc., for their cooperation.

The Lightning Warrior

The Indians call the great white wolf the Lightning Warrior because of the swiftness of his attack. But even the giant Colbolt isn't interested in the massive wolf until Sylvia Baird makes the beast's pelt the one condition for her hand in marriage. She thinks she is safe, but when he returns with not only the pelt, but the wolf itself, and demands his prize, Sylvia's only hope is a desperate flight for freedom. Colbolt sets out in determined pursuit, but he's forgotten Sylvia's newest ally. . .the Lightning Warrior.

___4420-X $4.50 US/$5.50 CAN

Dorchester Publishing Co., Inc.
P.O. Box 6640
Wayne, PA 19087-8640

Please add $1.75 for shipping and handling for the first book and $.50 for each book thereafter. NY, NYC, and PA residents, please add appropriate sales tax. No cash, stamps, or C.O.D.s. All orders shipped within 6 weeks via postal service book rate. Canadian orders require $2.00 extra postage and must be paid in U.S. dollars through a U.S. banking facility.

Name_____
Address_____
City_____ State_____ Zip_____
I have enclosed $_____ in payment for the checked book(s).
Payment <u>must</u> accompany all orders. ❑ Please send a free catalog.
CHECK OUT OUR WEBSITE! www.dorchesterpub.com

RONICKY DOONE

First Time In Paperback!

"Brand is a topnotcher!"
—New York Times

Doone's name is famous throughout the Old West. From Tombstone to Sonora he's won the respect of every law-abiding citizen—and the hatred of every bushwhacking bandit. But Bill Gregg isn't one to let a living legend get in his way, and he'll shoot Doone dead as soon as look at him. What nobody tells Gregg is that Doone doesn't enjoy living his hard-riding, rip-roaring life unless he takes a chance on losing it once in a while.

_3738-6 $3.99 US/$4.99 CAN

Dorchester Publishing Co., Inc.
P.O. Box 6640
Wayne, PA 19087-8640

Please add $1.75 for shipping and handling for the first book and $.50 for each book thereafter. NY, NYC, and PA residents, please add appropriate sales tax. No cash, stamps, or C.O.D.s. All orders shipped within 6 weeks via postal service book rate. Canadian orders require $2.00 extra postage and must be paid in U.S. dollars through a U.S. banking facility.

Name_____
Address_____
City_____State_____Zip_____
I have enclosed $_____ in payment for the checked book(s).
Payment <u>must</u> accompany all orders. ❑ Please send a free catalog.

MAX BRAND

TROUBLE IN TIMBERLINE

"Brand is a topnotcher!"
—New York Times

Barney Dwyer is too big and too awkward to be much good around a ranch. But foreman Dan Peary has the perfect job for him. It seems Peary's son has joined up with a ruthless gang in the mountain town of Timberline, and Peary wants Barney to bring the no-account back, alive. Before long, Barney finds himself up to his powerful neck in trouble—both from gunslingers who defy the law and tin stars who are sworn to uphold it!

_3848-X $4.50 US/$5.50 CAN

MAX BRAND

THE ABANDONED OUTLAW

No writer captures the American West better than Max Brand. And nowhere is Brand's talent more evident than in these three classic short novels, all restored to their original length, and collected in paperback for the first time. In "The Gold King Turns His Back," young Miriam Standard is more than capable of running her father's ranch, but finds she has much to learn about the Westerners' meaning of honor. In "The Three Crosses," an ominous prediction leads a cowpuncher to a showdown with a notorious gunfighter. And the title novel finds a young woman caught in the middle of a lifelong rivalry between two men, one of whom is an outlaw. Experience the West as only Max Brand could write it!

___4465-X $4.50 US/$5.50 CAN

Dorchester Publishing Co., Inc.
P.O. Box 6640
Wayne, PA 19087-8640

Please add $1.75 for shipping and handling for the first book and $.50 for each book thereafter. NY, NYC, and PA residents, please add appropriate sales tax. No cash, stamps, or C.O.D.s. All orders shipped within 6 weeks via postal service book rate. Canadian orders require $2.00 extra postage and must be paid in U.S. dollars through a U.S. banking facility.

Name_____
Address_____
City_____ State_____ Zip_____
I have enclosed $_____ in payment for the checked book(s).
Payment <u>must</u> accompany all orders. ❏ Please send a free catalog.

MAX BRAND

SLUMBER MOUNTAIN

Here, for the first time in paperback, are three of Max Brand's best short novels, all restored to their original glory from Brand's own typescripts and presented just as he intended. "Outland Crew" is an exciting tale of gold fever and survival in a frontier mining town. In "The Coward," a man humiliated in a gunfight finds a fiendishly clever way of exacting revenge. And in "Slumber Mountain," Brand presents a harrowing story of man versus the wilderness as a trapper fights for his life against the mighty wolf known as Silver King.

___4442-0 $4.99 US/$5.99 CAN

Dorchester Publishing Co., Inc.
P.O. Box 6640
Wayne, PA 19087-8640

Please add $1.75 for shipping and handling for the first book and $.50 for each book thereafter. NY, NYC, and PA residents, please add appropriate sales tax. No cash, stamps, or C.O.D.s. All orders shipped within 6 weeks via postal service book rate. Canadian orders require $2.00 extra postage and must be paid in U.S. dollars through a U.S. banking facility.

Name_____
Address_____
City_____ State_____ Zip_____
I have enclosed $_____ in payment for the checked book(s).
Payment <u>must</u> accompany all orders. ☐ Please send a free catalog.
CHECK OUT OUR WEBSITE! www.dorchesterpub.com